Centrifugal Force

Lisa J Lickel

Other books by Lisa J Lickel

The Buried Treasure Mystery Series
The Last Bequest
The Map Quilt
The Newspaper Code
Healing Grace
Meander Scar
A Summer in Oakville, with Shellie Neumeier
The Last Detail
"Three Rings for Alice" romantic historical novella in *Brave New Century*
First Children of Farmington for early readers
The Potawatomi Boy
The German Girl
The Saxon Boy
The French Girl
The Yankee Boy
The Irish Girl
"Gangster's Ghostcapade," a radio play in
A Wisconsin Harvest, vol II
Everything About You, romantic novella
Requiem for the Innocents
UnderStory
Fancy Cat mysteries
Meow Mayhem
Meow Matrimony

Centrifugal Force
Fiction

Copyright © 2017 by Lisa J Lickel
First edition

Published by Fox Ridge Publications
Hillsboro, Wisconsin

Cover Photo: adapted from mantasmagorical, www.Morguefile.com, free for commercial purposes
Cover font is Wabroye by gluk, www.1001fonts.com, and is licensed under SIL Open Font License, free for commercial use
Cover by Rodney Schroeter and Lisa Lickel

ISBN-13: 978-0-9967683-6-8
ISBN 10: 099676836X
Electronic ISBN: 978-0-9967683-7-5
Library of Congress Control Number: 2017918611

Centrifugal force is the virtual sensation of being pushed to
the outside while spinning, out of control. In reality, you're
losing your balance.
Gervas Friedemann

Freiburg, Germany

Fall, 1938

When the first storm troopers arrived in Freiburg that afternoon, Eli had hurried to pack the precious historical artifacts at their country estate and get them to his office in the city. He stood near the last of eight small trunks tucked inside the recess of the false wall. Rosa hunched nearby, weeping and cringing at the sound of shouting in the streets outside.

"They will take us away." Rosa lowered her faced and moaned, grasping the maroon velvet bag between her small, age-speckled hands.

Eli closed his eyes briefly, then shuffled to his wife. He hurt to see the roughness of the skin and her broken nails. "Come, Rosa, it has been this way always for our people. Thirty-five generations, almost a thousand years, our people have been removed from Baden. Yet we keep coming back." He patted her shoulders under the fine silk shawl from China. "They can liquidate our businesses, they can blow up our synagogues, but they cannot take away our souls."

The rat-a-tat of machine gun fire not far away made Rosa cry harder, if that were possible. "God will judge," Eli roared toward the door. He gentled his voice trying to comfort her. "We will return. If not here, then someplace better. We suspected this day would come. That is why five years ago I made the arrangements with our neighbors."

"It is my fault," she mumbled. "If Papa had not come from Poland, perhaps—"

"No, Rosa. Do not blame yourself. They will find a way

to take us all, not just the Polish Jews this time. You know that. No one is safe." He put his hands over hers on the velvet bag. "I must pack this now for the journey."

"Why do they care more for things than people? Why?" She released her favorite pieces of the collection to him, her dark eyes following while he tucked the bag carefully amongst the wrapped sculptures, tiles, and other less important jeweled trinkets of Italian art and dishes.

"They do not understand. God has darkened their hearts and minds." Eli closed the trunk and locked it. "You will wear them again someday. The earrings made your beauty shine." He pinched the trigger of the finished outer wall and lowered it like the cover of his roll-top desk in front of the trunks. No one could tell where millions of dollars of art lay hidden.

Rosa sniffed. "The rings were my favorites."

"Friedemann promised to protect them in Canada. I contacted him yesterday. He will come later to pick up these trunks. The other pieces in the museums now, well, we can only assume they will be safe from the Nazis."

"At least the Friedemanns can get away. Hide. Like…like—"

"Rosa, my dear. Hush."

Anger dried some of Rosa's tears.

The door to their antiquities business rattled and broke. Rosa screamed in the circle of his arms. Eli held her tightly, helpless against the five uniformed men who rushed inside brandishing weapons. In contrast, a Waffen SS major, by the markings on his sleeves, strolled after them, a self-satisfied smirk making his blondness even uglier. Eli stiffened.

"Regenbogen. These men are here to escort you to the trains." He tsked as he strode about the room, bare now of all but desk and chair, tapping the walls and floors with his stick.

Rosa began to wheeze. Eli gripped her waist in warning.

"No pictures on the walls, no rugs, no curtains." He shook his head. "I see you are ready for your vacation. Your pig frau is expelled to the Polish border as a special mercy. You, however, and ninety-nine of your kind, will enjoy the charms of Dachau."

- 1 -

The lingering echo and tingle of a quarter-century-old slap trembled along her fingers and tickled her palm. She clenched her fist to stop the sensation.

"Mom, here's another e-mail from that guy with the strange name. The one who keeps asking about you."

Rachel Michels closed her eyes, even though her grown daughter couldn't see her cower behind the front section of the newspaper. The paper rattled in her hands. Rachel lowered it.

"Hey, Mom—you there? You said you were going to take care of it."

"I said I would, Maeve." Soon as she could stomach the thought of telling Gervas to knock it off. He probably didn't even know who Maeve was, just that she had the same last name as a girl he once knew in Wisconsin.

The real question was why, after twenty-three years, he thought he had the right to come waltzing into her life. How dare he? "Just hit delete without opening it. I'll take your laptop in to work with me tomorrow, have Scott in IT purge the sender, okay? And I'll call Bob in security, see if we can trace it."

"I don't want to lose any of my stuff."

"You won't. Just copy the material you need and you can use mine tomorrow."

"I guess that'll be okay. I'll let them know at work, so they don't think I stole or wrecked their equipment."

Maeve, Rachel's surprise gift child, was all of twenty-two, with a newly minted bachelor of arts under her arm and the

4

owner of a condo—too many miles away for Rachel's taste —
in Cottage Grove, south of Madison. At least the advertising
company she'd interned for the last summer had hired her full
time. Almost any job that paid the bills was good these days
when so many graduates were struggling with the tanking
economy of 2011—which was shaping up to be nearly as awful
as 2010. It was worse in Europe, where the European Union
was voting whether to bail out member nations in economic
crisis.

Rachel stood and tossed the paper aside. "I'm going to fix
a cup of tea. Want one?"

With fingers poised over the keyboard, beautiful Maeve
looked up, two little squiggles of concentration crossing an
otherwise smooth forehead. Her daughter's long-lashed tiger
eyes blinked to focus. "Um, yeah, sure. Thanks."

Too far away, Rachel thought again. Fifteen point seven
miles, door to door. It had been just the two of them forever,
and now, well, empty nest couldn't come close to describing
the aching alone-ness and touch of fear that there'd be no one
to share the rest of her life. What Rachel's sister Ann had gone
through those years she'd been alone—no, nothing could
prepare a person. It was like living in a bubble, and suddenly
popped out on a cold rainy night with no plan, no training, no
advice.

Rachel pretended her smile worked perfectly and
practiced one before she turned and went to boil water. At least
her daughter's hair had returned to its natural, glossy brown
color. The various gruesome facial piercings she'd given herself
in college were healing. Rachel shuddered. If not for Ann's
husband Mark, who knew what would have happened to them.
So handy to have a lawyer in the family.

Carrying the mugs, Rachel set one down next to her

daughter. "I feel like I should be serving iced tea in July."

Maeve's grin made things right.

"It's a little cool tonight." She held up the steaming cup of mint. "Besides, there's nothing like home and something warm. Thanks, Mom."

Rachel crouched near the sofa, creaking in the knees. Maeve laughed.

"What are you working on now?" Rachel scooted her cheaters across her nose.

"New mug designs for a local businesses. They send their logos, and I give them some options, or if I need to, work with them to create a logo."

A ping sounded and a small window popped up in the lower right hand corner of the screen. Before she could stop herself, Rachel crushed the delete button so hard she broke her fingernail. She put the finger to her mouth. "Yikes. There goes my manicure." She let her voice fade at the look on her daughter's face.

"How did you know?" Maeve's expression was open-mouthed shock. "I don't remember telling you his name."

Too late. Rachel grimaced. "Sorry. Mother-hen instinct. I hope that wasn't a client. I can have Scott get it back."

"It just went to trash. But, no…it was him. Jer-Grr-Gervas Friedemann. However it's pronounced. He said he was looking for you, or at least someone with your name who used to work at Mendota. What's going on?"

Years of practice side-stepping reality hadn't quite prepared Rachel for this—the possibility that he would seek them out. She felt the heat rush to her face and knew she couldn't lie. But the truth belonged to no one except her. And him.

<>

Gervas Friedemann thanked the receptionist who showed him to a chair in the pastel-themed lounge at University Hospital. Americans were so vapidly indulgent with everything, even their waiting areas. He studied the innocuous floral print in a pink frame nailed to the wall. No real form or design. Machine cast? Spit out from something beige and metallic, no attempt to create a bond with its viewer, or capture a piece of the artist's soul? Perhaps one of their test creatures had painted it. He had seen the scrawls of apes and elephants. Fewer people were needed to do even the simple tasks that made life glow.

But that was exactly what he needed. People. A person, anyway. Something from a particular person to help his daughter Katrine. Machines had not yet been able to recreate bone marrow. Not yet. This University of Wisconsin had experts creating and recreating the microscopic elements of a person's genetic map. Katrine's diseased blood, but deeper, his own faulty genome, had betrayed the family.

"Dr. Friedemann?"

Gervas looked up at the tall young man in a white coat, his smooth hand held out. In greeting? Or helping an old man rise? "Yes. Gervas Friedemann."

"I'm Dr. Randolph, assistant to Dr. Kappers, director of the Stem Cell Gene Therapy program here at the William and Alexis Barton Institute. We've been expecting you. Please, come with me."

Gervas stood before shaking the hand and gripped it briefly. He followed the unlined face and vigorous steps of the one who held Katrine's fate. A boy doctor in gray shirt and tie under the pure clean laboratory coat. William and Alexis Barton? Who were they? Another thing distasteful about the States—such pretention everywhere. Naming rights.

The room where Randolph led them was not a typical office but a conference room with a large table, comfortable chairs, and blinds at the windows. Randolph gestured toward one of the high-back blue padded seats. "Please." He poured them each a glass of water, and sat next to Gervas. "Dr. Warner, another associate, will join us shortly. Unfortunately Dr. Kappers is out of town today. I understand you are interested in our ongoing clinical trial?"

<>

"There was an exchange professor at Mendota years ago," Rachel said. "You know we have that study program with Freiburg University in Germany. This probably has something to do with my work. If that's so, then he shouldn't be trying to contact you just because we have the same last name. Or he's simply confused. I'll take care of it."

Clicks and pops in her hips made Rachel gnaw the inside of her lip as she pressed herself upright. "Why don't you put your files on a disk and we can trade computers now?"

A flash of the old mutiny glinted in Maeve's eyes before she corralled it. "Okay."

As they traded machines and her daughter packed up to leave, Rachel wanted to erase the doubt Maeve wore. They walked outside to Maeve's car in the driveway. Crickets stirred the summer evening and gnats swirled under the lofty streetlamp. It wasn't cold, but not as hot as it could be, either. Blacktop, heated from the day, radiated fumes of the underworld.

Rachel rubbed her arms as Maeve stowed her gear. "I'm glad you came. You're always welcome to stay."

"Thanks." Maeve's look had a question. But then she smiled and hugged tight, leaning down slightly from her two-inch advantage in height, before she slid into her car.

Rachel waved at the taillights, wondering how the tables had turned in such a short time. She was the one who needed to prove herself to her daughter now. To show her that some secrets were worth keeping, even though outright lying usually did more harm than good by creating a false sense of security.

How far did Rachel want to root into the past? What good would it do, anyway? Maeve had turned out pretty well. Sure, she'd had some rough spots—who hadn't? Rachel had made many poor choices—some she'd even admit. The messages must be a mistake. Gervas didn't know what he was doing, how much things should have changed in two decades. Absent-minded professors were like that.

Scott would help her keep Gervas from her daughter. And all the office staff knew how to protect her privacy.

<>

"Yes," Gervas replied to the physician. Were all prospective patients given this preferential treatment of a private consultation? He handed over Katrine's file, with the letter of permission from her, as an adult, and her many doctors, giving him the right to discuss her case. "My daughter Katrine suffers from Fanconi Anemia, and unfortunately, many side effects."

"How old is she?" Randolph didn't look at him, but instead leaned across the closed file.

"Twenty-seven." Right there on the file, if you'd just look. What it didn't say was that she'd been born of Gervas's first marriage, nearly three decades of teaching, traveling, networking, study, international acclaim, and a second marriage, ago. He rubbed his cheekbones over his trimmed beard where Sylvie's ring had etched his face that day she'd learned of Julianne and filed for divorce. Katrine had been eight, Max eleven. A bad end to an interminable situation.

"She's been receiving excellent care," Randolph muttered when he finally began to turn pages. "I see an attempt at MSD was undertaken to slow the myelodysplasia."

Gervas would not entertain that discussion, though echoes of it slammed him at times like these. When he'd confronted his ex-wife, she told him why the matched sibling bone marrow donation, MSD, had failed. "That's because Max is *not* your son." Sylvie's voice had lacked the triumph he'd heard during her announcement, he realized later. She was not that cruel to flaunt their mutual and many indiscretions in Katrine's face, despite the vicious things they'd done to one another.

"Yes," Gervas said to Randolph. "The procedure had disappointing results."

They'd been desperate enough in those days, he and Sylvie and the doctors, to risk the transplant under less than perfect conditions. How did they say it, here in America? Close, but no cigar. Tumors had resulted in surgery that reduced Katrine's voice to a harsh rasp.

The doctor reminded Gervas somewhat of a house spider, spindly and nearly colorless, but capable of dispatching anything that got in its way. Randolph sat back and crossed his ankle over a knee. "Fanconi Anemia, or FA, presents with several disorders and may affect nearly any system in the body. As you know, it is inherited and often fatal, though it seems your daughter has escaped many of the debilitating birth defects, except for the heart, and then the tumors as a result of the failed bone marrow transplant."

Gervas held his breath and let this self-important American doctor get his ingratiating need to spew data out of the way. He supposed many of those students and colleagues who attended his lectures over the years felt so, and reaped his punishment as another step to get help for his daughter.

"In the decades since your daughter's diagnosis, we've…"

Always that American overconfidence. It had been the Swiss, Friedrich Miescher, who first isolated your genetic material, and the British who worked with it. A young woman doctor with a good German name, Catherine Freudenreich, was a current expert in abnormal DNA structure. Even though she was an American.

"Of the damaged genetic markers so far, we've been able to identify…"

And so Randolph spoke the words of the initiated, those invited to the specific chromosome party who could absorb the meaning of mesenchymal stoma cells and non-hematopoietic cells and insert them in conversation like so much *ex vivo* and *in vivo*; outside the living environment or inside a living host. Gervas knew all the words, the tests, the impossible treatments.

"Our trial's outcome is to provide a disease-free survival for patients who have developed conditions such as myelodysplastic syndrome," Randolph said.

Gervas narrowed his eyes.

"Should your daughter decide to enroll in and is qualified for our program, which has a number of years to run, she will receive free evaluation and treatment."

Of course Konrad Meissen, Katrine's lead physician, had already explained this. Gervas had wanted to see for himself, to meet these people and form an opinion based not on the coldness of letters and figures and numbers on a page, or impersonal computer screen.

Konrad had also looked Gervas in the eye and told him there needed to be someone unrelated, but still HLA-compatible. Neither he nor Sylvie were acceptable donors for this program, nor could Max be considered an HLA, or human leukocyte antigen donor. There were no other close enough relatives with similar genetics to help Katrine. Marvelous, the information people could discover today about human white blood cells and the substances on their surface—leukocyte antigen. A miracle to have such data at one's fingertips.

"Usually, a blood relative would make a better donor," the American doctor said, seemingly echoing Konrad's Bavarian accent.

A blood relative. A blood relative. A blood…

"But there are ways to work with unrelated, HLA-compatible donors."

The door to the conference room opened to a similarly-coated young woman. Randolph and Gervas stood. "Dr. Warner," Randolph said, eagerness and pleasure creating a sense of adultness, of *knowingness* in his being. Once, Gervas would have enjoyed such a lovers' secret. Now, he wanted no more distractions to come between his daughter and her existence.

As they repeated the situation so that the new doctor could catch up, Gervas studied the pair, their professional and intimate body language proving their interest in themselves and the research they both apparently loved. Would this pose a problem? Could he trust them?

"Professor Friedemann." Dr. Warner smiled. "Thank you for taking the time to come and meet us. I feel confident that something can be done to alleviate your family's suffering."

At last. Gervas allowed the warmth of her certainty to flow through him. Someone understood. Yes. It was good. And just.

"You won't remember me," she said, giving a faint toss of wavy brown hair behind her shoulder and jingling earrings that looked like coins. "I was in the exchange program for a summer semester, from Mendota to Freiburg. I took your cultural anthropology course and nearly changed my major."

"I'm glad you didn't," Gervas responded, allowing a small twist of his lips.

Mendota again. And memories, back twenty-some odd years, nearly the time of this young woman's birth. No…a little later, obviously. The underlying reason of his visit to Wisconsin, which, unfortunately, had little to do with Katrine and everything to do with the family honor.

If he didn't find her, that young woman who had taken her revenge on him all those years ago, more than his daughter—an entire coalition of nations—would suffer worse than this disease of one person's blood.

2

As Rachel made her way to the IT dungeon at work the next morning, Maeve's laptop clutched in a death grip, anticipation, or anxiety perhaps, warred with her common sense. Scott Warfield had asked her out twice since he started on the job a year ago, and both times she'd had legitimate reasons to say no. Her sister Ann's six-month wedding anniversary had been a big deal. Since Ann's stroke, her husband Mark went out of his way to make every milestone count. The other time Scott asked had been the occasion of moving Maeve to her new place—news which lit a curious gleam in his eyes.

Today Rachel would try asking him out. Coffee, maybe lunch. She hadn't dated because of Maeve, she told anyone who asked. Excuses. Each click of her heels on the tile took her closer to Scott's office. Everyone liked him. He obviously loved his job, but not in the computer nerd way.

His lights were on, the door open. Whirring and keyboard clicking noise came from inside and she hesitated. A quick sliding footstep and the juggle of the doorknob made her dance back.

"Oh. Hi, there, Rachel."

Rachel couldn't help ducking her head after staring at the upward curve of his lips. She felt the flush, too. Good Lord, how old did a person have to be to grow out of perpetual angst? But she'd never had a chance to do anything like this, this stepping over the line of her comfort zone, this leaping without planning every detail—at least, not since…him. What a disaster that had been. Deep breath. "Morning, Scott. I hope

I'm not catching you in the middle of something."

A genial grin reached his eyes, something Rachel could legitimately focus on. "No." He hadn't had time to roll up the sleeves of his white dress shirt like he usually did. He gestured for her to enter his office. "Come on in, tell me what I can do for you."

Business first. Give her time to work up the nerve. She held out the laptop. "This is my daughter's work computer. Someone is sending her messages, and I, we, hoped you could figure out a way to keep him from doing it anymore? More than just block sender, I guess, is what I mean. Purge him from her accounts and keep him from finding her anywhere on the internet?"

Rachel liked the concerned vibes from him. She knew his age and birthdate from his office records but not a whole lot else. He would be fifty later in the summer, and had not listed a spouse. He wasn't buff from over-compensating on workouts, or paunchy, so he must do something to keep fit. His work history had listed a couple of decades in the military, a good career in itself.

"Do you want me to notify the police?"

"Huh…oh, um, no. He—I—the messages weren't dangerous. Just annoying."

"I have her permission to take a look?"

"Yes, of course. She wants you to help if you can."

"Okay."

They stood there until Rachel realized the moment had grown awkward. "Oh! Right. When you have time. Don't let me take up any more…we both have work to do."

After they'd taken two steps toward the door, Rachel took a deep breath. "I want to thank you—"

"No problem. Always happy to help a colleague."

Too late. Rachel groaned inside. He must have found someone more willing to date him. Do something! "Would you like to have lunch with me?"

"Sure."

Rachel stared, hoping she hadn't misheard. The crinkles around his eyes seemed to agree with the "sure."

"So, today all right?"

"Yep. I'm off between twelve thirty and one thirty. Is that okay? Meet you in the cafeteria?" he said.

"No." Oops. "I mean, how about I take you over to…to…" Name, *name*. "That Greek restaurant, over on…well, I know where it is, anyway. I've heard it's good."

Scott's expression was cautiously pleased. Maybe a little puzzled. "You want to do that?"

She nodded. A little too vigorously, but that didn't stop his slow-growing smile. He clasped her arm under his elbow and walked her out of the office. "Well, you know I'll have to reciprocate, then, don't you?" He let her go and mock-saluted.

Rachel watched him walk down the hall, rolling up his sleeves. He whistled something from Disney. And left a whiff of man-scent in his wake, probably just his deodorant, but the breezy smell made her want to stand there until it was gone. Something in his saunter had her wondering if he was a good dancer. The last time she'd danced was at her sister's second wedding, and she'd loved it.

She looked at her watch and rushed back upstairs. Nuts. Five minutes late for the first meeting of the day.

<>

The Olympus Grill. Rachel recalled the name of the restaurant during the meeting on revised benefits for the full-time janitorial employees. At least she didn't have to look like a fool in front of him, blabbering about knowing the way, but not the name. Once there, Scott entertained her during lunch with stories of teaching people how to use computers. "It shouldn't happen so much anymore, now that systems and programs are becoming standardized. But keyboards. One time I answered a call from a second grade teacher who whispered she needed help immediately, she needed me to come to her desk as she couldn't move."

Rachel chuckled, more in response to his enjoyment of the story than sympathy with the victim of the tale. "So, did she have her hand stuck between keys, or something?" She captured a chunk of feta with an olive and forked it into her mouth.

"Worse." Scott shook his head. "She had her hands on the keyboard, a pinky each on the control and alt buttons. When I got to the room, she was practically in tears. 'This is a new keyboard,' she said, apparently forgetting I had installed it for her the day before. 'I can't find the delete button. It used to be right up there. And now it's gone. What do I do?'"

Laughing out loud, Rachel sat back. "You can't make this stuff up."

"Nope. You run into all kinds of folks when you're in a big organization. Some you have to show the 'on' button, and some you have to wait until they mess up before you can show them the right way." Scott tossed his napkin next to his plate. "This is great. I wouldn't have guessed you like Greek food."

Truthfully, it hadn't been Rachel's favorite. At the time Maeve had mentioned it she thought it had sounded exotic and impressive. "My daughter said it was good. So, you were working in the public schools? What made you come to Mendota?"

The hesitation was so fleeting, only someone like Rachel who'd had to become adept at reading a formerly secretive and rebellious, strung-out daughter would have picked up on it.

"Things changed," Scott said. "Public schools are heading toward privatization of many services." He picked up his glass and smiled grimly. "Maintenance, lunch programs, summer school…"

"Technology," Rachel added. "I get the picture. I was just in a benefits meeting. We're hanging on to our janitorial staff by a thread. And pretty soon they'll be using avatars to teach classes." Something elusive hung between his words. She probably shouldn't have interrupted him. She couldn't ask about his past military history without revealing she'd snooped through his files, though of course it was her job to do so before hiring him.

"So, I was happy to come to Mendota." He drained the last of his lemon water and twisted his wrist to check his watch.

"Well, we should head back." Rachel waved him off when he reached for the check. "My idea, my treat." She signed the receipt and allowed him to open the door for her on their way out. "Thanks."

On the short ride back to campus, they shared friendly observances about Madison. A nice picnic and summer concert on the capitol lawn sounded perfect for their next…outing. Whatever. Scott promised to call. They hesitated near her department before parting ways.

"I should be able to give back your daughter's computer tomorrow."

"Great, thanks. I hope it's not been much trouble."

"Na." He winked. "I learned a few tricks about blocking certain types of communications over the years."

"I guess there's a lot of stuff students shouldn't accidentally get into."

"Ri-ight." He waved and disappeared toward IT.

Rachel hummed on the way to her office, where her blinking inbox let her know she'd been missed. She picked up a letter opener and sliced the first envelope of a dozen pieces of correspondence while she scanned the e-mails. She stopped midway through the first envelope and ignored the subject lines of the messages to lean closer to the large screen of her computer. In the bottom right-hand corner was the alert icon she'd set up to keep track of Gervas's online activity. The nerve of that guy! Now he was posting on Mendota's online bulletin board for information on Rachel Michels who used to work at the college in the late '80s. *Seriously? Five hundred dollars for information?*

His post was beyond creepy. She'd either call the cops or call him herself and make him pay *her* the money. Swiping his little precious family bauble all those years ago hadn't come close to what he'd really cost her. Not that five hundred bucks would make a dent toward the pain he'd caused. First, she had to get that online bulletin board post down. Some student would be sure to say there was a Mrs. Michels working in the administration office.

She threw the letter opener onto her desk and reached for the phone. "Scott!" His name came out in an angry hiss before she stopped herself and cleared her throat. "Sorry. I'm just so mad. That creep has posted on the Mendota Forum, looking for me." She rubbed her forehead while she listened. "Yes, the same one on Maeve's…I don't know…yes, you're right, I should call the police. But in the meantime, can you take it down? Great, thank you."

Rachel copied the phone number from Gervas's ridiculous plea for information in a shaky hand, screaming at herself all the while, before the post blinked out. Scott was quick. Wondering why she thought she had any business copying Gervas's phone number, she pushed back her chair and threw her now-contaminated pen in the garbage can and crumpled the Post-it with the number—a US number—to send after her pen. He must be using a temporary cell phone while he was here. She paced, taking deep breaths, unable to let go of the note. Hopefully no one had paid much attention to Gervas's post in the twenty-five minutes it had been up. Would he notice its absence? How soon?

A sharp tap on the door was all the warning Scott gave before walking into her office. She whirled and nearly tripped over her feet.

"Are you okay? You sounded almost panicked." Scott reached for her hands and she automatically backed away.

Rachel stared out the window, rallying her composure. "I apologize. I don't know what's gotten into me. I don't think he's dangerous—"

"Are you kidding?" Scott folded his arms. "He's offering cash. What did the police say?"

She quirked her mouth and faced him. "You got up here so fast I haven't had time."

"I can back you up with some stats." He raised a brow and nodded toward the phone. "Like, let them know Friedemann started to search your name and address six weeks ago. From Germany."

"How…why did you—that's none of your business." For a second Rachel's sight dimmed and she had to remind herself to breathe. That long? So it wasn't just a whim of Gervas's.

"Guilty. What do you have to hide, Rachel?"

"What? I beg your pardon." Rachel dragged out the words. "Thank you for your help, Scott. Don't let me keep you from your work."

"He must want something awfully badly to come all this

way." Scott completely ignored her hint that he was crossing the line of privacy. "You're sure it's nothing to do with the school? Maybe he needs some records. You must have dealt with him earlier."

"I said…" Rachel sat and picked up the letter opener. "Thank you." She stared at the pile of letters and plucked up the half-opened one, thought, and summoned a softer voice. "I appreciate your concern." She raised her eyes to his. "I'll do some checking in the files later. Maybe you're right. But there are plenty of proper channels he could have gone through."

Scott let his arms fall to his sides. "He seems desperate, and that usually makes people do crazy things." At her door, he looked back, expression gentle, hopeful, kind. "I want to help you."

Much as she thought she was ready for a relationship, her earlier outburst frightened her. What if she had lost the ability to trust anyone? Relationships needed trust. "Okay. I-I'm sorry for my tone. I appreciate your offer. I'll see if I can figure out what happened when he was here before."

He nodded and pulled the door shut behind him.

Rachel crossed her legs, hugged herself and admitted her true fear. Scott was smart. He could easily look through the campus files, searching for Professor Gervas Friedemann, PhD, and know exactly when he'd been on campus the first time with the international exchange program, and later lecture and book tours. Scott could look at the numerous publicity shots of him in various world-wide arenas, giving lectures, speaking. It wouldn't take him long to do the simple math. And if he met Maeve, the rest would fall into place. Maeve looked almost exactly like Rachel's sister, Ann, except for the color of her eyes. No member of the Michels family had eyes like that, though Maeve's were edged with the Michels blue around the iris.

Scott assumed Rachel would call the police and report Gervas for cyberstalking. She should. After she checked some files and got some specific dates. It wouldn't hurt to document Gervas's searches, either. *Okay, pull yourself together.* Get through the mail and anything else that looked urgent. Pull some past international exchange program files, talk to Dr. Carlson, Mendota College's president, about this…situation, and see if she wanted the police involved.

It might be a cop-out, but it was the best she could do now. Rachel pulled the top drawer of her desk as far as it would go and released the false panel in the back. The little maroon velvet bag was still there, tightly cinched. She glanced at the door. Silverfish-quick, she shook the object onto her palm. Years. It had been seventeen years since she'd looked at the gold band with the elaborate filigree, and large red and blue polished stones. A piece of antiquity, Gervas had said. Long before gems were faceted.

The buzz of her phone made her jump. She thrust the jewel back into its hiding place and slammed the drawer. Taking a breath, she answered her call.

3

Gervas stared at his computer screen. Gone. His post on the college website had vanished. What did that mean? He rested his chin on his knuckles. Perhaps he'd committed some illegal act when he typed his public request for information. The offer of money had been distasteful, but time was rushing past. He had not applied for any type of visa for this trip. The Visa Waiver Program gave him up to ninety days for travel and tourism. But staying in this hotel was not something he wanted to do for more than two weeks. If he couldn't find her or a lead on her current whereabouts by then, he'd find some other way.

He rose from the small wooden desk and pushed aside the room darkening curtains, as if looking for a police squad to appear in the parking lot, officers looking to charge him with a crime. Information was all he sought. Combing through public auctions and sales records, museum acquisitions had yielded nothing. Of course, one small artifact might not be worthy of mention, even if it was twenty-five hundred years old.

Since his attempt to reach the five persons with the name Michels as part of an e-mail address had failed, he needed to explore his options. Rachel might not live in the area anymore. Maybe she was dead, though he'd done a search through obituaries and death records. She probably married and no longer went by the name Michels.

If only that one name had worked. Maeve, the Irish warrior queen. Intoxicating. After the girl's first reply, the rudeness of the return questions, who was he and what was he doing contacting her on a business address, Gervas had been somewhat hopeful that she'd actually have some information. He soon realized by her response and avatar she was much too young to have known Rachel. Her reply was sarcastic and crude; no one with whom he wanted to associate.

Then why had he reached out again a few days later? An emergency vehicle siren made him look out the window again. Two police cars and an ambulance streaked past, out on the road known as the Beltway.

Options. He glanced at the fat telephone book again, knowing it was useless. The large numbers of Michels listed was only a small portion of those who actually answered to the name. *Rachel, Rachel, where are you?*

He should have started his hunt for her at the college, but memories and pride had held him back. Rachel would not have shared how they'd parted that last time; she was not that type of person, and he'd moved on from teaching the exchange semester in the United States. Foolish, to be fearful at his age and in this stage of the game. Gervas gathered his rental car keys and the room card and walked down the carpeted rose and green patterned staircase to the parking lot. Time to visit the campus. On the way, he allowed himself the luxury of dwelling on his memories. Of course he'd been captivated by her enthusiasm, their eagerness to discuss the topic of his seminar when she'd been a student. Socialism, the ever-flowing dynamics of Europe and the artificial cultural lines drawn. Wars…the ultimate freedom of reaching out into the universe and the discoveries that went with it had been put on hold due to economic crises, and the attempt to curtail disaster with the European Union.

Nothing would curtail disaster, of course. Gervas didn't need to hear from his brother, Manheim, a Federal Minister, to know that Germany would not be dragged into the abyss created by other nations who could not reign in their budgets. Portugal, Greece, Ireland. Rescue had been difficult. Manheim whispered of the coming vote to abandon the Union, even as new members like Estonia were adopting the euro. So closely divided were the members of the Bundestag that secession was possible. Manheim's vote was crucial. Abandoning the Union would certainly cause a ripple that would shred modern Europe, and the rest of the civilized world.

How would Gervas lecture on this topic? If the world knew how close the planet was each day to utter ruin, how would the people react? Rachel Michels had been one of the livelier student debaters, back in the mid-1980s, during his lectures. They'd met twice outside of the classroom, both times in public for coffee, but he would not have stopped himself if she'd offered more. His wife, Sylvie, was more discreet about her unhappiness in the marriage than he, and these "time outs" of his lengthy travel and teaching assignments was the only thing holding the fragile threads of their public life together. That, and the children.

Four years later, he'd returned on a book tour, arranged with the help of Rachel, who had not continued into academia, much to his disappointment. Having graduated, she'd stayed working at the college.

Gervas drove into the parking lot of the administration building at Mendota College. The maple trees had grown more stately in the intervening years. He climbed out of the American-made Japanese model car, anonymously gray, and closed the door. He toyed with the key, reluctant to move, caught up in memories. Two enormous lawn cutting machines glided along the grass. The breeze wafted that scent of mown field. Rachel had liked the aroma. Few people milled about the campus since the main academic year was in hiatus. That last time he'd been here, speaking and signing books in various places for that week, Rachel said she'd remained every bit as enthusiastic about current world affairs, as she escorted him to his readings. Before he'd left home, Sylvie had threatened to leave him again, and though he knew she never would for she liked his money too much, the whole battle had wearied him.

Rachel made up for it, revived him, and reminded him of everything he loved about the realm of studying and learning. There had been other affairs, naturally, but none matched her passion of the mind as well as body. Gervas studied the two-story building. It had been expanded since his last visit. Red brick facing hadn't added any charm. Was she inside, now?

He shook his head. Of course not, or her name would be in the directory. The three Rachels listed had not matched either age or picture, or job. Rachel would not be a mathematics professor, or a food service worker, or a dormitory advisor.

At the wall map inside the main entrance, Gervas paused. Student Services? General Administration? Office of the President? He should have called to make an appointment. After his gaff with the online student bulletin board, however, he'd be fortunate to walk into the building at all. General Administration, then, and an apology.

A young girl in a sleeveless, faded orange top with a haircut that appeared to have been done with children's safety scissors looked up at his entrance.

"Good morning, sir. What can I do for you?"

At least some manners still existed. "Good morning. My name is Gervas Friedemann, and I—"

"Ohhh, Professor Friedemann! I'm in Soc 312 this summer, and we're reading your book!" She squinted. "At least, I think it's you. I just love the class. Professor Lambert is always quoting your lectures. It's so cool."

Gervas waited to see if there would be more outbursts from the girl before attempting to speak again. "Thank you. I—"

"Of course it's you. How silly of me. I mean, how many Gervases are there. So that's how you pronounce it? You must be tired if you came all the way from Germany. So, how can I help you?"

This time he didn't pause. "I wish to locate a person who used to work on campus. Her name is, or was, Rachel Michels." He gave the blonde a casual study that made her smile a little cat smile. "Probably before you were born." The girl's smile dropped instantly.

"You must mean Mrs.—"

"Thank you, Melissa." At the new voice, the girl's eyes widened. Apparently she had not heard the approach of the heavy-set brassy-haired woman, either.

"Mrs. Atwater. The professor, here, he's," her voice lowered, "Gervas Friedemann, the famous author, by the way," then raised, "wants to make an appointment—"

"I'll take it from here. Thank you," Mrs. Atwater told the girl.

"'K. 'Bye, Professor." Melissa sauntered to the back of the office.

"What can I do for you, Professor Friedemann?"

Gervas transferred his gaze from the sight of Melissa standing on tiptoes in her sandals to the florid face of the woman who took her place. "Mrs. Atwater, I believe? It's been a number of years but I hope you can help me."

"It has been a long time, Professor. Welcome back."

Subtle currents of disapproval led Gervas to believe she

knew about his post on the student board. "I'm looking for Rachel Michels, and I hope you or someone can help me."

"I'm sorry. We have strict privacy rules. I can't help you regarding personal information. Is there something else I can do for you?"

Gervas slid his glance toward the orange-shirted Melissa who faced him. She bobbed her head slightly toward the hall.

"Miss Michels had been so helpful the last time I was here to set up a stop on my lecture tour. I just thought I'd stop and say hello while I was in town."

The Atwater woman remained stone-faced. Gervas dared not look anywhere else than her puffy expression and small dark eyes when her coral-colored lips parted. "Were you looking for another tour stop for a new book? Perhaps the Madison Area Arts Board would be able to—"

"Thank you, but no. Good day." Gervas allowed himself to smile, nodded at her and Melissa, turned and walked away, but not before spying a partially open office door with light spilling along the hallway. There was no name plate.

4

Rachel took a breath and wiped a bead of sweat gathered at her temple. Peggy had made it out to the front desk just in time. Rachel heard her, now, telling the summer girl who was part time manning the desk and part time filing that personal information was never, ever allowed out of the office.

"Just take a note, Melissa. Do not even hint that personal records may be available, not even for references. Those requests go to Human Resources. But all you need to do is tell the person you'll take a message. Understood?"

Rachel pictured Peggy's light blue eyes, an outer layer of iceberg blue when she was annoyed, targeting the girl.

"Yes, Mrs. Atwater. He seemed so nice, though. And he's a superstar, sort of. Why couldn't I tell him—"

"That's all, Melissa. I must ask you to protect Mrs. Michel's privacy under all circumstances. Both here and outside the office. We explained the situation when you were hired last month. Can you perform this job or not?"

In her office, Rachel felt Melissa's pain, saw in her mind the girl's round blue eyes and the fluttering of her lashes, the slump of her taut young shoulders. Peggy's lesson had to be driven home, though the damage was done.

"Yes, Mrs. Atwater. Of course I can. I'm sorry. I just didn't see the harm."

"Remember, even if you see him later outside of this environment, you cannot give out any information, personal or otherwise, about the staff. I advise you not to discuss the professor's visit with anyone. It's possible he may be stalking

Mrs. Michels, and you wouldn't want anything to happen to her, would you?"

"No, of course not. Is he really dangerous? He's so famous and all." The girl's voice had risen to a squeak. "Should we call the cops?"

Peggy's answering tone remained firm and level. "It's not necessary at this time. That will be all, Melissa, thank you."

A few seconds later Peggy returned to Rachel's office.

"He really came here," Rachel said. She cleared her throat. "That was close."

Peggy resumed her seat and picked up the legal pad with her notes.

"I probably should have just changed my name."

Peggy raised a brow.

"I know, I know. Maeve's all grown up now. I have nothing to be afraid of anymore."

"Why is he here, looking for you?"

"I suppose it was the last place he left me. He could have sent a letter."

"I think he did." Peggy harrumphed. "A rather expensive one at that." She leaned back and smirked at Rachel. "That post on the student board, looking for you? Are you really worth five hundred bucks? He must want something badly."

Rachel's heart raced and stumbled while she tried to keep an impassive expression even in front of her close friend. "I guess. I can't imagine what, though. It's not like we parted under happy terms."

"My ears are forever blistered," Peggy agreed.

Rachel reached across the desk to clasp Peggy's wrist briefly. "It's a good thing you weren't any harder on Melissa. She still might say something to Maeve."

Peggy's face hardened. "Hiring a friend of your daughter

might not have been the best idea."

"She's done a fine job so far. Have you had any complaints?"

"No." Peggy rose and paced a tight little circle behind her chair, her bulk making Rachel feel claustrophobic. "What if he does find out about Maeve? He could easily track her down at her job if Melissa can't control her gift of gab."

"Maybe it's time to stop thinking I have anything to hide. Did he look deranged, or dangerous? Like he'd hurt her? Or me?"

"No." Peggy sat again. "Just older. Still intense, but maybe not quite so much. She has his eyes. That's not something you can hide, even with contact lenses. I bet even Melissa could figure it out if she tried hard. You should talk to the police, tell them he's harassing you and get a restraining order."

"That would pretty much be an invitation to show him where we live, then, wouldn't it?"

At Peggy's squint, Rachel sighed. "I'll think about it. Thanks for rescuing me all those years ago. Us, I mean. I've been grateful for your friendship and loyalty. Always."

"I know. Now, where were we?"

At four thirty Rachel admitted her concentration was shot and took a load of paperwork home for the evening. The work she'd been doing for the past twenty-odd years had definitely lost its appeal, though the thought of looking for another job at her age nauseated her. She passed a parked city squad car, which made her think about involving the police in the bulletin board incident. Peggy had been the second person to mention calling them, after Scott. Gervas upset her, and though she'd been concerned when he contacted Maeve, she'd been more curious and, well, snide, not afraid. Proud, really, that she'd managed to hide so well for so long. Hiding in plain sight, waiting all these years for him to come crawling back… Who was she kidding?

It wasn't hiding if no one was looking, right?

By the time she pulled into her driveway ten minutes later, she'd talked herself out of calling the police, had almost made up her mind about whether or not to confront Gervas, and decided not to meet Scott on the capitol lawn for a concert if he ever asked.

She called Maeve. Since her daughter's friend had met Gervas, Rachel knew it was only a matter of time until the truth came out, and it was time for "the talk." A nice dinner and a heart-to-heart would clear the air. Then she'd hunt down Gervas, and neither of them would hopefully end up in jail.

A whispered hurry-up call with Maeve knocked Rachel off her high horse.

"Can't, Mom. Sorry. Don't know how long this client meeting will last. Call you later."

What else could Rachel do but acquiesce? "Okay, love you," she whispered back and closed her phone. She set it on the counter. Pacing, she ran her hand along a framed photo of her sister Ann on her wedding day. Were there any legal ramifications in store for her if Gervas knew he had an adult daughter? Ann's husband, Mark, was an attorney. Rachel picked up her keys and purse again and headed back on the road for a drive through the summer rush hour of Madison traffic to the west side and her sister's home.

Mark answered the door, though Rachel spied Ann in the hall. Ann had graduated to a cane last month as her strength and balance slowly righted after her stroke. Mark's hair had developed attractive gray wings, though he wasn't even forty. Love did that sometimes. Unfair for it to be debonair in men and aging in women.

"Rachel!" Mark and Ann said in unison.

Rachel refrained from rolling her eyes, but the smirk couldn't be controlled. "My favorite sister and brother-in-law," she said. "Are you very busy? I didn't call, I know."

Mark simply ushered her in and disappeared back toward the kitchen.

Ann took Rachel's arm and leaned on her some as they shuffled into the living room and sat on the couch.

"You're a little tired today," Rachel said. "I should have called."

"I'm tired every day, and of course you're always welcome." Ann had to work her mouth around the r's, as the stroke had affected control of her facial muscles. At least the drooling had stopped and her smile was even-sided again. "Physical therapy this afternoon, that's all. Grueling." Ann shuddered and smiled. She tilted her head and studied Rachel. "What's up?"

Ann was first-born, delicate-looking with a figure kept smooth through swimming, and hair professionally attended. Maybe their eyes and cheekbones were similar, and if Rachel could have afforded it, their hair would be the same texture and color. Looks were nothing to mourn, to regret. Ann wasn't any more perfect than Rachel, though it didn't feel that way. The deep heat of shame and fear and defiance of what she was about to reveal crept up the back of her neck and along her cheeks.

She ducked, closed her eyes, and took a deep breath. "I have to say this before I change my mind. Twenty-three years. It's finally happened." She opened her eyes and begged her sister to understand. "The past has, has…oh, it's so cliché, I can't believe it."

Rachel got up and paced to the mantel where family

photos scattered along the surface amongst bric-a-brac and a lighted string of miniature white bulbs. She rested her forehead on her hands in front of Maeve's graduation picture. Sweet, fruity potpourri stung her nostrils and she took hiccupy breaths, trying to stem the tears she'd never allowed in front of her sister. After a moment, Ann's hand touched Rachel's cheek.

"Mark brought us some tea. Come, sit and tell me about Maeve."

Rachel clasped Ann's frail hands after they resumed their seats and she'd had a sip—Maeve's blend of rosehips and wild mint. "How did you know it was about Maeve?"

Ann just smiled and glanced at the photo.

"Okay, yes, well. Mom was the only one who asked about…um, this is hard. I promised myself I'd never, ever talk about it. But, now. Ann, I'm scared, and I don't even know why."

"Do you want Mark here?"

"Yeah."

Mark came in response to his wife's quiet summons on a pager. He sat across from them. "Someone call for an attorney?"

Rachel choked out a short laugh and wiped her eyes which had begun to leak. "I don't know. Probably just family support."

"You've always had that," Ann said.

"I know. I haven't appreciated it out loud very much. But…you know."

Ann nodded back, patient, mellowed after her ordeal with her former husband Gene Ballard's family, her own health issues, and new marriage. They'd loved and fought as sisters, but had each other's back. Mark studied the dark empty fireplace, still, hands clasped around his knees, waiting.

"Okay, I'm ready to talk about Maeve's father." Rachel cringed as their eyes drilled her. The smile on Ann's face broadened slightly, as if she *knew* what was coming. Mark looked startled for a moment, the defense surprised by submission of a piece of suppressed evidence, then regained his composure.

Catching her reflection in the surface of the shiny coffee table, Rachel spoke to it, softly but clearly, as if she'd rehearsed the story, though she never had. "He was a professor from Germany with the exchange program, and returned later on a book tour. I loved him. I thought I did, anyway, or I never would—just a few…times, only one night it went too far. Anyway, now he's back. And I-I don't know what to do. He contacted Maeve through e-mail, just searching for people named Michels. Neither of them knows about the other. I'm pretty sure." She waited for an interruption, a barrage of questions. When they didn't come, she raised her face to look at Mark's compassion, then her sister's sorrow.

"I never told him," Rachel said. "You see, I thought…really thought, and it's so stupid, I know, classic naïve me, but I wanted, I wanted someone, the right someone, who was just mine." She bowed her head again. "He was so alive, you know, so passionate, and in so much private pain over his estranged wife and kids. At least I believed that. He said she constantly threatened divorce and disgrace for the family name, and he was always giving in to appease her, though she was unfaithful too. I thought that he'd finally let her go, you know, if he had someone like…me."

Ann's cool hands folded around hers. "It's okay, Rachel. I understand. Believe me, I do. We've never condemned you."

"I know." Rachel sniffed and looked at her. "Maybe it

would have easier if you had."

"What did you tell Mom?"

"What?"

"You said the only one who'd asked you about Maeve's father was Mom."

"Oh, right. I told her it was someone who tricked me but I'd never see again. She cried. I was mad."

Mark spoke up. "So, what can I do? Is he threatening or bothering you?"

"He's trying to," Rachel said and told them what Gervas had done so far. "I don't know if he has any parental rights, or can claim I defrauded him, or something. I don't know the terms. Mostly, I just want to keep Maeve…safe."

"But you said you never told him about her," Mark said. "Do you think he found out some other way? If he's made specific threats, you should go to the police to make a report on the cyberstalking. Are you sure this is about Maeve at all?"

"He hasn't made any specific threats." Rachel looked briefly at her folded hands. "I just don't want him around. I don't know what he wants, really. We have no money, unless he thinks you can pay him off."

"Us?" Mark lifted an eyebrow. "We're more than comfortable, but not blackmail-worthy."

Rachel let a grim twist cross her mouth. "I understand. Just pulling at straws here. I've worked so hard all her life to protect my daughter from him."

"Who?" Ann said. "Is he some criminal?"

Rachel grinned, realizing she had yet to say his name. "Gervas Friedemann."

Mark whistled. Of all people, he would recognize the name. "The author of *Reframing World Social Order*?"

"Among others."

"Somebody famous, I assume." Ann used her dry voice. "Only the brightest and best could be the father of my niece."

"Wow, his work has been so hot, especially now with all the trouble in the European Union and economic problems," Mark said. "He's been lecturing. So, is he here for another book tour or something?"

Rachel shook her head. "I haven't heard. Frankly, I haven't even been paying that much attention to the news this summer. Just headlines. Anyway, how can I keep my baby safe?"

Mark mirrored her head shake. "That's the problem, Rachel. She's not a baby. Not even a minor. There's nothing you or anyone can do unless you can prove she's in physical danger, and then the authorities can only issue an injunction if she requests one."

"She can't know about him!" Rachel leaned back and closed her eyes, allowing the panic to wash over her until she trembled.

"Why?" Ann asked. "You said you didn't know what you were afraid of. Do you know now? What makes you think he would hurt her?"

"Or you?" Mark put in.

"Nothing," Rachel whispered. "It's just me, afraid of losing…control. She's all I have—all that's just mine."

<>

When Rachel got home as the city lights winked on at dusk, the blinking answering machine caught her attention. She'd left the cell phone on the counter, typical. Somehow she knew. She trembled when she pressed the button and listened to Maeve say she wouldn't be coming that night. She was going out with her friend Melissa, and would call tomorrow.

Too late, too late, too late beat in time to her pulse.

- 5 -

Three days before Gervas was to fly home, he received a curious e-mail. He sat at the desk in the hotel room attempting to put the outline for his latest book in order when the new mail alert popped open.

"If you are still available, I would like to meet you. I warn you, however, that I can't give you any information about Rachel Michels."

Signed M. Michels.

Maeve, the girl who'd responded with such passionate defense to his earlier blind messages. No apology for her earlier rudeness. Still. "When and where?"

"Flagpole in front of the capitol, 6:15 tonight. I'll carry a copy of *Reframing.*"

He chuckled but resisted responding, "I'll bring my gold pen."

So, now he stood in front of the state capitol building, acting like a German tourist in his—how did they put it?—golden years, waiting to meet what would hopefully be a young woman for…he didn't know. The worst case scenario? He'd gotten himself involved in some sort of American sting operation to find sex offenders, and a sentence to Guantanamo Bay with the terrorists. Ah, the imagination of a writer. He should turn to fiction.

Gervas had struggled over what to wear to this—what?—set up. The warmth of the day precluded his preference for a jacket. He did not expect to do anything than perhaps have a drink if she wanted to move from this public spot. So busy, it was, with crazy people rushing home from their jobs, or other tourists snapping photographs and jabbering away. He heard at least six different languages, Japanese and Chinese, even Russian, and of all things, Swahili. He turned his face aside when a group of other Germans strolled in front of him, led by a tour guide explaining the close ties between Wisconsin and Germany, as so many of their people had immigrated during the mid-nineteenth century.

At least he had the good sense not to wear sandals. He carried nothing, though had shoved a small notebook and pen in his shirt pocket, a short-sleeved one, he wore with his tie. He looked at his watch and tried to maintain an amiable expression. Gervas had arrived early and now she was late. He planted his feet and lifted his face to watch the US flag flutter weakly.

Despite all the commotion of people around him, he sensed her presence at his right shoulder. Gervas studied her face, eyes hidden by dark sunglasses, before noting a copy of his book cradled loosely in her hands. A black leather bag was slung over her left shoulder. Her navy knit dress hung in graceful folds about her slim figure, which stopped just below his 178 centimeters. Back to her unsmiling face, surrounded by shoulder-length straight dark hair. He inclined his head. "Miss Michels? I am Professor Doctor Friedemann."

He waited, allowing her to study him, then looked her in the eye. At least, he assumed so, since he couldn't see behind the black-tinted lenses.

Her hands tightened around the book. "Professor… Doctor…"

"Professor."

"You were sending messages, contacting anyone with the last name of Michels, right? Not just me?"

"Correct." He refrained from repeating the content of his request. She knew very well what he wanted, as he'd been clear in his messages, and he suspected she could help him, which meant staying in the States longer. He made a mental note to change his flight when he returned to the hotel.

"You knew m-Rachel Michels a long time ago?"

"Yes."

Maeve raised the book to her chest, hugged it.

Sympathy warmed Gervas. He wanted to assure this young woman that he meant no harm, but he didn't understand the nature of her distress. He scanned the vicinity. A couple had vacated a nearby bench and he gestured toward it. "Shall we sit?" She nodded and followed him. When perhaps thirty seconds passed, he said, "Has something happened to Rachel?"

The girl shook her head. "No, no, nothing like that. I just didn't know what to expect. My friend Melissa said she'd met you. Gushed about it, actually."

The helpful desk girl from the college. Yes, but such a coincidence was hard to understand. "You and she are friends?" he replied in his best active listening voice.

"She's taking a class." Maeve held out the book she carried. "I'm not sure why she…never mind. Anyway, when I said that was strange because I had an e-mail from you, she told me…told me…"

Gervas started to tune out, the suffocation of disappointment sighing along his veins. Just another young person, how did they call it? Groupie.

"I looked for your schedule online, and I didn't see any tours, and new books, any lectures, but there was nothing listed. Are you sick, dying, or something? Is that why you're here, looking up people? To make amends, or something?"

A reporter! He stood, breathing deeply now in anger and frustration. "My public relations firm schedules interviews. I have nothing to say other than I am in perfect health." He turned and strode away.

<>

The hotel room was too small that evening to contain Gervas's anxiety. Katrine's physician had left a message that he'd begun the paperwork to enroll her in the medical study at University Hospital. Sylvie, characteristically, was being uncooperative releasing enough funds from the trust, but Max, her son, assured Gervas he would take care of the matter. Strange to think of the boy he'd raised to a man had not been a product of his genes. At thirty, Max had done well so far, becoming an engineer, and on the point of asking his sweetheart to marry him. Sylvie needed to be shut away soon, for she was becoming a danger not only to herself. So far her family had shielded her from prying public eyes. Gervas, an ex-husband, had no rights in the say of her care, though he would never allow her illness to affect Katrine's well-being. He had to trust Max.

The call from his brother Manheim fenced Gervas at the edge of a steep cliff. With the time difference, Gervas had a seven-hour window into the future. It was two o'clock in the morning at home.

He answered the buzz of his cell phone. "You are up late, Manheim."

"The discussions are heated, as you can imagine. Two dozen people holding the fate of the world in our hands. Gervas, the decision weighs me down. Today we had to consider a vote of no confidence in the Chancellor."

His brother's sigh vibrated from across the world. "Does the vote have merit?"

"I don't know. Even the president has contacted some of the ministers."

Germany's Federal President was something more than a figurehead, something less than an autocrat, though held the power to dismiss the Cabinet and even the Chancellor. Gervas knew better than to ask Manheim's position in the matter.

"At least we delay dissolution from the European Union," Manheim said. "The euro continues to downgrade. I don't know what's to become of the other member nations who will find it difficult to remain economically viable, even if Germany stays. We cannot bail out everyone."

"We are no longer feudal lords," Gervas muttered. "Though sometimes I wonder."

"*He* called again. The office this time, though he was careful. Crafty in his choice of words."

Gervas paced the small room, wishing for the first time in decades he could smoke. He pushed the curtains aside, wandered onto the small balcony, and looked down at the small picturesque lake. Mendota, like the college. "I thought I had a lead today," he said at last. "I don't think it will play out."

"I need to tell him something to appease him."

Regenbogen, the lone descendant of the family who'd formerly lived adjacent to them, wanted more than the return of a valuable piece of history given in haste for safekeeping one night in 1938. He wanted revenge, subliminally couched in words of justice for his family. In reality, justice for the Jews, not something Gervas was prepared to deal with. The Friedemanns could not pay for the death of not just their neighbors, but for all the horrifying acts of Nazi Germany. Except the Friedemanns had sat out the war in Canada—along with their own treasures, and those of the Regenbogens.

After the war and the Friedemanns' return to their home,

no one came back to the estate next to them. Through his few remaining years, Gervas's father took care of their neighbor's valuables. Gervas and Manheim learned of them from their mother who blithely decided fifteen years after Father's death that since no one had claimed them, they might as well be enjoyed. Mother had always appreciated a fine show of sparkle at the lost and good causes she attempted to rectify through post-war gala fundraisers and the resulting newspaper photos. So long ago.

"Gervas, what should we do?" Manheim's voice cracked over the phone.

We? What should we do? "What was his message?"

Seventy years later, a Regenbogen had come forth to claim the property and the treasures. Max returned the jewelry Gervas had given Sylvie upon their marriage. But one piece was missing, part of a documented set, and for this, Regenbogen would publically discredit Manheim and force his resignation from the Cabinet.

"He knows of the precarious nature of the discussion of the Union, though I do not believe he heard of the no confidence vote. That might buy us some time. He has contacted the Louvre for a display in the new year. He expects to meet in August. We have until the fifteenth."

Gervas hitched a breath and clutched the wrought iron railing surrounding the balcony. So soon. "I will continue my efforts, Manheim. Perhaps we can find some replacement."

Manheim replied to his ridiculous comment with a soft click.

They both knew there was no replacement.

6

"I can't do that!"

Rachel stood at the front door of her home, watching her daughter walk up the brick path, phone glued to her ear, wailing into it. She must have had a meeting today, and dressed more formally than usual in a pretty dark blue dress Rachel had never seen before.

Maeve stopped at the lamppost, waved, and pointed to the phone.

Rachel nodded and backed away from the glass door. A late-for-Midwesterners supper, cold pesto salad and drinks, her daughter's favorite cheese, a veggie Jack, and crackers, waited on trays in front of the leather sofa. Their favorite TV program was due to come on in ten minutes at seven o'clock, a reality thing they hooted over and ragged on. It kept them bonded and Rachel was grateful Maeve made the time.

The black-cased laptop kept her girl's place warm. Rachel sat next to it, toying with the strap. Scott had finished debugging the other day, and Rachel told her right away, but Maeve had put off picking it up. Something important must have been going on to cause the tension in her voice, and the delay over reclaiming her precious work computer.

Scott had brought it up to her office, along with a daisy and an invitation for supper on Saturday. Rachel had said yes, wishing she didn't feel so jittery about it, wishing she didn't think his smile seemed feral. She was almost ready to come out of the quicksand she'd so carefully stood in for the past twenty-five years, not moving a muscle so it wouldn't suck her under.

Was Scott the one who could pull her free?

The front door slammed, making her jump.

"Sorry, Mom. Didn't mean to scare you. Lost? Daydreaming?"

Rachel managed a weak grin. The TV program didn't take away as much of her tension as usual as they watched young women scheme their way into a fake marriage proposal.

During a commercial, she refilled their glasses. When she returned, Maeve was texting furiously but put the phone away when Rachel came close.

"Work? By the way, you look really nice today. Must have had an important meeting." Rachel grimaced inwardly, hoping she hadn't come off too helicopter-mom.

"Work? Oh, right. Yeah, I had an important meeting."

"You must have missed your computer."

"Right, yes, I did." Maeve stared at the case near her feet.

Rachel's heart sank. "Something wrong?"

"Wrong? At work? Oh, no, nothing like that. Look, it's back on. What do you think that bikini girl will do this time?" Maeve wheezed out a laugh and slumped against the sofa, drew her legs up under her, and focused on the screen.

Grabbing the remote as soon as the last scene faded to commercial, Rachel leaned toward her daughter. "So, do you want to talk about it?"

"It, Mom?" Maeve pursed her mouth and folded her arms. "I'm not having trouble on the playground."

The edge of the remote bit into Rachel's palm as she tried to keep her expression concerned but not hyper-alert. She didn't think there were drugs involved this time. At least, she prayed not. "I'm here for you. You know that."

Maeve's eyebrows smoothed out from the wrinkles she'd made with her frown. "I know. You and Aunt Ann."

No jealousy, Rachel repeated to herself. She forced her lungs to keep emptying and filling at an even rate. "I'm glad you have her."

Maeve scooted sideways and laid her head on Rachel's shoulder. "And you. You put up with a lot from me. I'm sorry you're worried, but there's no need. I'm just trying to track someone down. That's all. A…a colleague."

Rachel wrapped an arm around her daughter and drew her closer, breathing in the scent of her hair and the aroma of the stress of the day. Now that Maeve had moved out, Rachel would never belittle empty nest syndrome again. The tumultuous college years that had forced them apart physically when Ann agreed to let Maeve stay at her house were over. Rachel had been ready to kick her troubled daughter out and now refused to begrudge her sister's love. After all, who could love Maeve any better? She cleared her throat. "Can I help?"

She didn't miss the little shudder that ran across Maeve's shoulders and wished the clock could turn back twenty years.

"Maybe sometime, but not now." Maeve sat up and flipped her hair over her shoulders. "I should get going. I've got work."

Rachel wouldn't press her to stay overnight as she often did. Maeve stopped mid-reach of the laptop bag. "Oh, that guy from IT fixed this, right? What's his name again, Scooter?"

Laughing at her daughter's unsubtle hint and wicked grin, Rachel curled back into the sofa cushions. "Scott."

"Do you have something to tell me?"

"Maybe." Rachel looked at the black screen of the television, nerveless at the thought of her upcoming date.

"Mom?"

Resetting a smile, Rachel hugged herself and studied her daughter's concerned expression.

"It's all right, Mom, you know. You can date if you want to, now that we're all grown up."

"Dating, hmpf. I think I'm too old."

"I'll help you." Maeve clasped Rachel's wrist with chilled fingers.

"Ooh! Are you cold?" Rachel stood. "Let me get you a sweater."

Maeve matched her shift to standing. "Nope, just sitting still too long. It's still eighty degrees out there, I bet. And don't change the subject. Melissa said he brought you flowers."

"One flower. A daisy."

"Hmm." Maeve eyed her, smirking. "Innocence."

"Excuse me?" Rachel widened her eyes and snorted.

"That's what it means in the language of flowers. A daisy represents innocence."

Rachel paced around the coffee table and picked up their plates and glasses. Maeve grabbed crumpled napkins and a stray spoon and followed her to the kitchen. "So, do you like him?"

"I don't really know him."

"But you're going out with him. Again."

Sending a stern none-of-your-beeswax look didn't stem her daughter's sassy expression. Rachel set the plates in the sink and turned, gripping the edge of the counter behind her. "All right, what do you mean?"

"Melissa said you got back late from lunch the other day, and that Scott was with you."

"You and Melissa must have had quite the night out." Rachel narrowed her eyes. "I might have to have another conversation with her."

At Maeve's gaping response, she laughed, though did keep in mind that she'd have to watch herself. Maeve's friend hadn't done anything to merit a reprimand, but it was good to know what things were being said outside the office. Apparently Gervas's impromptu visit was still under the table. "So we had lunch. I wanted to thank him for taking care of your computer."

"Shouldn't I be the one doing the thanking?" Maeve raised a brow.

Rachel moved past her, out of the confines of her galley kitchen, back into the living room. "I was the one doing the asking for help, that's all."

They stood by the sofa again, in silence, for which Rachel was thankful. Judging by the heat on her neck and face, she must have looked like she'd been caught red-handed holding the lid to the cookie jar. *Mercy, Daughter.*

Her silent plea worked. "I love you, Mom." Maeve merely slung her purse over her shoulder and grabbed the computer. "So, it's all fixed?"

"What?"

"The computer? The e-mail?" Maeve held the laptop bag by the handle, though her face had paled and her lips trembled.

"Yes." Rachel pulled her into a hug, wanting to protect her from everything nasty in the world. "That guy won't be bothering you anymore. I promise."

7

Gervas stood at the machine in the airport in Madison, securing his boarding pass for his flight home. He was bone weary, defeated, and desperately running scenarios through his mind to come up with some placation for Regenbogen. Either way, the Friedemann family name was smirched—the truth was often uglier than any lie. If Gervas admitted the ring had been stolen years ago on a teaching exchange, and had never filed a report with the authorities over such a priceless item, more questions would come. Yes, yes, the other pieces were there, thanks to Max. But the ring—one of two with different gems—completed the set since it matched the stones in the necklace and bracelet. The priceless set of ancient Etruscan jewelry had been well-documented during its years on loan to various museums around the world. It was important enough that its disappearance during World War II had been noted, but with all the valuable art stolen and lost or destroyed by the Nazis, no unusual effort had gone into tracing it.

Only old Eli Regenbogen and the Friedemanns knew the real story.

Gervas printed the pass and then wandered to the coffee counter where he bought a cup of an aromatic Peruvian blend. One thing about Americans—they occasionally got the coffee right. He passed up the muffins and pastries. Too much fat and too sweet. Not ready to sit, he stood idly, leaning over an open fold of the *Capital Times*, when he felt her presence.

"Doctor—Professor Frie-Friedemann. Please, there's something I need to ask you."

"Miss Michels, I have nothing to tell you. I'm on my way home. You can call my agent if you need more information for your story."

He refused to give her the courtesy of looking at her, though he heard the nervous shuffle of her sandaled feet, the clutching, shifting of her handbag. From the corner of his eye he noted a bright patterned short skirt and yellow blouse.

"Story? Oh. I'm not working on anything like that. Please. It took me a couple of days to track you down again, and I can't…I just need to know, all right?"

Gervas sighed and rubbed his forehead. He slung his carry-on bag onto a bench and faced her. She wore those large sunglasses even inside the building. No cane, so she must not be blind. "Yes, yes." He waved his arm. "I am your captive audience, apparently. What must you know that only I can tell you?"

As she slowly reached with both hands for the sunglasses, he had that odd sense of real time slowing. He tensed, preparing himself for the scar, or other deformity, hidden behind them.

Maeve pulled the glasses from her face.

Contacts could have lied, but he detected no sheen of unnatural lenses. Even if it wasn't for the color—the same as his but for the outer ring of blue—the odd little peaks of hair along her temples, the subtle point of the bow of her upper lip that came into focus, all these things added up. Now he saw Katrine's delicate oval-shaped ears close to this girl's head, his mother's painted porcelain coloring, yet Rachel there, and not there, in her cheekbones and nose.

Rachel, Rachel, what have we done?

Her lips were moving, confirming the truth he already guessed subconsciously. "…my mother."

He looked down at the boarding pass he still clutched with numb fingers. "Let me cancel this."

<>

They didn't speak as Maeve drove them away from the airport. By focusing on the short list of things he'd have to do, Gervas kept himself in check. He'd had affairs in the past, but no reported children—unlike Sylvie who'd had Max. Gervas still had a paternity test done, despite the failed match with Katrine's transfusion, which confirmed Sylvie's claim. But now. This daughter. Could there have been others? He glanced at Maeve, skillfully negotiating the traffic—this daughter he'd helped create. She looked healthy, cultured. There were empty holes in her earlobes. Her fingernails were of medium-length, unvarnished. No rings. Her mouth pursed in concentration.

She turned the car into a park on the lake. He didn't know which lake this was—Mendota or Monona. They sat in the car with the engine quieted, and stared out of the front windshield at the late afternoon sun sparkling on the wave crests. She said she had questions—a question. He'd wait until she spoke first since he wasn't sure of his voice yet. The feeling had returned to his hands, the shock wearing off. He should be ashamed instead of pleased; this he knew, but this little nod to his virility boosted his pride. Rachel… He almost missed Maeve's low-voiced comment.

"She never told you, did she?"

Gervas didn't consider dissembling. "No, but to be fair, neither did I ask. We did not part well."

Maeve leaned her elbow on the steering wheel and looked at him. "I don't understand how she could have… I mean, she's always been so, so…rigid. About wrong and right. Aunt Ann said she wasn't ever wild, even when they were kids. Did you…was she…"

The girl's cheeks flushed crimson and she faced front again, gripping the wheel tightly in both hands. He had to think about the purpose of her questions, and truthfully, struggle somewhat to recall the events that led up to his and Rachel's intimate encounter. He'd never had to face himself like that, and it hurt, both that he couldn't remember everything about Rachel, and that he could remember everything he felt. Regret, first—on so many levels. That Rachel misunderstood his intent, but also that she had the power to make him want to leave Sylvie, which he hadn't done. That Rachel had never been with another and he had taken something precious from her. That she had been so deeply emotionally wounded when he wouldn't change his scheduled return to Freiburg. That he had not missed the ring until somewhere over the Atlantic, woken from sleep, its familiar weight gone from his hand which, in the turmoil of leave-taking, he'd not noticed. Assured by a call to campus housing that no one had turned in a ring, he knew that Rachel, who'd admired and pried its story from him, had taken it. Could he begrudge her the trophy? Reclaiming it meant more promises, more lies, more effort than he could afford, with Katrine showing signs of a mysterious illness.

"I did not force Rachel," he finally said. He hoped their daughter would understand. A mutual passion. Mutual but unequal.

He missed another of Maeve's questions. "Hmm? I'm sorry?"

"Did you love her?"

"Yes." Still, he dared not ask where Rachel was. If she was still alive.

"You must have done something to make her not want to tell you about, about, the…the baby. About me."

Oh, yes. Yes he had. This innocent young woman seemed

far removed from the way adults treated each other. Gervas fiddled with the strap of the bag at his feet. At least she'd caught him before he'd checked the rest of his luggage. It now lay in the trunk of her vehicle. He twitched his mouth. He couldn't imagine what Rachel would want him to say.

"You really didn't know?" Her soft voice reminded him he hadn't responded.

He turned to her, wanted to touch her hand, but refrained. Not yet. First, build trust. Earn it. "I may be a cad, but I would never abandon a child. I would have been in your life somehow, some way. Of this I must reassure you a thousand times over."

Maeve cocked her head so the hair fell across her cheek.

Gervas had a flashback, seeing Rachel look at him like that during a happy moment, and he smiled. "We cannot bring back the past, nor do we want to live in it," he said. "But we can make decisions about the present. Perhaps the future. I would be honored to have the opportunity to get to know you now."

Her eyes became shadowed, her expression pinched. She fingered her earlobe and took a stuttered breath. Gervas's heart melted even more. What had he missed? Did she suffer from a malady such as Katrine's? He had yet to know a single detail about her life, yet vowed he would do anything he could for her.

"Would you like to know anything about me?" he asked, trying to put her at ease. He grinned when she faced him. "Not just public information." He waved a hand at a picnic table.

"Okay."

She followed him the short distance to the table where they settled across from one another. Sunlight, dappled through maples and birches, made her hair glisten and her skin translucent in places it touched. The air was thick, promising rising storms later, though cloudless now. Vegetation from the lake gave off a sweet, rotty odor. He watched a man unload a motorboat while his small son skipped around, eager to turn the crank which allowed the craft to slide alongside the dock. He'd never taken Max on such a ride, never learned how to operate a motorboat.

"Are you married now?" Maeve asked.

He got the feeling she knew the answer to that, though his last divorce had been fairly quiet. A test question. "No. Julianne and I divorced fifteen years ago." Gervas looked her in the eye. "She was my second wife, for a short time. We had no children, and I have not married again."

"Your first wife? You were married when, when you and Mom…um."

The unusual flash of shame caught him by surprise. "Yes."

"Didn't you love her? Your first wife?"

Ah, child. "Sylvie and I had always expected to marry someday, from the time we were in the nursery. No, it wasn't an arranged marriage and we were not forced into a wedding." He shrugged and watched the man on the dock buckle the little boy into a blue life preserver. "It suited us, and it kept the family lineage intact, as well as our bank accounts."

"You're rich?"

Gervas laughed at her wide eyes. She'd left the sunglasses off when they sat in the shade of the tree. He studied the blue around her honey irises. "It is old money, well-enough managed, I suppose, though the economy these days…" He shrugged again. "How do you put it? The falling money rates did serious damage."

Maeve waved at a pesky insect buzzing her nose. "You're famous, too, I guess. With the books and lectures and interviews."

"I guess. Much noise, little profit."

"Do you have children from your—other marriage?"

Gervas tried to keep his affable face in place but felt it slide.

Maeve must have picked up on his distress. She reached out first, to touch the back of his hand. "I'm sorry. You seem to be sad. You don't have to talk about it."

He shook his head and covered her hand with his other one. Her hands were smooth but cold. "My daughter, Katrine. I can see a little of her stamped in your features. A son, Max. He's an engineer and soon to be engaged." No need to drag this girl into family issues.

"You must be happy about that. How old is your daughter?"

"Twenty-seven."

Of course she did the calculation in her head; anyone would have known by looking at the way she glanced down, slightly unfocused. "She was five, then."

"Yes, yes. Her mother had begun to show signs of dementia by then. Sylvie has become unstable."

"Maybe I understand a little better," Maeve said softly. "Did my mother know?"

"No, it was a private family matter."

"I think she might have understood."

Gervas squeezed her hand and let go. He leaned back. "And now? Would she understand now?"

- 8 -

On Saturday afternoon, four hours before her dinner with Scott, Rachel stood in front of her open closet, rifling through her dresses. Maybe she should wear slacks, though lately the size of her derriere had been giving her grief. She needed to exercise more, she knew it.

Start with footwear. Her favorite sandals always gave her confidence. Tarnished silver color, the Bjorns had been on deep discount and were classy enough to go nearly everywhere. She'd never been much a clothes snob, but lately, since she no longer had to support a collegiate daughter, money was not as tight.

Dress, pantsuit? Scott hadn't mentioned a specific place he was taking her. Better wear something fairly neutral. Nice earrings always worked to spiff up anything.

An hour later she'd dithered over four outfits, taken them out one by one, worn one around the house in the sandals, then took it off and hung it back up. Maeve hadn't answered her phone. Who else should she try? Peggy. Mom. Ann. The list of fashion advisors was short.

Peggy's phone went to voicemail. Calling Mom just didn't feel right. Rachel wasn't sure what she'd say, how serious to make this date sound, after she admitted it was a date.

Ann answered on the fourth ring. By the time Rachel had sputtered out date, Scott, clothes, and started sniveling, Ann said she was on her way and hung up. Rachel flopped backward onto her bedspread and waited.

Rachel heard the kitchen door open. Her sister had

arrived. Mark wasn't crazy about her driving around Madison alone, but Ann was careful and stayed away from the busiest of streets. Rachel lifted herself to her elbows and grinned at the sight of her older sister leaning on the jamb of her bedroom door. She brought a fanciful cane painted with leaves around tree bark, one of a collection she used with outward good grace, but Rachel knew she hated. At least she could still swim, something she'd always done for exercise and enjoyed.

Ann came into the room, raising one eyebrow. "There's no pile of clothes."

Rachel raised herself to her elbow. "I put them back."

"And you don't know where he's taking you?"

"Nope."

"How long until he picks you up?"

Rachel squinted at the clock. "Two hours and forty-five minutes."

Ann's smile warmed to brilliant and she beckoned. "Time to shop."

An hour later, Rachel had said no to the nice young sales girls in two different stores. One had held up a broom skirt that stopped above her flabby knees, and layers of tank tops. She'd also said no thanks to the clerk who showed her a high-collared, long-sleeved retaliatory old-maid outfit. Then Ann stared at a window across the wide aisle of the mall. Rachel followed her sister's halting but determined gait through clumps of teens and families to a store with modest colored, well-designed and flowing clothing. And lots of scarves and gold jewelry, something Ann loved. But that number on the mannequin, the one with loose slacks buttoned at the ankles, would go with her sandals. Silky gray the slacks were, and with a fuchsia-colored top that hid the worst damage of a desk job. Rachel was pleased. Ann fussed with the angled collar of the blouse and suggested some clunky earrings which Rachel declined. Everything else worked and Rachel breathed a sigh of relief.

When they passed a Chinese restaurant on the way out Ann bit her lips and covered her mouth. "You're okay?" Rachel asked, realizing how long they'd been out. "Not overdoing it? I'm sorry, I shouldn't have—"

"Don't be ridiculous. I'm always here for you." Ann took a long shallow breath. "Except when I'm not." She frowned and toyed with the clasp on her handbag with her good hand. "I've just been feeling a little weird lately. Don't say anything, okay? To anyone?"

Rachel frowned and opened her mouth.

"Not even that sweetie pie daughter of yours." Ann plunged on. "She's been a God-send for sure. We couldn't have gotten to this point in my recovery without her."

"It's been good for her, learning those things she never wanted to bother with at home." Rachel ticked them off on her fingers. "Laundry, cooking, cleaning."

Ann laughed. "It's just easier to see how necessary chores are from someone other than your mother." She flipped open her watch pendant necklace. "Just enough time for a bubble bath."

<>

Rachel paced in front of her house, fifteen minutes before Scott said he'd come. Despite her best efforts, she couldn't rid her thoughts of the last time she'd been involved with a man. She had no business comparing them, either, as they were nothing alike. Not in age, nationality. Looks. She stopped pacing, folded her arms, and tapped her sandal on the pavement. Maybe they had some similarity in passion for work. But not in the same way. Gervas had an amazing grasp on the state of world cultures, economies. He'd been a persuasive lecturer, debater, speaker. Rachel snorted. A little too persuasive. At least she'd exacted revenge, stealing something from him the way he had from her.

Funny, she never would have pegged herself as a vengeful person.

Scott liked his work with machines, communication systems. Willing to do a favor at the drop of a hat. Concerned for both her and her daughter's well-being and safety.

She let her arms drop to her sides and took a firmer grip on her purse when Scott brought his red Fiat to a stop in her short driveway. The top was down, of course. Marty Westman from next door, out watering his flowers and new trees, gave a curious nod and wave.

Boring Rachel Michels fed the neighborhood gossip with a juicy tidbit. Great. She greeted her date, who'd gotten out of the car. Scott's grin asked whether or not he should wave too, and she shook her head at him with a mini frown when he opened the door for her.

"Top up or down?" he asked with one brow raised and a mock leer when he reached for the ignition. At least she hoped it was mock.

"Down's fine."

As he came to the first stop sign, she said, "I wasn't sure what you had in mind for a restaurant." He was dressed business casual and Rachel relaxed a bit.

He named a place out in the country near Mount Horeb which Rachel had heard about. "Okay with you?"

"Sure. Thanks."

Toward the end of the entrée course, the subject of Gervas and his quest came up.

"What did the police say about his harassment?" Scott

asked casually, while picking up his coffee cup and bringing it to his lips.

Rachel stiffened and tried to force her shoulders to relax. She wiggled in the chair and dropped the rosy colored linen napkin from her lap to the floor. Searching for it and picking it up gave her some breathing room, though she wouldn't use the napkin again, and ended up putting it on the seat of an empty place at their table. "Thanks for your concern, Scott. I'm grateful for what you've done to help Maeve and me. When I went over the facts in my mind, it seemed like overkill to report him to the police."

"Overkill?"

"Well, he hasn't done anything—"

"Rachel, he's cyberstalking your daughter and actually offered money—a large sum—for information about you."

"But you took care of the messages, right? Blocked them?" Protecting Maeve was the most important issue for her now. Not these confusing feelings of wanting to end the loneliness, now that Maeve was finally in a house of her own.

Scott set his lips in a straight line. The good thing about being independent, Rachel thought as she tossed back the rest of the water in her goblet, was that she didn't have to put up with adult sulks or temper tantrums. And she wasn't about to explain herself to this stranger.

The waiter glided to their table, dessert menus in hand. "We have—"

"Oh, I couldn't," Rachel cut in. She smiled at the young man. "Thank you anyway. Could we please have the check?"

He nodded, grabbed their plates and moved away.

"You know the man, don't you?" Scott's low voice wasn't a surprise, and Rachel was glad he'd asked her in public. She sighed, knowing he wasn't referring to the waiter. The ride home was bound to be long.

"I remember the professor's last visit to campus."

Scott gave a fake little groan and slight smile. "Oh, don't tell me you were one of his groupies."

The waiter slid the check in front of Scott and handled the transaction at the table. Scott stood, pulled back her chair, and kept his hand at her back as they wound through the tables to the exit. Warmth and pressure should have been comforting, if they had come from someone she loved. Now, Scott's hand guiding her seemed controlling and Rachel had to force herself not to squirm away.

What had she been thinking, wanting to date? Meeting someone like this, having to make small talk with strangers, then having to decide how personal to get. She just wasn't the dating type and wished she'd brought her own car instead, so she could leave.

"Do you want me to pull up?" Scott asked when they stood outside.

Twilight had fallen. Rachel swatted a mosquito. "No, that's okay." They walked in silence to his car. Scott pulled out of the parking lot with a spray of gravel. He drove for several minutes, taking the winding, tree-lined road faster than Rachel was comfortable with, but she didn't say anything.

After the first four-way stop, Scott slowed down. He still clutched the steering wheel in both hands, but glanced in her direction. "I apologize for getting too personal. Of course it's none of my business."

Rachel bit her lip as she considered what to say. "In a way, it is. I invited you into my problem when I asked if you could block him from my daughter's computer, and when I asked you for help with the campus online bulletin board. And I appreciate your concern." She pulled her hands away from each other, where she'd been folding them in nervous twists. She gripped the shoulder belt. "I did know him, yes, though it was so long ago. And I wasn't exactly a groupie. I was doing my job."

Scott flexed his hands on the wheel, making the leather squeak. He whistled in one quick breath after another through his nose until he sighed. They were walking a boggy line, unsettled, unsure of where to go from here. Rachel decided to give him another chance instead of telling him when they got home that she wasn't sure a relationship outside of work was something she could do. He'd earned favor with his concern, which didn't seem to be coming from some kind of crazed jealousy factor. She didn't want to annoy him, either. Now she understood more than ever the trickiness of dating coworkers.

"I'm worried about your safety," he finally said.

"Thank you. I am grateful." Rachel knew what she would do before Scott stopped the car in her driveway and came around to walk her to the door. She'd not left the outside light on as it drew insects she didn't want to gather on her door. She led him to the side door off the kitchen and unlocked it. He didn't try to kiss her, though Rachel admitted she would have let him. Anything to erase the subtle presence of Gervas, who seemed to invade her personal space as if he was physically here.

"Please keep me in the loop," was all Scott said.

She let out her held breath. "Good night." She closed the door but didn't turn the lock until he was in his car. That would have been rude, and Rachel wasn't a rude person. Though she was about to be. She turned away from the door, kicked off her shoes and booted up her computer. While she waited through the welcome screen, she got out the phone number from Gervas's message, seeking her. Time to confront her past.

Gervas chased another mosquito from his cheek.

"Come home with me," Maeve said across the picnic table.

Overhead lights had come on to emphasize the night. "Are you hungry?" he asked instead. "Let me buy you dinner."

Maeve shook her head. "I can cook for you. I've been helping my aunt. She was partially disabled last year when she had a stroke, but she's been showing me how to cook."

He was getting tired and must have allowed some hint of skepticism to show through.

"I'm not too bad, really," Maeve said. "You were planning to be on an airplane, or at least nearly home to Germany by now, weren't you? You stayed for me. The least I can do is feed you and offer you a bed. I have a guest room."

And so Gervas agreed to accompany Maeve to her home in a nearby suburb, though he thought it wouldn't be right to stay with her. If anything, she must have neighbors who would gossip over such a thing as a strange older man keeping a lovely young woman company. He would not allow her reputation to suffer. Besides, he wasn't ready for so much bonding.

He studied the curve of her cheek as she drove along the city streets. They'd passed a different hospital complex, not the one with the research program for Katrine, though he didn't stop the drift of his thoughts. Would this research be the one to cure her?

Maeve came to a red traffic light and faced him during the wait. "Do you need anything before we hit the freeway? Like, maybe stop somewhere for a restroom break?"

So considerate, was this girl. Rachel had done an excellent job raising her. "No, thank you. You live alone?" He should have asked before. She grinned and gunned the engine when the light turned green.

"No roommates. It's nice to have my own place, thanks to the family. They made a big down payment for me when I graduated from college."

Family was important to her. A good sign. He sighed and shifted in the small car seat.

"It's not far," Maeve said. They'd moved into a rural area, traveling south. He couldn't see much in the dark, but she was right. Only a short time passed before they reached the outskirts of another community. Maeve waved her right hand. "Welcome to Cottage Grove."

A good-sized store was lit up. "Piggly…Wiggly?" Gervas rolled the letters around his tongue. "What kind of place is this?" He'd never really spent much time in the local businesses, even when he'd lived in Madison while teaching for a semester exchange. He hadn't needed to shop for anything but souvenirs, and had visited mainly cultural centers as a guest.

Maeve laughed. "It's a grocery store. For food? Very nice. I'll take you there some time." She zipped past quiet streets with large buildings, some of which had balconies on upper levels, and turned into a neighborhood that appeared to be mostly condominiums.

Gervas's unease grew at her comment. How long did she think he could stay? He'd been on his way to meet his plane, surely she remembered that? He hadn't seen a hotel nearby. There had been so many in Madison, grouped together in clusters block after block, that it hadn't occurred to him there would not be any out here. Maeve had come to a halt in a short driveway, pushed a button on her visor and crept into a garage.

"Home sweet home." She pushed another button and he heard the latch of her trunk release. She had his suitcase unloaded before he opened his door. "I have a washing machine and dryer."

He moved as if underwater, exhausted with the flood of information bombarding him. An attempt to gain control of his environment and circumstances was going to be impossible, he conceded. Besides, he needed to find Rachel and couldn't bring himself to barrel into the subject like some oaf. Maeve was reluctant to say anything other than her mother was fine.

"You'll like the guestroom." Maeve chattered as she tugged his carry-on bag up the short flight of stairs from her garage into her house. "It even has its own bathroom." Her voice echoed from inside. Gervas took a deep breath and followed her with his larger suitcase and computer case.

An hour later he sat at a round cherry wood dining table, eating a pesto salad, which he conceded was quite delicious, and drinking cold water. Americans loved their ice, and air conditioning, something he learned to appreciate as well during the summer heat and humidity. Maeve set her fork on her empty place, picked it up again, tested the points with her fingers, and bit her lips. Gervas went through his mental catalog of safe conversation starters, which were too few as he preferred robust discussion among colleagues about the current state of the world. Since he'd never had to attempt to put a newly-discovered adult offspring at ease, he was at a loss. They'd already discussed her job. The meal was tasty. The weather pleasant.

"Did your aunt teach you this recipe?"

She stopped playing with the utensil and raised her brows, quirking the corners of her mouth. "Yes, she did. I can make the sauce from scratch easily now. It's not that hard. Did you like it?"

He nodded at his empty plate with a smile. "Very much so. Quite delicious."

The broken ice seemed to restore her tongue.

"Good. I was worried. I didn't know what you like to eat." She rose and began to clear the table, shaking her head at him when he followed suit. "No, no, I got this. Can I make some coffee? I have this machine…no? Okay."

Her kitchen was small, bounded by overhead cabinets and counter space, the washing machine and dryer whirring quietly behind slatted closet doors while she continued to chatter about her recovering aunt.

"I have a confession," she said from the other side of the counter.

"Oh?" Gervas hoped she hadn't called the state department or some nonsense in order to hold him in the States. Maybe she'd called her—

"I called work and said I had a family situation, that I needed Monday and Tuesday off."

Alarm tingled along his cheekbones. "I don't want you to get into any trouble."

"No, no. It's all right. I said I'd make it up the next weekend. We have this new client, and a generous deadline. I already started on the project. I want to have some…some time with you." She came around the corner, hesitant, serious. "Look. I know I sort of kidnapped you from the airport."

He nodded, afraid to say anything that would hurt her.

"You're not about to have an expired visa or anything like that if you stay a few extra days? It won't cost you anything. I'll even cover any cost for changing your tick—"

"Stop!" Gervas held up his hand. "Of course you will not. If I hadn't been so thickheaded when we first met, we wouldn't be in this situation." He grimaced and turned away, glad Maeve hadn't interrupted. The dryer stopped its noise and it became unnervingly quiet. "I was on my way home, yes, because I gave up hope looking for something."

Maeve took his hand and pulled him into her living room. "I want to help you." She gestured for him to take a seat, and curled into an armchair near a soft green sofa. "Please tell me what I can do."

Ah. At last, the opening he'd been seeking. "I need to find your mother."

Disappointment crossed Maeve's face and her lips drooped as she tucked her hair behind her ear and laid her cheek on her knee. "I wanted you to myself for a while first," she said in a soft voice. "She's kept me from meeting you all of my life, and I want to know why. It's not like you're a criminal who was in prison or something. Right?"

He snorted. "No prison." Maybe not physically imprisoned. "I don't have any easy answers for why your mother said nothing about me. I think Rachel felt I'd cheated her. I had." He stopped and thought. "I won't lie to you, but some things are private. Maybe she'll discuss it with you herself after I've had a chance to meet with her."

His daughter raised her face. He saw her desperately searching for some way to keep her dignity, to keep the ball in her court. He'd do everything he could to help her, but he had no control over his government's call for a vote to leave the European Union, and Regenbogen's revenge. He'd never risk Maeve's relationship with her mother because of his past mistakes. Maeve didn't deserve to be mixed up in his mess.

"You said you'd given up hope looking for something. Let me help you find it."

"It has to do with your mother."

Her lips pursed. Gervas had a sudden window into this girl's personality. Mutiny. He smiled. So maybe she wasn't as sweet and pure as he'd thought.

"As long as she doesn't know about us," Maeve said.

Us? She sounded more like him—the old him. He canted his head, sure they were through deciding whether to walk the dark path and taking the first steps along it. The old ache and longing for Rachel hit him hard in the gut. Surprised by the intensity of the feeling, he stood. "Love. I suppose I am the least qualified person on the planet to discuss such a thing." He sighed, touched a framed photograph of Rachel and Maeve on the end table, straightened, looked at his daughter. "Let's just say that making a good number of mistakes has taught me that keeping promises outweighs keeping secrets."

At her puzzled expression, he smiled wryly and waved his hand at her. "Case in point, eh? I have obviously lost much more than you by not being a part of your life, though I may also not have been a good father as you imagined." He hurried on when she opened her mouth. "No, no regrets, remember? I must tell you some things now."

Gervas sat on the couch again, closer to her. "Some of this information is vague for a reason, a very important reason, and I must ask you not to say anything about it to anyone, not even your mother, and certainly not your exuberant friend, yes?"

At her wide-eyed nod, he smiled again for reassurance. Daring, he took her hand and squeezed it. "I told you a little of my—our—family, of my father's passing, my mother, and my brother, Manheim. Of Manheim's work as a federal minister. And you know about some of my work. I retired from regular teaching last year, though I will still teach one course the next semester." Pausing, he measured his next words. "It is no secret that the world is in turmoil, economically. The European Union has suffered some, shall we say, growing pains?"

Maeve's eyes narrowed. "I read a little about how hard it was to adopt the euro." She wrinkled her nose. "I had to, for a business credit."

"Yes, that's part of the problem. And of course because commerce and trade are on a global scale like never before, problems in one country are more easily able to effect problems elsewhere."

"Like what's happening in the US with the banks and car makers. The bailout."

He nodded, pleased. So few young people paid attention these days. "The US is in a position to do more to help itself than some other countries."

"Like Germany?"

"Germany is at a crucial point of making important decisions that will also impact other nations."

"And your brother is part of that?"

"Correct."

Maeve squeezed his hand and then sat back, frowning. "But what does this have to do with something you're looking for? What could my mother possibly have to do with Germany's economy?"

Gervas leaned back and crossed his legs. "Now I must take you back in time, to World War Two, although the real story is much older than that." He studied her expression to determine her level of patience. Polite interest. Perhaps not the same passion as her mother, but he had yet to get to know this new daughter. Quickly, then, to avoid losing her interest. "My parents lived beside another prominent family on the edge of our city, a family named Regenbogen. The Regenbogens were Jews, but not many of us—how is it? Well-to-do, cared about such things. Not only were they Jewish, but they were collectors and sellers of antiquities. Old Eli Regenbogen enjoyed sharing some of his collections with the great museums around the world. He loved being a showman, I believe you call it, holding galas to open exhibits. I believe he even came to Milwaukee in the nineteen twenties."

He saw Maeve's eyes begin to glaze so he reached for his phone and clicked through the photographs until he found the right one. Enlarging the picture, he passed the phone to her and watched her study the group of items. She hovered her finger over the screen and enlarged the photo again.

"You see," he said, "when it became apparent that things might go very badly for people of Jewish descent in Germany, the Regenbogens asked my father for help. My parents agreed to take their neighbor's most valuable possessions for safekeeping, at least until after the war." Maeve was still studying the picture. "The Friedemanns went to Canada in 1938, and did not return until 1945. The Regenbogens were not there. Their estate was owned by others after those times, and broken into pieces and sold."

"I recognize this." Maeve tapped the screen, then met Gervas's eyes, their matching amber color both comforting him and grieving him for all they'd lost. "Your family kept the valuables, then, didn't they?"

Disgrace warmed his ears. "My brother was born in 1946 and I in 1950. Our father passed away in 1955, and it was not until 1970 that our mother spoke of the treasure kept in a bank vault. She gave some to Manheim for his wife, and showed me some—*that*," he pointed to the phone, "for my future wife. Sylvie had the necklace and other items, and one of the rings. I often wore the other. I suppose to remind me of the power and wealth of mankind's history. It was priceless, and I was full of pride then."

Maeve's knuckles turned white where she clutched the phone. "But I've seen this before." She pointed to the screen. "The ring."

Chill replaced the heat and ran down into his lungs, icing his blood. So, then, his assumption about Rachel's theft was confirmed. Careful. He cleared his throat. "You have seen it?" he echoed.

"I used to play dress up. One day I got into Mom's jewelry box. I think it was the summer I was five." Maeve smiled, then drew her brows and twitched her mouth. "I haven't seen it since, though."

Gervas measured his breaths, waiting. The light dawned across her face.

"You gave it to Mom?"

He squirmed. "Not exactly."

She muttered something under her breath. He wasn't sure, but it sounded like "Way to go, Mom." He deserved nothing less.

"Something happened, though, right? To make you want it back? Not all the Regenbogens were gassed by the Nazis?"

He held himself still while she handed back the phone and closed her eyes. So much damage that era had done. The arrogance of the Nazis would remain forever. Upon occasion he was glad his family had removed themselves from the evil.

"That must be a mistake, there, on your phone." Maeve frowned, though her eyes remained shut. "I thought it said 500 BC. That 'circa' means 'about,' doesn't it? They must have meant, like, 1500 AD.”

"There was no mistake."

Maeve leaned against the cushion. "BC?" she whispered. "Twenty-five *hundred* years ago? And now the guy wants it back?" She opened her eyes.

"Yes."

"He must be about ninety years old. But I don't blame him. It's a simple design, but beautiful. What happens if you don't give it to him?"

"Simon Regenbogen is a great-nephew of the owner. Nevertheless, he is the rightful heir." *And a cheat and a swindler.* "His claim appears to be legitimate and I want to return his property." *Must return it, and soon.* August was close. Gervas glanced at his watch with the date. July 24.

"Let me think where she might have put it."

He breathed a sigh of relief when she dropped the questions. His phone lit with an incoming call. Gervas studied the number, one digit different from Maeve's.

"Excuse me, please. I must take this."

Gervas held the phone away from Maeve's line of sight and walked outside, down toward the street. He spoke his name into the phone and waited.

"Rachel. Michels," the voice on the other end responded, softly. "I understand you want to see me."

The only light in Rachel's house came from the computer screen. Dark felt comfortable, like hiding. She curled up on her sofa with her phone pressed to the side of her face.

"Rachel."

His voice tickled her ear, intimate and belly-warming. She had heard him speak the other day in the outer office of course, and had recognized him as surely as if they'd left each other last week instead of decades ago.

"I admit I had given up hope of finding you," he said. "I was on my way home."

Clenching and unclenching her toes, she shifted and sat straight. If he was on the plane already she wouldn't have to see him. It was better that way. "I'm sorry I missed you. Perhaps the next time you're in the States we can talk."

"Oh, I can talk now. In fact, I have something to discuss with you."

His voice had taken a brittle edge, causing a ripple of unease to vibrate along her skin. She moved the phone to the other ear. "Wh-what would that be?"

"Give me your address. I can be there shortly."

Whoa! Rachel stood and hurried to lock the front door. "I thought you were on a plane. What is this about?" Her tone was sharper than she wanted it to be and hinted at her level of distress.

"Rachel, it is a matter of some urgency. Please let me—"

"No! You can…" *Where? When?* "The office. Come to the admin building at Mendota, where you…where…you know the place. I'll meet you there. Seven a.m. on Monday morning." She closed the phone with a snap, turned it off, and buried her head in her arms. Shaking, she let the tears fall. What had she gotten herself into? *Calm down, calm down.* He didn't have her address. The privacy measures she'd taken so far had worked.

He wouldn't harm her; she wasn't afraid of that. He needed something from her so it wouldn't make sense to do anything that would keep her from being able to give it to him.

Taking deep, even breaths, she got up and paced, shaking her arms and twisting her neck. Who could she call? Not Scott. Not after tonight. She had no idea what she would say to him after he'd shown how upset he'd been to learn she had known Gervas before.

Maeve. Maeve mustn't know.

Dad. Her deaf, limping but proud veteran father would do anything to protect her, but she couldn't go there. Someday she'd confess to them. They'd been so good and supportive.

Peggy would come in early on Monday for her. She was certainly intimidating, but were the two of them enough? Enough for what? Seven wasn't that early, come to think of it.

Rachel twirled and paced until she stumbled into her coffee table and plopped into a chair, rubbing her knee. It occurred to her that she was still allowing him to hurt her emotionally, and it had to stop. He must need the ring. Maybe he'd lost everything in the economic crisis and needed it for the money. Maybe…

Maybe, nothing. She got up and turned on three lights. If she wanted to know what he wanted that badly, she'd have agreed to meet him earlier. Rachel had a bigger problem. If she admitted she'd stolen the ring, could she go to jail? She had a feeling she was going to need a lawyer. Mark was going to get an interesting call tomorrow.

Shutting off the lights again, she double-checked the door locks and headed for her room. On second thought, she'd meet Mark and Ann at church. She should be safe there. Even if she wasn't in any trouble for now. At least, she hoped not.

<>

After a calmer night than she'd expected when she went to bed, Rachel was at the toaster, humming while she watched her English muffin, when the sound of fumbling and clinking at her kitchen door made her heart jump. She backed away, slowly, while the door opened as far as the chain. Whoever was behind it was out of sight of the glass panes.

"Mom! What gives?"

Rachel breathed out and bent over, clutching her throat. Then she straightened and walked unsteadily to the door. "You scared me about to death." She pushed the door all the way shut, unchained it, and opened it again, turning before Maeve could see her shaking.

"You never set the chain." Maeve walked in and tossed her purse on the table. "Your toast is burning."

The smoke alarm gave a piercing wail as smoke billowed to the ceiling. Maeve calmly drew a chair under the alarm and pushed the silence button while Rachel unplugged the toaster and opened the window.

"You haven't replaced that toaster yet?" Maeve climbed down and set the chair in its regular place. "You know what you're getting for Christmas, then, don't you?"

Rachel uh-hummed and waved at the smell and smoke. "I hope you didn't come for breakfast."

Her daughter shifted from one sandaled foot to the other. Her shorts and tank top weren't regulation church wear. "And you obviously forgot it was Sunday."

"Yeah, well," Maeve muttered. "Um, I see I caught you

on your way out."

Rachel smirked and turned to the refrigerator. "Guess I'll just grab a quick bowl of cereal. I have a few minutes. You're not coming to church?"

"Not today."

"Something I can help you with?" Rachel poured some stale flakes in a bowl, grimaced, then splashed milk over it.

"Not today. Just have to look for something I think I left here. You don't want to be late, do you?"

Rachel leaned her back against the countertop and ate her breakfast. Three years ago, she wouldn't have fallen for Maeve's underhanded, sneaky ways to do something to take advantage of her, like stealing money out of her purse, raiding the medicine cabinet in this house as well as her parents'. Emptying Mom and Dad's scanty liquor cabinet. "Returning" merchandise if she found a sales slip. Maeve's eyes were clear, though her expression wavered between peace and faint impatience. There was a problem, but probably not that serious. Rachel scraped the bowl and put it in the sink. "You're welcome to borrow anything. Why don't I help you—"

"I'm not sure where it is, so I don't want to bother you. I'll start with the basement."

Rachel gathered her purse and keys. She had enough worry not to get sucked into this one too, and decided to back away, not ask anything else, and trust. "Okay. Are you going to be here for lunch?"

"I'm not sure."

"All right, then, I'm outta here. Call me if you need me."

"Say hi to Aunt Ann and Mark."

"I will. I love you."

"Love you, too."

"Lock up if you go before I get back."

"Don't worry."

Rachel frowned as the sound of the door closed tightly behind her. She welcomed the brief respite from worry about her other problem, but as she mentally switched gears to church and seeing her sister and brother-in-law, she forgot to look behind her while pulling out of the driveway. Squealing brakes on her right had her shooting forward again. *Sorry, sorry.* At least she hadn't hit the other car. She glanced at the kitchen window, hoping Maeve hadn't seen her gaffe.

She crept out the driveway again, slow and carefully enough to make her driving teacher proud.

When she arrived at church, Mark was alone in their usual aisle. With a couple of minutes to spare before the opening music, Mark whispered that Ann wasn't feeling well and had stayed home.

"Oh, no. She seemed a bit off the other day when we were shopping."

"She thinks it might be a touch of flu." Mark smiled. "It's good to see you here."

"I know." Rachel rolled her eyes and started clapping when the song leader started the first tune. "I've got to get back in the habit of coming. Can we talk later?"

He twitched his lips. "Sure."

After the service, Rachel followed her brother-in-law to a park with an enormous play castle, swings, and a small koi pond surrounded by little ones and their parents. A food vendor cart catered to families. They got a hotdog and popcorn and sat on a bench.

"Something tells me you're not just here for the company," Mark said when they finished chomping the dogs.

Rachel scrunched her silver and red hotdog wrapper and aimed for the metal waste container. She missed. "Yeah. I'm so transparent I'm invisible." She got up and tossed in the wrapper, helping Mark's rim shot over the edge as well. She scrambled away from the smelly bin and the bees that buzzed out when the trash hit the pile.

"So, okay, I left out part of the story," Rachel said, not looking at Mark. "You know, about the professor and the baby."

Mark been the one with the most faith when he'd first showed up in Ann's life, and a great example to all of them. His fragile side was laid open when Ann had her stroke. In a way, the resulting emotional breakdown saved Maeve when she stepped up to help. Still, Rachel felt raw about admitting the seamy things she'd done. Having a baby out of wedlock…well, forgiven, done with. But, theft? Of a priceless historical artifact? Gervas must have put some kind of spell on her, for the goody-two-shoes Rachel had been in high school, even in college, would never have even considered either of those things.

She shivered as a cloud passed across the sun.

"Rach?" Mark asked.

"Right. Sorry." Rachel rubbed her arms and sat next to him again.

"There are only a couple of crimes that have no statute of limitations, and I have a hard time seeing you committing either one."

Rachel made up her mind. "Okay, here's the deal. When Ger—he—left, I took something of his, something important. I was so angry." She realized her hands were fists and she struggled to relax. Mark's arm came around her shoulders. "I don't even know myself," Rachel whispered. She cleared her throat.

"Let me give Ann a buzz, tell her we'll be home in a little

bit, okay? I want to hear you out, but I want to make sure she's all right."

Rachel leaned against his shoulder and let tears fall. "Yeah, of course."

She realized a minute to collect her thoughts would help both of them.

Rachel sniffed and straightened as she listened to Mark. He let his arm fall away from her shoulder and hunched forward. "Yes, okay. Sip some tea. You had toast? Okay, try to rest. We'll be back shortly. Yeah, I love you. See you later."

Mark leaned back, slid sunglasses on and said out of the side of his mouth, "So, what did you steal? Plans to create international lasting peace? The first draft of his next book?"

"A two thousand and some-year-old artifact. A ring he used to wear."

Whistling, Mark asked, "And he never called you on it?"

"Maybe I thought he would…well, that I expected him to come back. Or at least call and ask. Maybe that's why I took it in the first place."

"He must have wondered where he lost it. He probably filed an insurance claim."

"It's not like that. The story behind the jewelry is rather sordid."

"Sordid?" Mark leaned back and crossed his legs and turned to face her. "Okay, start from the top with what you know. Why did he carry around such a valuable item? Did he steal it first?"

Rachel twined her fingers. "Sort of. He used to wear this unusual ring. That second time he was here, you know, after I was working on campus, we grew, um, close. I admired it, asked him about it." She shook her head. "It was part of a set he inherited after his father died. Something to do with taking care of some Jewish neighbors' valuables for them during World War Two. Of course, it wasn't healthy to be Jewish during that time, certainly not in Germany." She stopped, took a deep breath. "Anyway, when the neighbors weren't…available to reclaim their treasures afterward, the Friedemanns just kept it. Gervas said this set of jewelry was Etruscan, part of a set that was often on loan to museums."

"Part of a set? From a museum?"

"Well, not *from* a museum. The neighbor was rich and had lots of artifacts. Their shop was *like* a museum, Gervas said."

"And the professor never called or wrote to ask if you happened to know where he misplaced this ring, you said?"

Rachel shook her head. "I never heard from him again. Until, you know, last week."

"Maybe he never admitted it was lost. He might have had a copy made. Or maybe the one you, um, have is? You have it now?"

Rachel gave him a helpless look and nodded.

"Is yours a fake?"

"I don't think so."

"Well? Where is it? Did you have it appraised?"

"Of course not. I didn't want anyone to know about it. It's in my desk at work. I keep the drawer locked."

"All this time?" Mark took off the sunglasses to look at her.

Rachel imagined the consternation that look would cause an accused criminal in court and shuddered, hoping he would see it her way. "I was too scared to keep it at home. Maeve got into my jewelry box when she was a little girl, and I was afraid it would get lost."

"You didn't get a safety box at your bank."

"No. There was so little money to go around as it was."

"Theft of a museum-quality artifact." Mark tapped his chin with the sunglasses. A plastic disc whizzed close to Rachel's cheek and she ducked.

"Sorry!" A couple of ten-year-olds and a Saint Bernard rushed after it.

Rachel righted herself. Mark was still lost in thought. "So, he might not have reported the loss?"

She chose to treat his question as rhetorical.

"The theft of a theft, no chain of custody…" He continued to muse.

The sun warmed her face. It felt so good.

"With all the recovery of stolen Jewish art going on, I'm not sure what to think," Mark said eventually. "I'd have to do some research. I know some people. Of course the art was stolen by the Nazis. Were the Friedemanns…er?"

"No!" Rachel faced him. "No, they were in Canada during the war. In fact, Gervas's brother is in the German parliament, their government, that is. He's sort of important, I think."

"Hmm. This gets deeper, then. With the economy collapsing all over the world, everyone's feeling a pinch or two. Desperately seeking missing jewels might be some indication of family trouble, but what it might have to do with the government, I can't imagine. Unless the original owner had stolen it. But that doesn't make sense. So, you think your professor might want this artifact? And if you admit you stole it, some indication of possible consequences if he presses charges?"

"Yes."

"Rachel, I had no idea." Mark started laughing.

"What?" Annoyance raised her voice to an unattractive level and she snorted.

"You're the responsible one."

"Hmpf." She folded her arms. "I am. I'm just not responsible for some of the things they think I did."

Mark's phone chirped and he checked it. He swallowed. "Maeve. She's with Ann."

"Is she all right?"

"Let's go find out."

"No. I don't know, Pro…Ger…um, no. I looked everywhere around the house—the basement, my old closet. I even found the key to her jewelry box."

Maeve's voice over the speaker phone sounded tinny and worried. Gervas paced in her condominium's small front room. "You tried. Don't you think it is time we were honest with your mother?"

"No! Not yet. I can look other places. In her office, too. Please, not yet. Once she finds out that we've met, she'll be so mad. I know her. Everything will change. Let me…can't we just wait? I'll ask my grandparents if they have any of her stuff at their place. Oh, they sold their house and moved, but I know one other place to check. I'm going over to my aunt's house now."

Her voice crackled. He picked up the phone and took it off speaker, but the call had ended. Her hesitation over how to refer to him wounded, though it was not his fault Maeve had never known him. Had she ever called another Father?

In the small kitchen, Gervas poured water into a glass and downed it. Of course he had nothing to say to her since he planned to meet Rachel in the morning. He still hadn't worked out what, if anything, to tell Maeve. She had taken the day off work, so how was he going to explain that he had an appointment? So early in the morning? Maybe she was a late sleeper. He'd arrange for a taxi, be back before she knew he'd left.

Not a good example of a father figure. He had no other

choice right now than to sneak out if he wanted to earn Maeve's trust. A truly oxymoronic situation, but she knew how her mother would react better than he. Gervas paced, looked out the window but decided not to go outside. He checked for messages, then got out his computer and tried to focus on work. When Maeve returned, he vowed to pay attention to her, do what he told her earlier, get to know her as a person, as a child he should have raised himself.

<>

Rachel was pleased to see Maeve's car in front of Mark and Ann's house. She parked behind her daughter while Mark drove into their garage. When they met in the hall, she glanced at Mark's clenched jaw and kept silent.

Maeve's voice rang from a three-season porch off the dining room. "We're in here."

Ann lay on a sofa, blue washcloth across her forehead.

"No, don't get up," Mark said in an exasperated voice, laced with fear. He knelt next to his wife and glanced up at Maeve.

"I just stopped in." Maeve shrank back and let go of her aunt's hand. "I wasn't doing anything. She was throwing up."

"I'm all right." Ann was obviously irritated but didn't move.

Rachel hid a smirk at the taut lines of disapproval alongside her sister's mouth. They'd talked earlier about whether a discreet tuck and lift around the jaw and neck would be considered plastic surgery. Ann wasn't really the drama queen Rachel had once considered her. Sisters were a support system like no other, when it worked, and a pang hit Rachel as she regretted raising Maeve as an only child.

"I'll call the doctor," Mark said.

"Don't you dare." Ann pushed his hand aside, grabbed

the washcloth from her forehead, and sat up. "Much as I'm glad Maeve came along, and thank you, dear, no one would have known about this little episode. I was just nauseated, that's all."

"From what?" Mark took her arm and helped her get to her feet while Maeve pushed a silver and porcelain-handled cane under her hand.

"Stop fussing!" Ann brushed hair from her cheek and met Rachel's eyes, pleading for some peace.

"Sister time." Rachel waded through Mark and Maeve. "Let's go up and change clothes. You two can make tea. Did you find what you were looking for?" she asked Maeve.

"Uh, no." Maeve didn't meet her eyes.

Rachel planned to worry about that later. Ann refused the chair lift and Rachel didn't press. She refrained from speaking on the careful shuffle up the stairs. Once in the bedroom, Rachel was shocked by Ann's thinness. "How long has this nausea been going on?"

"Just a couple of weeks." Ann leaned her head and shoulders inside her closet. "I have a regular appointment with my doctor next month." The clink of hangers accompanied her words. "And I'm not moving it up."

Rachel sat on the queen bed, deciding how hard to press her sister into changing her mind. Ann emerged with a clean blouse, buttoned halfway, which she pulled over her head. Rachel watched her struggle with the buttons but knew better than to offer to help.

"It's probably just the new meds," Ann finally said when the last button was set. "Something I ate. The change of life. Who knows."

"Too long for something you ate. Change of life? You mean menopause? You're only...how old?"

"Oh, stop it. It'll happen to you too, you know." Ann shook her cane and tried to frown though her lips kept twitching the opposite direction. She lowered herself to the bed and joined Rachel's chuckle.

"You're not even fifty. Aren't you concerned? How often are you sick?" Rachel patted Ann's hand, the one with the diamonds and sapphires that probably caused her imbalance troubles.

"It's just been a couple of times." Ann leaned on Rachel's shoulder. "I called the nurse, who checked on the medication. She said that I might need to adjust, that's all. It could make me a little dizzy and tired, too, which is true. Don't worry." She pulled back and stared at Rachel. "Have you thought about telling Maeve? You know, secrets, and all." Ann laughed. "Not that I'm throwing stones or anything."

"No, you wouldn't do that." Rachel blinked, sighed, shifted focus. She caught their reflection in the mirror over the dresser. Two women in their late forties, trying to act like there was not a thing wrong in their lives.

"Who's throwing stones?" Maeve asked from the door. "May I come in?"

Rachel's heart skipped. How much had her daughter heard? What exactly had Ann said?

"Sure," Ann said and rose. "Thanks for being here, and I'm so sorry you caught me at a poor moment. Did you need something? I never got the chance to ask before." Ann took Maeve's arm and headed back down the stairs. "Coming?" she asked Rachel over her shoulder.

"Yes." Rachel followed in their wake. She hadn't told Mark to keep her secret. Ann hadn't asked her to keep her nausea a secret. Maeve hadn't told anyone, apparently, what she was looking for. Another secret. Everything had been fine before Gervas showed up. Somehow all these things going wrong were his fault.

No, it wasn't a rational thought, but Rachel was beyond caring. He was to blame and the sooner she got rid of him, the better. Tomorrow morning couldn't come soon enough. She rubbed her hands together in anticipation of all the things she would tell him.

- 12 -

Rachel paced in front of her car in the parking lot of her office, not yet ready to go in, having realized this early in the morning, she'd have to let him in, anyway. She had arrived a half hour earlier than she'd told him to come, needing more time to rehearse. She wanted to be practiced, aloof, and mature when she lit into the cheat who'd basically ruined her life.

Fair?

The sky had just begun to lighten, and was now thick and oppressive with summer humidity.

It made her sweat. If she didn't have to meet him, she wouldn't be sweating. Rachel touched her neck with a handkerchief to blot the moisture.

What else was his fault?

He'd made her stay in this job for all her life, catering to students who couldn't make up their minds, getting them out of academic messes, finding them money they should be earning themselves.

She glared at the taxi cruising up the drive. That better be him, though it wasn't his style, allowing someone else to drive.

The cab drew closer. Rachel grabbed the handle of her car, realized it and pulled away. Put her hands behind her back. Clenched her car key until it bit her palm. Looked at her feet. Looked up again. There he was, getting out, handing money to the driver. Black dots danced until she took a deep breath.

"Rachel."

"I don't faint," she said before her knees gave out and Gervas lowered her to the pavement. She didn't think she completely lost consciousness, just got lightheaded. Maybe she caught something from her sister.

"Better?"

Gervas held a paper cup of water in front of her lips. Rachel blinked at the pair of workpants-clad legs next to her. Clark, a maintenance staffer. Great.

"Yes. Sorry. Thank you." She took Gervas's hand, swallowed the memory of the last time he'd touched her, and stood. Clark nodded, glanced at Gervas, back to her, and then walked around the side of the building. Rachel watched until Clark disappeared, avoiding the moment she'd have to look at Gervas.

His breathing changed; an intake that meant he was going to say something. Rachel had to beat him to it. Regain control, not look weak. She had been the one to call the meeting. "Right, then, shall we go in?" She was thankfully still in possession of her keychain, though at the door she'd unlocked and held open, she saw her purse in his hands.

She took it and led the way to her office, motion-sensor lights clicking to life as they swept by. She waved at a chair. Panic rose. "I'll just go get some coffee started. Be right back." Why was he so quiet?

At the sink in their break room, she stood, filling the glass pot and trying to subdue the emotion that threatened her need to rail at him. She shivered when she felt him behind her, reaching around her shoulders to shut off the water and take the overfull pot. He poured enough into the machine and prepared the grounds.

No more excuses. Rachel took a deep breath and allowed herself to look at his face.

Peggy was right. His features hadn't changed that much, but life experiences had marked his soul.

She'd drop the part about her sister's illness being his fault.

"Gervas. It's been a long time."

The coffee seeped through the filter, the welcome aroma reminding her to breathe evenly.

"Yes, Rachel. Twenty-three years."

An edge to his voice made her narrow her eyes.

"You are a hard woman to track down."

His near perfect English held its formality. She swallowed at the memory of ripeness, intimate whispers in her ear of the soft rush of the "w" and lengthened "oo" sound when he said the word "woman." "You certainly tried hard enough. I like my privacy."

"Apparently."

"You scared me with some of your tactics. My friends and family said I should call the police." Rachel checked his expression. Good, she'd made an impression, judging by worry lines.

"Did you?"

"No." She poured them each a cup of coffee, resisting the urge to add cream, and handed him one. He could add his own. It was safer to talk here than in her office where the ring might come to life and try to escape her desk in an attempt to get back to its rightful master. She mentally rolled her eyes. Right, so now her life was epic. "Let's talk here."

They sat at one of the round tables.

"What do you want, Gervas?" Even she winced at the baldness of the words, but she wasn't backing down. She sipped the hot coffee as she stared at him over the rim, blaming the heat for making her tear up. She couldn't blink away the blueness, the hurt, the anger, she saw in his eyes.

"Rachel. So unkind. That is not like you. Like my memory

of you."

She pursed her lips and waited while his expression sorted itself into pensiveness, as though he, too, changed his mind about what he originally planned to say.

"I wrote to you. Two letters."

That was not something Rachel expected to hear. She clenched the mug. "I didn't get any letters. When? How did you know where to send them?"

"Soon after our parting. They were returned with a note asking me not to contact you."

Rachel frowned. "Who did that? Who would do that?"

He shook his head. "I wouldn't know. I also tried to telephone. Hang ups."

She studied the way sadness grew along the creases of his eyes and down his cheeks.

"I would never have stayed away if I'd known about her."

Numb. Rachel's feet were too numb to move, to get up, to run to her office and slam the door, and pretend Gervas was a dream. Of course Melissa said something to Maeve, who could never, ever, let things rest.

Commotion in the hall and outer office told her it was nearly eight, time to go to work. Humming from Melissa made Rachel vow to strangle the girl later.

Rachel curled her toes inside her shoes. "Maeve knows? You…you met. You talked to her." Rachel lurched to her feet, knocking her mug over.

<>

Gervas grabbed napkins and blotted the river of coffee. "What are you trying to hide?" he called as she fled. He tossed the wet napkins in the waste basket and started for the door.

"Oh, good morning, Mrs. Michels," Gervas heard a youthful female say in the outer office.

That young person who was Maeve's friend.

He hesitated. Maeve had been right about Rachel's reaction to the news of their meeting. He hadn't wanted to tell Rachel until he learned the fate of the ring, and had certainly not planned to blurt it out first thing. But what made her so upset?

Complications. Always a disaster, whether he was the responsible party or not. If Father had not agreed to protect their neighbor's treasures, he wouldn't be in this mess. Gervas wiped the spilled coffee and threw the soiled napkins in the trash. He washed his hands. Of course, if the Etruscans had never made jewelry, none of this would have happened.

If he hadn't met Rachel, Maeve wouldn't have happened. Life was off-balance, out of control in a way he'd never imagined when he first promised Manheim he'd find the ring and appease Regenbogen, save the family honor, allow the vote, protect the Union. Save the world. He shook his head.

But to learn of the other consequences of his actions changed the nature of the quest. Or did it? Family honor was still first. Rachel must not have the ring anymore. Disappointment burned through him. Of course it was right of her to get rid of something that would continue to remind her of their liaison. It was their child she'd wanted to keep secret. But why? He would never have allowed them to be in want. Rachel had taken so much from him. Why couldn't he be angry, furious, have it out with her and get it over?

Gervas slapped his hands against the stainless steel and pushed away from the sink. He headed to Rachel's office. First, she must tell him for certain what she'd done with the ring. Then he'd fix the other problem.

A few steps down the hall brought him face to face with the Atwater woman. They measured each other.

"Good morning, Professor. May I show you out?"

Gervas had never heard a voice on the other side of the calls he'd made to Rachel, decades ago. But this raspy breathing…yes, it had been this woman, Atwater, who had hung up. He gave in. "Thank you. I am certain I can find the exit." Fuming would serve no purpose and only waste energy. There would come a right time and place to confront Rachel. Hopefully without the police or the apparent bodyguard.

As he waited for a taxi, he even chuckled. If Manheim had such an Amazon for protection, Regenbogen would have backed down in a moment. Perhaps the woman could be persuaded to take a trip to Germany and sort out the unfortunate presumptions on the part of their blackmailer.

Rachel was fortunate to have such a champion. But he still needed to get around this misguided personal cop to talk further to Rachel. And for that he needed Maeve's help. Maeve must encourage her mother see that the ring needed to be returned if she still had it. Afterward, they'd work out the rest of the awkwardness.

The encounter with Rachel had not taken very long. Gervas watched the parking lot slowly fill as people came to work. He received a few curious stares and one offer to help him locate the correct office from a harried-looking woman, which he politely declined. While studying a bud on a rosebush filled with red tea rose blooms, someone bumped into him, hard enough to knock him off the curb. A muttered apology as the large man passed annoyed Gervas. He pulled his hand from the rosebush and watched drops of blood well up from multiple scratches. At least he had a clean handkerchief to press against the stinging wounds as his cab arrived.

The taxi took him back to his daughter's home, where he found her awake, and pacing with his cell phone in her hand.

Ach, he'd forgotten to take it with him in his haste. "Maeve, I apologize for simply leaving like that. I hoped I would be back before you woke."

"You could have left a note or something." Maeve continued to stand there, wearing loose-fitting pants with multi-colored balloons and a plain tee shirt. Her hair was mussed. Her agitation made him feel badly, but he wasn't sure what else to say to ease her discomfort.

She held the phone in his direction, but not to simply hand it over. She wielded it like a weapon, accusing him. "You had a call. I answered when I saw the last name was the same as yours—that it was Katrine. I wanted to talk to her, you know, get to know her. I never had a sister and I just wanted to know her."

Gervas reached behind him for the support of a chair. If Katrine's health continued to fail, all the priorities would have to be rearranged.

"I think she must have wondered if I was your girlfriend, or something." Maeve resumed pacing, her bare feet slapping against the wood. "I didn't want to just blurt out that I was your daughter, you know. But she didn't seem to care who I was. You have a lot of young girlfriends?" Maeve shook her head. "Never mind. Cheap shot. Her English isn't as good as yours. I told her, no, not a woman companion. I think. I only had two years of German in junior high. Then she wanted to know if I was part of the sick study."

Gervas touched his forehead and closed his eyes. *Katrine, what were you thinking?*

"Sick study? Gervas, she's sick. Why didn't you say anything? You should have said something. What if she dies before I get to meet her? She's my only sister. Isn't she?"

13

Rachel trembled, clenched her hands, and stared at the desk drawer in front of her. She imagined the ring glowing, bouncing in its bag. In her mind the picture shifted to a hand adorned with the ring. The picture widened until Rachel saw the hand belonged to Maeve. A gunfire rap on her door made her heart leap into her throat. Before she found her voice, Scott plunged into her office.

"So, he was here?" Scott planted his fists on his hips. "You talked to him? Alone?"

Rachel swallowed and stood, slowly, to give herself time to calm down. "Good morning. How can I help you?"

By the way his lips thinned and his eyes glinted, Rachel knew she'd handled his ire all wrong.

"May I remind you he's dangerous? He's a stalker willing to pay good money to find you."

Rachel came around her desk. "So, he found me already. We had a talk. I think we're done here." She moved past him toward the door in the most obvious hint she could offer to get him to leave. Right now the mild-mannered German professor was the least of her troubles. How could she be so wrong about men? Hopefully Maeve hadn't inherited her gift of incompatibility with males.

"I don't understand." Scott didn't budge.

Rachel had to turn around to face him, putting her in a vulnerable position with her back to the door. Just like a game of chess where the pawns were all wiped out. Where was her rook? Peggy?

"I asked you to let me help you, to keep me informed. I have a bad feeling about this whole thing," Scott said.

His chest rose and fell in syncopation. Rachel looked away, out her window, hoping the right words would appear and she could parrot them. This was one reason workplace romances rarely worked. Not that they'd gotten to the romance part yet.

"Thank you." Rachel pursed her lips and forced herself to meet his eyes. "I've asked you for some favors, and maybe it seemed like I owed you."

An impatient shake of his head made her pause. "That's not it, and you know it."

"I don't, really, Scott. I have no idea how to handle this."

"You had a child. You must have been with someone. Unless—"

"Dangerous ground here. None of your business." Fury replaced any sympathy Rachel tried to muster. "This is too far over the line. I need to get to work, and so do you." She walked back to her desk and turned her back on him. "I'll thank you to keep our relationship professional."

When the door clicked, she slumped into the chair and put her head in her hands.

"I know your vacation doesn't start for another ten days."

Rachel squeezed her wrists and groaned. "Peggy!"

"But I really think it should start today. You've got a lot of sick leave and personal days. I know your schedule. I'll cover for you."

Rachel didn't raise her head, for tears had mingled with the sweat on her cheeks. "You may be right," she mumbled.

"There's no 'may' about it. Go on, now. Get out of here."

At that command, Rachel lifted her head and wiped her face. "Um, well, I've got—"

"I have your number," Peggy said, and turned on her heel. "I'll be back in five minutes and you'd better not be here."

Rachel scrambled to pick up her purse and jot a couple of notes. At the forty-five second warning before Peggy's return, she ripped open the desk drawer and the false back and seized the velvet bag. It did, indeed, feel warm in her palm.

<>

Gervas reached for his cell phone. He could not scold the girl for her curiosity, for her loneliness, which was in part his fault. She'd been locked in a cage of only childhood all her life and had no idea how to behave now she was free. She didn't admit she'd revealed her identity to Katrine, or had she?

"What did you tell…Katrine?" At the last second he substituted "Katrine" for "my daughter."

"Katrine is such a pretty name," Maeve said, pacing again. "I always hated my name. You know how many disgusting variations kids can make out of such a simple one-syllable word?"

"I've always loved the name Maeve, from the Warrior Queen. Did your mother tell you why she gave it to you?"

Maeve stopped and glared. "Like you said, warrior something or other. And fairies. You know how bad that can be for a little kid? When the older kids call you names and you don't even know what it means at first? Or why everyone else is laughing?"

He should have been there for her. Fairies? There was some childish interpretation out there, probably, of the story. Some animated version. "Are you familiar with the poet William Butler Yeats?"

Maeve sniffed and stopped. "The name is familiar."

"He wrote a poem about a legendary Irish queen who lived about the time of Christ in Ireland, and ruled the land for sixty years." He wasn't going to tell her about the five husbands—she could look that up herself. "She was someone I'd studied and lectured on at the time, in regard to succession, legend, and mythology of culture." Gervas cleared his throat, realizing the next revelation was too intimate. "Your…Rachel, liked her." He shrugged. "Perhaps that's where your name came from."

"It could be worse," Maeve said. "It could have been Mathilda or Hespera."

"Or Brunhilda or Gaia."

Maeve's smile came on slow. "Demeter. Ursula."

"Freya. Although that wouldn't be so awful."

"Would you have let your wife give that name to Katrine?"

Gervas shook his head. "Katrine is a family name on Sylvie's mother's side."

"Oh." Maeve folded her arms and turned her face away. "I didn't tell Katrine who I was."

"Maybe we can do that together," Gervas said. "She is to begin a medical trial at University Hospital. Apparently her doctor discussed it with her, since it seems to you she knew about it."

"I think it was…but I'm not one hundred percent sure. 'Krank,' right? Sick? 'Krankheit' for sickness?"

He smiled at her. "Yes."

"But then, medicine, *medizin,* is almost the same."

"Correct. English has many roots in other Indo-European languages."

Her return grin showed her sly side. "Ah, but perhaps contemporary words have their roots in modern American English, eh, Professor? Like, most scientific words in other languages are almost always English."

So much like her mother. "I think you know that you are correct." He hitched a breath. "But now I have a confession. It is time for damage control."

Maeve put one bare foot atop the other and cocked her head. "This is going to totally ruin my day, isn't it?"

"Probably."

"Can't it wait? I had some great plans, you know, for just the two of us. Tour some around Madison, go out to the country to a vineyard. Have lunch at a little natural foods place." Her face fell solemn when he deliberately didn't respond.

Gervas hated to tell her, but each marching hour could not be slowed. "That was just one of the reasons I came to Madison—to look into the study for Katrine. Yes, she has a rare illness. But she is in good hands at the moment. You couldn't find the ring, and I thank you for trying. But you may guess where I was this morning."

"You went to see my mom."

He nodded.

"You told her you'd met me."

It wasn't a question. "Not deliberately. I could never betray you like that. There were other things to discuss, but we didn't get far."

"So, now what?" Maeve put her hands over her ears, then smoothed her hair. She turned away toward the coffee maker.

Gervas pulled off his jacket and started to lay it across the back of a chair. Something wasn't right with the side pocket. What had he left there? He frowned and pulled out a folded sheet of paper, opened it, and read, "I know what you're doing. It won't work. Go home."

"What's that?"

Maeve appeared at his side. "Here, sit down." She pulled

out the chair, pushed his shoulder downward. Then she leaned over the same shoulder and read. Her warm breath tickled his ear. "Where did that come from?" she asked. "What does it mean?"

"I don't know." The first chill had exited Gervas's spine. "And, I don't think I understand." He gave the page to Maeve and pressed his fingers against his eyes. Then he looked up. "That man!"

"What man?" Maeve had turned the paper around.

"What are you doing?"

She pinked. "Um, checking for something. I don't know. Like a watermark or something."

He didn't laugh. "Someone bumped into me. Rather hard. While I was waiting for the taxi. I didn't even think anything about it, but he must have put this in my pocket."

"Wow. Like reverse pick-pocketing." Maeve nodded. "What did he look like?"

"He wasn't very tall. Somewhat wide." Gervas squinted, trying to see into the immediate past. "Light colored hair. More…angry, I guess. I was upset after speaking to your mother. He didn't stop. He actually knocked me off the step." He held up his hand with the scratches.

"Oh. Right. I'm sorry. I should have noticed that right away. Let me get you something to put on that." Maeve had started off, but turned back. "Scott. You were at Mom's office? Yeah, must have been him. Just a sec. Be right back."

"Scott?"

"Wait," she called from the bathroom, where he heard her open and close a cabinet door. "Antiseptic. Bandages."

The scratches had begun to burn and itch. Gervas raised his hand, but held it away to better focus. Glasses? He patted his shirt pocket, found them and put them on. "There's a thorn or two. Do you have a—"

"Tweezers?" Maeve had appeared again. She handed the metal pincers to him. "I had a run-in with that bush earlier."

"You said a person's name," Gervas reminded her. "You have a suspect?"

Maeve squirmed. "Well, he's the head of the IT department. And, um, he's going out with Mom."

She was smoothing the bandage across his hand when he jerked.

"Sorry," she said. With a look into his eyes, hers softened in sympathy. "I don't think it's serious."

He rose. "Your mother should be happy."

"Wait." Maeve followed him into the living area. "She's not. I've always known that she wasn't a happy soul, but I didn't know why. I let it affect my life. I did things I'm not proud of. I blamed her for not having a…"

Maeve's wounded expression stabbed him. "Go ahead, say it."

"All right then. A father." Maeve grimaced and folded her arms. "But then again, it *is* her fault we didn't know each other."

"Maybe not entirely," Gervas said. "One of things your mother and I discussed was the fact that she never received my letters or phone calls."

"Really?" Maeve squealed and flung her arms around him.

He laughed and hugged her, surprised. "What is this emotion? So confusing." He held her away. "What makes you happy about such a thing?"

"Don't you see? She was waiting desperately to hear from you. When she thought you didn't care, she grew bitter."

The girl gave a dramatic sigh.

"Unrequited love. The best kind." She rubbed her hands

together. "So. I have to think."

"Maeve, Maeve. Many years have passed. I must remind you of my primary mission."

His daughter flapped her hand at him, summarily dismissing him. "Yeah, yeah. Saving Europe. I know. Don't worry. I'll make her give you the ring. I'll just grab a quick shower first."

Gervas felt emptied by the vacuum of her abrupt absence. Scott? Rachel's lover…friend? Was the note a threat? But regarding what? Rachel? Had she told him about the ring and its importance?

His cell phone rang. A quick check of the screen showed his brother's name.

14

Gervas automatically calculated the time. Three forty-five in the afternoon. Had they voted? His fingers tingled and felt clumsy as he stared at the screen while the ringtone clamored. He had failed his family honor, his brother, his country. The shame of it bowed his head. He put the phone against his heart before accepting the call.

"Manheim, *Entschul*—"

"Nein, nein. No need to apologize. I have bought some time."

"But how? Regenbogen—"

"Not him. I had to do this, Gervas. You must understand, but I had no other choice."

Gervas's gut twisted. "What did you do?" he whispered harshly, one ear on the sounds of water running from the bathroom.

"My vote—it seems I am not the only one with questions about the future of Germany's current course. Two others, whose names I will not mention, agree with me to stall."

Gervas clutched the phone. "Why? Why would they do that?"

"There is more happening behind the scenes than I—than either of us—imagined. Regenbogen's little ring is nothing compared to what has been uncovered. Edsel's book, you know, the one that came out recently? The rich American who lives in Italy and tracks treasure?"

"Yes, yes," Gervas whispered. The water in the bathroom had shut off. Maeve would be finished any minute. "What does that—"

"It seems some items Regenbogen claims are in question."

Triumph in Manheim's voice drew Gervas's brows together. "Are you—"

"Wait!" The background voices were muffled through the phone that meant the receiver was covered. "Gervas…are you there?"

"Ja. What is happening?"

"Be careful."

His brother's voice crackled with static. "The signal, Manheim. I can't hear you."

"…other issues. The cultural minister…falling euro…mis…. They want to keep it secret, Gervas. You must…align the vote. Do not…they will use any means. There is another who…questionable…trust…"

"Manheim, trust who? What?"

His only answer was the dial tone.

Gervas shook the phone. "Trust or not? Who?" He wanted to call back immediately. Maeve reappeared. He put his hands behind his back like a guilty child.

"What's up?"

"You startled me," Gervas said with a weak chuckle. He stuck the phone in his pocket.

Maeve cocked her head. "I heard you talking. Was it about me? Was that my mom?"

"No. I was not talking to your mother, nor was I talking about you." He twitched his mouth and rocked on his heels. "My brother called, but I couldn't understand him very well. Bad connection."

"Sunspots."

"I beg your pardon?"

"It's when some plasma blasts free from the surface of our sun," Maeve explained patiently. "The energy that makes it to earth messes with our atmosphere and communications."

Gervas was certain sun spots could explain many things but not the collapse of the economy. Maeve had slipped into flip-flops and was toweling her hair. She flipped it back, ran her fingers through it and beckoned. "Are you ready?"

He allowed the energy of Maeve to pull him along, out of her apartment and into her car. Katrine had never shown this robustness. What would she have been like had she not been so ill? Gervas wished the two could meet under different circumstances. They were similar enough to become friends and to challenge each other in positive ways.

He shifted in his seat and heard the paper in his jacket pocket crinkle. The note…what else could it be but the man of whom Maeve spoke—the computer fellow. Manheim's message, garbled as it was, left lingering doubts. Gervas was reasonably certain the note was not in his pocket this morning before he left, yet just because he had not noticed it earlier did not mean it wasn't there. The note seemed to indicate he was being watched. He looked at Maeve, working the little car through busy lanes of traffic. How much merit did these mysterious warnings have?

Not to trust, Manheim had said. Or to trust? Gervas rubbed his forehead. What had Manheim meant about Regenbogen? Had they perhaps misappropriated the jewels or other items in the collection to begin with? Trust…not to trust… Manheim's warning made little sense. How or why would anyone care about Gervas's business in the States? It seemed the stakes had just been raised.

Maeve faced him after she came to a halt at a red traffic light. "I have to stop at my aunt's house. I had a call earlier when I was getting ready. She's been sick, and I need to see what I can do to help them. You can meet her and her husband. You'll like them, I know."

There wasn't a choice available, apparently. "Okay," seemed a safe, neutral response.

The light changed and she charged forward. Her hands tightened on the wheel. "Um…what do you think? Should we…should we say…anything?" Her tone rose on the question mark.

Gervas tried to summon any memory of Rachel mentioning a sibling. "About what? This is your mother's sister?"

"Right." Maeve glanced. "She didn't tell you about Ann?"

"Perhaps."

Maeve prattled on about Rachel's older sister, a cousin and grandchild. Gervas tuned out somewhat, thinking of Max and Justine, his fiancé. There would more than likely be children. Could he still count them as his grandchildren?

"They saved me, you know."

Gervas came out of his reverie quickly. "Excuse me?" He realized that while he'd allowed her to ask personal questions, he had asked very little beyond the most basic aspects of her life. "You were in physical danger? When?"

"I made some poor choices," she said without inflection. "I was pretty rebellious when I hit college. Did things I regret. Mostly." She flashed him a spritely look and squealed through an intersection.

He clutched his shoulder belt.

"Anyway, I went to camp out with Ann for a while. But it was Mark who pulled me out of the dumpster when I couldn't get my act together."

Proud as he was of his English and idioms, Maeve had left

Gervas in the dust. Before he could ask for clarification, she whipped around another corner and stopped in front of a sturdy two-story home with mature trees gracing a wide yard. The same kind of trepidation of meeting his former wife Julianne's family for the first time clutched his stomach.

"Come on. Mark probably knows about your books, anyway. He's an attorney, very intellectual, very cool. You'll like him."

Maeve exited and slammed her door before he even unclicked his seatbelt. He followed slowly up a walk winding to a recessed front door. A maple tree hid much of the house. Birches whispered as he moved past them.

"Mark! Hi, I have a surprise for you and Aunt Ann. First, though, how is she? The flu?"

Low murmurs followed. Gervas reluctantly trod the path until he reached the alcove with a screened door being held open. In welcome?

"Coming?" Maeve beckoned. "Mark, this is Professor Doctor Gervas Fried—"

"Friedemann. Yes, of course." The tall, dark-haired man in blue jeans and short-sleeved gray shirt speaking to Maeve smiled and offered his hand. "Please, come in."

"See, I knew it," Maeve whispered as he walked into the foyer behind her. "Of course he heard of you."

Mark merely smiled, sending a piercing look to Maeve and back to him. He didn't appear surprised, though perhaps his attorney training allowed him to hide his emotions. Gervas had a feeling Maeve's uncle knew something of his identity but wanted to give Maeve the option of introduction.

"The professor is visiting from Germany," she said. "I guess you figured that." Maeve halted. "I—we..." She gestured at Gervas. Mark raised a brow. "Oh, no. We're not…um…where's Ann?"

"She's lying down upstairs. Would you like something to drink? To sit for moment?"

"No, no," Maeve said. "You had a list of things I can pick up? And you wondered about my schedule?" She rushed her few questions, as though she'd changed her mind about wanting to share her news and would rather leave. "When are you going in to work?"

"Maeve. How lovely you came." A slender woman stepped gingerly down the staircase, gripping the handrail. "And you brought someone. Hello. Welcome. Won't you come and sit down?" She arrived at the bottom of the steps; a lovely presence and unmistakably related to Rachel. Perhaps more delicate features, more lithe in pale pink slacks and loose blouse. "I'm Ann Roth, Maeve's aunt."

Gervas took her hand gently. "Gervas Friedemann."

"We have heard of you. It's nice to meet you."

Mark ushered them into a living room where they all sat looking at the floor, or casting side glances at each other. Mark broke the silence. "I have to be in Atlanta for a few days later this week." He glanced at Maeve. "That's why I'm not going in this morning. We wondered—"

"*You* wondered," Ann offered a grim smile.

"If you could spend a couple of nights here. If it wouldn't be an imposition. Ann hasn't been feeling well, but we don't think it's contagious."

"It's not." Ann crossed her legs and leaned forward on the short maroon sofa.

"I could," Maeve said, looking at Gervas. Still, he said nothing, afraid of giving away information that might discomfort her.

"The thing is," Maeve said, "is that, um, Gervas is staying

at…oh, no! It's not like that," she said to Ann's pale, sweaty face.

"Excuse me." Ann rose and slipped out of the room. A door down the hall closed firmly.

"Mark, please, has she been to the doctor?" Maeve asked.

"Not yet."

Gervas thought him overly concerned. The woman's condition didn't appear that serious, and he wondered what the fuss was all about. "I should wait in the car," he said, and pushed to his feet.

"Wait, please," Maeve whispered. "Mark, Gervas is my father."

Mark turned his face from the direction of the hall toward Maeve. He hesitated, glanced at Gervas, who held his breath, and nodded. He checked the hall again quickly. "We know."

"You do?" Maeve squeaked.

"Yes." Ann stood in the doorway. "I apologize. Maybe some ginger ale?"

Mark rose immediately. "Yes, of course," Mark said. He touched Ann's cheek in a way that made Gervas feel utterly alone. "Anyone else?"

Maeve looked stunned, as pale as her aunt had been earlier. Gervas leaned forward in his chair and touched her knee. "Maeve?"

"I just…how did you know? Did everyone know but me?" Belatedly she added, "And him?"

Gervas wanted to put his arm around her to comfort her, so wounded she looked, like a little girl whose secret was stolen.

Mark glanced at Ann and left the room, presumably for the kitchen. Ann sat next to Maeve and took her hands. "Your mother came to us recently and told us. I promise you, we did not know before that." Ann moved her gaze to Gervas.

The question in her eyes was one he could answer. "I was unaware as well. I swear to you that had I known I would have taken responsibility."

That was apparently not the answer Maeve's aunt sought. Her lips tightened and her eyes narrowed briefly before she looked at Maeve again and made an effort to relax. Her smile was brittle. "Are you all right?"

"Well, yes," Maeve replied. "I just wanted to be the one to tell you."

Mark returned and handed a glass of bubbly liquid to his wife. "Does your mother know that you have met?"

"Yeah, but you can't say anything to her."

"I don't think that's what your mother would want," Ann said as she took cautious sips from the glass.

"She kept this from me all my life. She probably went ballistic when she found out. I just want a chance to get to know him first."

Gervas began to feel invisible and risked Maeve's wrath. "I am not in favor of more secrecy."

"Rachel had some concerns," Mark said, with a swift shared look at Ann.

"About what?" Maeve jumped up. "Like, what? Is she gonna sue him for child support or something? It's not like he's some kind of criminal or crackhead who's been in jail. Come on, let's go."

Gervas sighed as he watched her stomp out the door. Her theatrics weren't lost on her aunt and uncle, either, as they frowned after her. He'd never apologize for others, but he could on his own behalf. "I believe my ride is leaving. These are not the circumstances I wished to meet Rachel's family. But I hope you believe that I would never do anything to hurt either Rachel or Maeve."

"Rachel was frightened," Ann said hurriedly in a low voice. "She wondered if you had any legal claims on Maeve."

Mark had leaned forward while his wife spoke, his face a mask of inner consternation.

"There is nothing I ask of my newly discovered daughter than the chance to get to know the dedicated young woman she has become, obviously loved by a family whom she loves in return." Gervas got to his feet. "I hope we can talk again before I go back to Germany."

"I'll walk with you." Mark caressed his wife's shoulders and followed him to the front door.

"Thank you for your hospitality. I hope your wife feels better soon."

"Thank you. I hope we can meet again under different circumstances." Mark ushered him out. "Wait." They stood on the stoop. Gervas looked toward Maeve's automobile in the driveway and was relieved to see her still there, sitting in the driver's seat and staring straight ahead with a blank face.

Mark lowered his voice. "Listen, Rachel came to see me last Sunday. Privately." He stared at Gervas who could not look away, heartsick at Rachel's fears. How could she possibly think he'd do anything to hurt either her or Maeve?

"She told me about the ring."

Ah. Gervas felt as though the oxygen had been sucked from his lungs. He resisted the urge to gag as he dealt with this turn of events. Surprise and dismay made him clench his fists. "What, specifically, did she say, if I may ask?"

"She explained how it came into her possession," Mark hedged.

"Is it still in her possession?"

"You never reported a loss to the authorities?"

"I did call the college to ask if such an item had been found." Gervas felt calm return to him in increments. She still had it.

"What would happen should you regain ownership?"

"Ownership has never been the heart of the matter," he said. "Until now."

"Oh?"

Gervas decided to take this man into his confidence, perhaps as Rachel had done. She obviously trusted him. "Rachel has nothing to fear from me, should she be in a position to return the ring."

Mark nodded, his eyes never leaving Gervas's face.

Maeve honked her vehicle's horn. They both turned, shielding their eyes. Gervas waved.

"I think your ride is ready to depart," Mark said with a grin. "We should meet soon to discuss issues. Perhaps with Rachel?"

"The sooner the better. There are…issues…that are rather urgent. Do you have experience with international law?"

15

Rachel drove home the long way, which meant she circled Madison twice on the beltline before taking the Fish Hatchery Road exit to wind back through city streets to her neighborhood. The thought of running away to South Dakota was too tempting for her to stay on the highway with the signs for I-90 in her face. Though that wasn't a bad thought—just taking off. "Run, run, run, as fast you can, you can't catch me, I'm the gingerbread man."

Maeve used to love chanting that with her when they read the story. The gingerbread man trusted the wrong people. She glanced at her purse on the floor of her car where Gervas's ring lay. She should just give the ring to him and get away for a while, clear her head. She had his phone number, but not the guts to call him again. Would he press charges after all this time? Where would she end up if she was convicted of theft? Maybe Mark would help her.

Nah…such a chicken. She couldn't keep begging others to bail her out. Though she did have a bone to pick with the person who'd returned Gervas's letters and refused his phone calls all those years ago. Would she have read the letters or spoken to him? Would it have made a difference in their lives if she had? That was a good case for personal cell phones, about the only bit of technology she truly welcomed these days. Once, Rachel had been certain he would leave Sylvie. And so he had, but married another. So much for the great love Rachel had only imagined. What a fool she'd been. No better than a statistic. She'd done the best she could to protect her daughter from someone who had hurt them so badly, who'd left them stranded, alone to bear the burden of being fatherless, husbandless. A philanderer.

She looked at her fuel gauge which had begun to ping with a low fuel warning. A large gas station with a green sign was up ahead. She signaled and pulled in.

Payment choices—inside or out? Credit or debit? Rachel looked at the building, which advertised pastries and pizza and beer. A coffee and a donut? Sure, why not.

When the car gobbled all the fuel the tank could hold, Rachel shut off the pump and went inside to make more decisions. Peggy was so right, Rachel thought as she stood in front of the glass case arrayed with fat and sugar in multiple formats. One vacation, desperately needed.

"Raspberry and cheese danish, please," a man's voice from over her shoulder told the woman behind the counter.

Rachel inhaled. The chill of shock ran down the back of her skull through her torso. "Scott! What are you doing here?"

He narrowed his eyes as he studied her. "I didn't mean to scare you. I'm probably doing the same as you, picking out breakfast on my first day of vacation. My favorite pastry." He reached a long sturdy arm across her to pluck his from the attendant. "What can I get you?"

This guy just never took a hint that she didn't want to see him outside of work. Rachel now had to choose whether or not to make a fuss. Why was life so complicated? She hugged elbows. "I'm just here to window shop," she said. "And pay for gas. Hope you have a nice day."

At the register she handed over her credit card, trying to ignore the fact that Scott was right behind her, close, inside her personal space, almost touching her back. She scurried to her car, got in and locked the doors before squealing away. One thing she knew—no vacation request for Scott Warfield in IT had been posted on the admin notes.

Highway 12 went west, but it was not a major highway. She shouldn't stay on it and risk having Scott catch up with her. Five miles blurred past. The county road to Cross Plains was ahead. She'd take that, circle back. Then she closed her eyes briefly and chided herself. What was she scared of? Calling the cops was out of the question. Again. What could she say? *Officer, my colleague took unauthorized vacation and is following me. He's plying me with donuts.* A child's complaint. They'd maybe let her take out a restraining order. The newspapers were filled with stories of how much good that did.

Mark and Ann's house. Would he know about them?

What was she, nuts? This whole situation was nuts. Maybe she'd check in on Ann, ask her causally if she knew who returned Gervas's letters all those years ago, find out how she was doing, health-wise, and hide from Scott.

She shook her head at her multi-tasking when she was supposed to be on vacation.

<>

Gervas had that weird sense of falling through a hole in the world when Maeve came to a jarring stop in a parking spot marked "Administration" at the college building he'd left a few hours earlier. He had no desire to meet the hostiles again so soon. What war was everyone fighting? Which side was he on? So many fronts, so many sorties. Manheim and Parliament. Germany and the infant Union. He and Rachel.

"Come on!"

He balked at Maeve's enthusiasm and continuous directives to "come" as if teaching a new puppy. His shoulders tensed at the Atwater woman's disapproval when she saw him following his daughter.

"Peggy Atwater and my mom have been best friends since they were roomies in college," Maeve whispered as they approached the desk.

Ms. Atwater frowned, waves of antagonism rolling from her like backlash from a jetliner.

"We shared an apartment until Mom bought her own house when I was a little over two years old."

But now he understood better. Who, indeed, would have returned his letters and refused the phone calls on behalf of another? He suspected her, but this was not the time to ask. There were others who could have been guilty as well. He should not leap to judgment.

"I'm just here to talk to my mom quick," Maeve said as she moved toward the hall and Rachel's office. Gervas noticed the door was closed and the room dark.

Atwater stepped quickly for such a large woman to intercept them. "She's not here right now." Her frown turned to disappointment as she studied Maeve.

"She in a meeting?"

Maeve didn't get it. The fierce loyalty had been a fortress of protection her entire young life, and she'd never been aware she'd been in danger.

Atwater answered with another question directed at him. "What do you need now, Professor?"

"He's with me," Maeve cut in. "Where is my mother?"

"She started her vacation today. She didn't share her plans with me. I don't know where she is."

"Vacation?" Maeve's drawn brows mirrored her inner confusion. She looked from her mother's friend to Gervas. "I don't understand. She wasn't supposed to go on vacation until next week."

"She needed to get away."

Gervas watched as Maeve's eyes narrowed. There it was. The loss of innocence.

"From what?"

Atwater looked beyond Maeve to him.

"I think you know."

<>

Ann's house wasn't far. Two exits and then a few turns. Rachel moved over to avoid being caught in the exit only lane when a loud pop made her reflexively tighten her grip on the wheel, just in time from being forced to veer into a black panel truck. Her car wobbled and sank on the back driver's side. A flat. She slowed and signaled but another van was on her immediate right, keeping pace with her. Didn't the guy realize she needed to pull off? She slowed more. So did the van. Okay, then, the left side it would have to be. Other cars seemed to make room for her as she attempted to pull over. Not the van. Rachel squinted. The vehicle on the left was dark, too. No windows. Was it her imagination or did it seem to nudge closer to her? Was the driver going to make her stop right in the middle of a busy highway? She looked frantically in the rearview and side mirrors. This kind of stuff only happened on TV. Was she delusional? Was this a nightmare? Where were the cops when she finally needed them? Where was her phone?

Obviously nothing was right about this situation and Rachel made a choice she hoped she wouldn't regret. She stepped on the brake to the sound of squeals behind her. Sparks shot from riding the back rim while a red car careened right up to her bumper and cut off the dark van that had been on her right and trying to make a sandwich of her car.

She careened onto the exit ramp, silently thanking that daring driver of the small car and bumped through the intersection into a very welcome auto mechanic garage. A flash of scarlet zipped past and the wail of sirens floated down from the highway. When her tumbled thoughts came to a rest she realized who'd been driving that little red Fiat. Drat him. Scott had stepped in and practically saved her life. She'd think about why he'd shown up in white knight fashion later—like if her wits ever caught up.

Taking a huge breath, Rachel leaned on the steering wheel and turned off the ignition. Smoke from her shredded tire settled. She opened her door but stayed seated. A heavy-set man in a clean blue uniform approached cautiously.

"Looks like you need some help, ma'am."

Obviously. "Yes, thank you." Then, "Um…I can't seem to find my phone. Would you mind calling the police, please?"

This time she would *find* something to say about Scott's antics, tactics, whatever, and keep him away from her. The past five minutes were starting to feel dream-like and she wasn't entirely sure if the whole thing had been Scott's fault to begin with.

Apparently Madison's traffic enforcement safety team and State patrol were cooperating well that day, for it wasn't long before a cruiser drove in, silent. The officers didn't question her story of being forced to stay on the road even with a flat tire. They looked at each other with what Rachel hoped was corroboration. There had been plenty of witnesses all around, if only some had stopped to tell the police what they'd seen.

"Did you notice the make and model of the vehicles? License plates?"

"No," she said. "They were right next to me. I couldn't see the front or back. So many cars are alike these days."

"Okay, ma'am. And you claim a colleague from your job may be involved?"

Rachel cringed, changing her mind at outright accusation.

"I'm not sure. He followed me this morning."

"Has he threatened you in any way?" The second officer had a notebook out. He looked as young as Maeve, very serious. Rachel hoped this wasn't his first day on the job.

"Not really," she replied. "Do you think I could call my brother-in-law? I was on my way to my sister's house."

"Your brother-in-law?"

"He's an attorney."

The officers looked at each other again, sharing some mental telepathy beyond Rachel's senses.

"Sure. Let's do that. And maybe you'd better come with us back to the station. We can all talk there."

Rachel's second "ride to the station" went much better than her first, back in high school when she'd been leaving a party at a popular girl's house, sort of invited by a friend of a friend. She actually hadn't even gotten to the door of the house where music was erupting from every crack in the siding. Police vans pulled up right on her and Peggy's tails, rounded up the lot of them and made them ride with puking, reeking kids. Rachel wasn't sure which was more humiliating—having to call her dad to come and get her or the party girl's swearing she had no idea who Rachel and Peggy were and that they hadn't been inside her house.

Mark met her in the reception area of the station, dressed casually in jeans and gray tee, his jaw unusually shadowed. He looked nothing like a lawyer, and obviously hadn't been at work when he'd answered his cell and agreed to come help her out.

"I didn't mean to pester you on your day off," Rachel said. "Is Ann all right?"

"No problem." He winked and she knew he was thinking of their conversation of yesterday. Chagrinned, she turned her head and frowned when she caught sight of the familiar profile of a man across the room.

She opened her mouth and nudged Mark. "That's him," she whispered.

"Who?" the officer escorting said.

"I-isn't that Scott Warfield?"

"Let me check." The second officer showed them to a bench seat. "Wait right here please." The two of them strolled in the direction of Scott, with his back to them now, talking to another man.

"He's getting away," she told Mark.

Mark stood while she sank onto the bench. He patted her hand in a thoroughly irritating way. "Let's just wait, like the officer said."

A short time later they were ushered into a conference room. The man talking to the person who'd looked like Scott earlier entered and introduced himself as a detective. John Briggs assured Rachel that several witnesses agreed with her version of events and they were looking into the situation. Police had followed the suspect vans until they were lost, but they would keep searching and let Rachel know the outcome.

She should let them know of any other concerns. Thank you and good bye.

Rachel opened her mouth to ask a question but ended up closing it again when the door clicked behind the detective.

"Uh, thank you," the uniformed officer who'd been with them said, and guided them to the lobby.

"Version of events!" she complained as Mark drove them away after the too-brief briefing.

"That's what they have to say," Mark said patiently.

"I don't understand any of this. Was someone trying to…to actually hurt me?"

"What do you think about it?"

"I'm a little shook up. I don't know if it was a personal attack or because I was a lone woman and presumably an easy target, or if I imagined the whole thing."

"Several witnesses say otherwise."

"Don't tell Maeve."

His sidelong look as he turned onto their street made her defensive. "I don't want to worry her," she said.

"I think you should stay with us for a few days." He pulled into the garage, turned off the engine and gave her a cagey smile. "In fact, I'm going out of town and Ann could use some company. Maeve has already agreed."

"You think we'll be safe here?"

He smiled at her gently. "Yes I do. You two won't be alone."

16

Rachel clutched her purse, still worked up and glad not to be going home by herself. It seemed so much easier to be afraid in company than alone. She forced her shoulders to relax as she sniffed the familiar lemon cleaner her sister used on the kitchen counters.

"Ann, Rachel's with me," Mark called. "She's going to stay through the weekend?" He made it a question. Rachel nodded.

"How lovely," Ann said, coming into the kitchen from the three-season porch. She sent a strangely reproving glance at her husband. "Why?"

Rachel pursed her mouth and then replied, "I started my vacation today. Guess I just feel a little lonely."

"I'm glad you'll be here." Ann went still and white lines appeared on either side of her mouth.

"If it's an imposition—"

"Never," Ann said and swallowed. "But I thought your vacation was next week. Are we still going to Door County?"

Mark cut in. "Let's see how you're feeling first, okay?" He shook his head at Rachel.

Huh. As much as she didn't want to worry Maeve about the little incident on the road, he didn't want Ann to know what was going on either. Well, some sister time was good, no matter if, when, or where they were. And Mark had mentioned something about them not being alone. Rachel had almost forgotten her first mission when she'd started on her way here. She wanted to confront suspects who might have returned Gervas's letters—starting with her sister and parents. But with

Ann looking so peaked, Rachel would tone down the accusations she'd been working up to.

"We were going to have lunch," Ann said. "You'll eat with us?"

"Yeah." Rachel took a deep breath and looked at Mark. "Okay?" she mouthed.

He gave a short nod, almost hesitant.

"Where's your stuff?" Ann asked as she turned toward the refrigerator.

"Stuff?"

"Were you planning to raid my closets? What about a toothbrush?" Ann smiled.

"Oh, right." Apparently Mark hadn't even told her where he'd had to go to pick her up. The police station was the last place Ann would think. "I'll go home and pack my suitcase," Rachel said.

"Later." Ann leaned into the refrigerator to get something. "I can drive you."

"No. I'll take her," Mark said, softening the tension with a grin.

Ann put a glass bowl of salad on the table, and removed the plastic wrap cover. "Hmm, if I didn't know better, I'd say you two were up to something."

Mark cocked his head at Ann, grin growing.

"Uh-uh," Rachel said. "It's you two who are in cahoots to kidnap me."

"Maybe. Sit," Ann said.

"Let me just wash my hands, please." Rachel grabbed her purse, noticing the zipper across the top was open. She must not have closed it after paying at the gas station. "Oh, no!"

"What?" Mark asked.

"It's gone! It must have rolled out."

"We can run back to the mechanic quick and check," Mark said.

Rachel's breath caught and she had to take several shallow gasps.

"What are you two talking about?" Ann had paled again. "Mechanic? Is that where you called from?"

"Wa-wallet," Rachel thought fast. "I think maybe my wallet fell out of my purse."

"Just call the garage," Ann said.

"It's not far." Mark picked up his keys. "We'll be right back."

"All right," Ann said with a huff. "I can tell you're keeping something from me. You know my birthday isn't until September."

<>

Maeve was nothing if not tenacious. Gervas watched her mentally change goals. "Mom's probably at home, then. Thanks, Peggy." She turned as if to leave, but spoke over her shoulder. "Um, by the way, can you tell me where Scott's office is? I know they've been going out, and I wanted to say hi."

"He's not in today," Atwater said.

Gervas was not surprised. But apparently Maeve decided she'd had enough. She didn't have to issue her order for him to "come." Before he strode after her, he leveled a look at Peggy Atwater, posing like a lighthouse whose beacon had gone dim. "This is no longer your battle," he said.

"I can see that."

Gervas nodded and followed his daughter. The lines had been redrawn, but how fair were they? He still needed to know what Manheim had meant with his warning.

Maeve headed for the car, but to his consternation, she kept walking. "I have a key to the other entrance," she said. "I just want to look in Mom's desk while we're here. I have to go back to work tomorrow, you know, and I want to get to the bottom of this now."

At what must have been his stunned expression, Maeve spoke in defiance. "I have a key. It's my mom's office and I can be there."

"But not in her desk."

She snorted. "Then wait here. I don't like it that Scott's gone too. I want to look at her calendar. It's not like her to do something like this, and not tell me."

And of course, Gervas wouldn't know anything about what Rachel would or would not do. "I would prefer to be open with her."

"I would, too, now. But first we have to find her, and this is our best option at this point."

Gervas sighed. From what he'd seen so far, Maeve seemed responsible, though liable to a few lapses in judgment. She was young. She had power.

"I wish to—how do you say it? Stretch my legs for a few minutes. I will meet you at the car." He clasped his wrists behind his back and took the sidewalk along the campus, whistling.

A quarter of an hour later he strolled back to Maeve's little car where she sat behind the wheel. He got in and buckled the safety belt.

"It wasn't there," Maeve said. "I couldn't find it anywhere."

"Okay." Gervas had never believed it would be that easy. "What shall we do next?"

"I guess we go home. Where I grew up." Maeve turned the key and the car rumbled.

Gervas watched each turn carefully, noting street names

and intersections and some landmarks. He also noticed something in the side mirror which he didn't want to voice out loud until she slowed. "Is this it?" he asked quietly.

"Yes."

"Please, just keep driving straight ahead."

Maeve's grip tightened. "I thought I was imagining things."

So she had been aware as well.

"The dark van following?"

"For at least the last mile," he murmured.

"Longer," Maeve said. "Since a block from the college, I think. What should I do?"

"Stay calm. Can you circle the block three times? That would preclude coincidence."

"Yeah."

A license plate on the front of the van looked legitimate, but upon closer look was merely an advertisement. He jotted down the information anyway and replaced the notebook and pen in his pocket. He was so proud of Maeve's ability to keep driving without panicking. On the third circuit the van sped off in another direction instead of staying on their rear bumper to the street where Rachel lived. But when Maeve drove toward the house, she kept going anyway. Another small car had parked on the street and a man in dark pants and white dress shirt with the sleeves rolled up his strong-looking arms stood on the sidewalk in front of the house. The same man who'd pushed Gervas into the rose bush at the administration building.

"That's Scott Warfield," Maeve affirmed as she drove past.

<>

Rachel gripped the shoulder belt of Mark's car until her

hand cramped. "It's Scott," she whispered when Mark came within half a block of her house. "What's he doing here? I don't want to do this right now."

Mark stopped behind the red Fiat. "I do. It's time to take a stand."

He looked at her before he left the car. She couldn't move. Nothing would make her. She took her phone and held her finger poised over the number nine.

Scott put his right hand in his pocket which made Mark take a step back. Then Scott removed his hand, lifted his arms away and shrugged. He looked in her direction only once during the short conversation, which Rachel could only guess at. Her fault. She could still get out and join them. She put her hand on the door, but watched Scott drop something into Mark's palm. He walked quickly to the Fiat, got inside without looking at her again, and drove off.

Mark beckoned.

Thoroughly confused, she clutched her phone, got out and approached her brother-in-law.

"Here," he said, and held out his hand.

A little velvet bag lay there.

17

"Tell me what he said again," Rachel commanded Mark as she watered plants before leaving her house for the second time. The philodendron had been a gift from Peggy when Rachel bought the place. Twenty years ago.

"He said he only wanted to make sure you were safe."

"He's said that every time he shows up and creeps me out." Rachel grabbed a small carry-on bag and let Mark take the handle of her larger suitcase, crammed with the first things she snatched out of her dresser drawers.

"How did he get my ring?"

"Your ring?" Mark stowed the case in his trunk. "Did you lock your door? I didn't see you."

"It locks automatically." She went back to check anyway and returned to plop in the car seat, disgruntled.

"He said he wanted to check for other damage to your car, besides the tire, and happened to look in the window and saw something on the floorboards." Mark checked the mirror and pulled out.

"Why would he care about damage to my car? How did he know, unless he was involved? I thought he was going to kill me."

"By cutting off the driver of the van? Is that what you remember? Two vans trying to squeeze you?"

Rachel pressed her lips together and turned to look out the window. "Yeah. Maybe."

"He told me something else I have to check up on."

"Do I want to know?"

"Not yet. But if it's true, he might have saved your life back there on the highway when you got a flat. Which, by the way, he doesn't think was an accident."

"Great. What does he think…never mind." Rachel let her head fall against the restraint and closed her eyes. "I suppose he'll sit outside your house and protect me from whatever the whole time I'm on vacation."

"No. I'm canceling my trip to Atlanta and the police are doing periodic drive-bys."

She sat up. "You don't have to cancel the trip."

"Postponing, then. Besides, I'm concerned about Ann."

"Right."

"And there's something else, but I'll save it for later."

"You know what I think of surprises."

"Uh huh." He just grinned in his infuriating way.

<>

Gervas had Maeve circle around one more time before stopping in her mother's garage. She pushed the button that lowered the door automatically and used a side exit to the house. Gervas followed. He waited, searching up and down the street after Maeve unlocked the side door. Where had Warfield gone? Would the van reappear? He didn't understand who would drive after them like that, or what Rachel's suitor had been doing here. Perhaps American thugs had wanted to rob them. But now it seemed they were alone.

He remained on edge while he noted details of the small home. It had false red-colored brick decorating the lower half of the front underneath large windows. Maeve's call of "Mom!" echoed while he lingered on the stoop, reluctant to go inside. White siding matched similar houses set up and down the urban street. Mature trees, silver maples, clumps of dangling birches, and pine trees, testified to the age of the neighborhood, maybe fifty years. A black metal lamp post and decorative knee-high corner gate distinguished Rachel's yard from her immediate neighbors.

"I don't think she's here," Maeve said. "Come on in. Should I call the police about that van?"

Gervas climbed the concrete steps, gripping the black iron railing. He felt like a voyeur, disturbing the space of someone he had no right to spy on. He realized he'd been holding in a breath and let it out when Maeve dropped her purse on a handsome small kitchen table. "And what would you say to them?"

She stared at him. "I'm not sure, I guess."

"I made a note of the license plate, but the driver will probably remove or change it soon. Did you recognize the vehicle make and model?"

"No." Maeve looked as though she'd failed a final exam in one of his courses.

He chuckled and reached to squeeze her hands. "It could all be coincidence."

"I suppose." She turned away. "Anyway, I'm glad Scott was gone that last time we drove by since it looked like he was trying to find Mom too. I want to talk to her alone. Make sure she's okay."

From where Gervas stood, rooted to the shiny tiles near the door while Maeve walked about, he could see into a small living area, uncluttered, stuffed wooden and upholstered furnishings typical in American homes. Soft blues, a color she'd favored. A parti-colored knitted throw hung over the back of a chair. Peaceful in a way he couldn't put into words.

"Her car wasn't in the garage, obviously." Maeve had returned to the kitchen, shrinking the room with her energy. "Oh. Right. You've never been here. Um, did you want to look around?"

Gervas let his gaze rest upon Maeve. Calm cloaked him. "No. I see all I need right here."

She flushed and looked down before her bright eyes met his again. "Thank you." She turned and took two steps toward the door before she snapped her fingers and whirled. "So, I want to try one more place before I head to Aunt Ann's. Are you ready for more family?"

Gervas shook his head playfully. "A young man, perhaps? You have not yet spoken of a boyfriend."

"Nothing so freaky as that." Maeve beckoned. "Let's go. I'll lock up."

Once he was captive in her vehicle, she zipped back toward the freeway. "We're going to meet the parents. Grams and Gramps will be so happy."

Gervas put his hand over his eyes, squelched the groan and actually prayed it would be so. He much preferred a boyfriend encounter over a surprise encounter with Rachel's mother and father.

<>

Mark stowed Rachel's suitcase upstairs in one of the guestrooms of the home. Another door was open. Rachel assumed the mystery guest would occupy it.

She had an inkling who it might be when she spied a baby crib against one wall. She hadn't seen her nephew Ritchie and his wife Colleen since their baby David's baptism back in March.

As Rachel meandered down to the first floor, she contemplated what their lives might be now if her sister hadn't had a stroke. Thinking of whom, Rachel winced at the sound coming from the powder room. Again.

Mark hovered outside the door, elbow in hand, shifting

from one stockinged foot to the other.

"Don't you want to take her to the doctor?" Rachel asked.

"I made an appointment against her will for nine thirty tomorrow morning."

"Ah. When are Ritchie and Colleen coming?"

"You guessed?"

"Wasn't hard."

"Okay, so Ritchie has Friday off from his summer job at the rec center, but Colleen and the baby are coming tomorrow."

"Ann will love it. So will I. It will help take my mind off…you know."

At the sound of flushing, Mark grimaced. "I hope so."

Ann limped through the door. "Yeah, so lunch wasn't the best idea." At the sight of her crowd she gave a mock bow. "Nobody ask for an encore."

Rachel tried to laugh. "Let's find a good movie to watch."

Ann peeked at Mark. "I know just the one."

Mark held up his hands. "No, please, no!"

"P and P," Ann said.

"The long version," Rachel added.

Ann fell asleep in the middle of the first disc while Jane Austen's characters disgraced themselves so Rachel turned it off. She studied her sister's sleeping face, pale, with prominent cheekbones and blue veins showing along her eyelids. Purplish gray showed under the lowered lashes. Rachel's heart ached for her. Ann had done so well regaining her speech and range of motion, and now this setback.

Rachel looked up to find Mark leaning in the doorway, eyes on his wife. Rachel rose and led him to the kitchen. "We need a few supplies. Let me do some grocery shopping."

"I don't want you to go out alone right now."

A jolt at his words made her realize she'd pushed aside her earlier fear. The ring, cocooned in its velvet bag, bulged her side pocket and she fingered it. "I'll just go to the minimart, two blocks away."

He set his large hands on her shoulders. "Wait until tomorrow when I take Ann to the doctor. You can take my car during the appointment and come back again. It's safer if you're using a different vehicle in a different locale."

It made sense, though Rachel struggled against the feeling of being ordered. So used to not having to answer to anyone, she had to tamp the automatic disagreement. She swallowed. "Right. Let's do that. I'll make a list and talk to Ann later."

"Talk to me about what?" Ann wobbled into the room. "You shouldn't have let me fall asleep. I have to stop doing that or I don't sleep well at night."

Rachel grabbed a pen and pad of paper from the kitchen desk. "Just planning some meals and picking up some treats tomorrow."

"While we're out," Mark added.

"At that appointment you're forcing me into," Ann grumped. She fluffed her hair which had flattened on one side. "Maybe we could do a spa day. I'm sure that's all I need."

"Sure," Rachel said. "Sounds great." She looked at Mark. "Uh, what about—"

"Some ingredients for paella," Mark cut in. He narrowed his eyes at Rachel.

"I'm not sure I'm up for that," Ann said, looking queasy.

"Is the BRAT diet still in for upset tummies?" Rachel asked. Maybe he'd changed his mind about asking Colleen and the baby to be here. "That's what I used to feed Maeve, you know, when she was sick. Bananas, rice, applesauce, and tea."

"Yeah, get that," Mark said. "So, you ladies done with the

movie for now?"

"Not on your life," Ann said. "In fact, you'll have to rewind to the place I fell asleep."

"Do you even remember where?" Rachel asked as they returned to the living room.

"Who cares?" Ann giggled. "Hmm. Mark? Bring me something?"

"What?" He'd followed them, tagging on like he wasn't sure he had anything better to do.

"Ginger ale? Potato chips?"

His face lit as though he'd been given a great honor. "Anything!"

After he left, Ann asked, "So, what's in your pocket, Rach? Can I see?"

<>

Alice and Ray Michels, Rachel's parents, had moved to a nearby community where they lived in a low-rise building along the picturesque Wisconsin River.

"Two towns merge together," Maeve explained as she drove along a wide street with a view of the water on one side and huge old homes on the other. "Prairie du Sac, which is French for Prairie of the, um, something or other, and Sauk City. I worked up here at a restaurant on the weekends when I was in college."

His stomach gurgled when she said the word, and she'd laughed. "Well, it is lunch time and I wouldn't mind stopping in."

Lunch at the little place with a deck overlooking the river ate up another hour. The Blue Spoon was popular and it took some time to be served the quite good food.

"It's just a couple of blocks, but I guess I better drive," Maeve said. "Let someone else park here. We can go for a walk later, see if there are some eagles about."

They took up the next few minutes talking about the eagles that nested and stayed in the area. And then Maeve parked and got out.

Gervas followed his daughter around to the front of the building where she pushed one of at least three dozen buttons in a large panel. He listened to buzz and static over a voice asking for identity.

"It's me, Grandma. Maeve. I wanted to say hello and introduce you to someone."

"Of course. Come on up."

A click signaled she'd unlocked the outer steel door. They trod up the stairs, three floors, and emerged into a hallway lit with wall sconces. Maeve led him several meters until she stopped and knocked on a door. It opened.

Gervas looked into Rachel's future face, softened and folded in smooth lines, and wrinkles around eyes that looked into his soul when they met his. Her surprise lasted nanoseconds, her recovery serene.

"Grandma!"

"Maeve, darling, how wonderful to see you. Come in, come in. And bring your friend."

Gervas entered, pulled along in Maeve's invisible wake, and waited to be introduced.

"Grandma, is Grandpa here? I want to tell you something."

"Your grandfather is down on the dock, as usual," Mrs. Michels said. "Although he knows it's the middle of the day and the fish aren't biting." Mrs. Michels turned toward Gervas and lifted a brow.

Maeve took the cue, though stumbled. "Um, then, well, I wanted to tell you both at once. That is, let me present, well, this is Professor Doctor Gervas Friedemann. My—"

"Father?"

Gervas felt small under this woman's scrutiny, although he didn't believe she tried to be hostile. He had to say something, at least try to offer an explanation. To apologize.

"Frau Michels, please allow me to thank you for allowing me, us, to come. It is only recently that I have been made aware of the fact of my—" he changed in mid phrase at the thinning of her lips—"that Maeve is my daughter."

"I can see it in your features." Mrs. Michels's expression turned to sympathy when she looked at Maeve. "All these years. Does your mother know?"

"Yes." Maeve flushed.

"Well, then." Mrs. Michels swiveled and placed on hand on a chair back and leaned over it.

"Grandma, are you all right?"

"Yes, yes." She straightened and waved toward the living area with a wide window on the river. "Go and sit. I'll bring us something to drink. Lemonade. It's been such a warm summer."

The sweat at the back of Gervas's neck cooled when he went to look outside. "What a lovely view."

Maeve joined him. "This is the only place Gramps would consider moving when they decided to sell their house. I have to warn you, he's very hard of hearing."

Gervas frowned. "He is difficult to listen to?"

His daughter laughed softly. "No. I meant that his hearing is poor. You'll have to speak loudly to him."

"I see."

"Stubborn coot." Mrs. Michels set a tray of filled glasses on a low table near the sofa. "It took some convincing, but he got new hearing aids. He understands better now."

Maeve and Gervas sat and took the lemonade.

"So, tell me about yourself, Professor? Doctor? From Germany?"

Gervas put the glass on the table. "Gervas, please." He took a steadying glance at Maeve. "Yes, I live in Germany. Freiburg. I am mostly retired now, teaching only one class a semester."

"And what is it you teach?"

"Socio-economics."

"Grandma, he's famous. He lectures all around the world. He's even advised countries who want to join the European Union. And guess what, he's from an old, old family. They even have a crest!"

When had she discovered that? Gervas shifted, discomfited. "Well, I do not know about famous."

"Grandma, we need your help," Maeve jumped in again. "What do you remember about a ring Mom used to have? I remember seeing it when I was little. It was gold, with a round red stone."

Mrs. Michels frowned. "Ring? Your mother never liked jewelry. I don't remember any such item."

"Do you still have anything of hers? Boxes of old stuff, or something? Maybe in storage?" Maeve got to her feet, as if prepared to pounce and tear open any box her grandmother might have secreted. "We need to find it."

"We?" Mrs. Michels frowned again, the good feelings sucked back out of the room. "What's this about?" She faced Gervas. "Why, exactly, did you come back? And what are you doing, sneaking around behind my daughter's back? I don't like—"

"I'm home!" A male voice punctuated a door slam. Gervas rose, having quickly been reduced to a teenager, one-third of his years, not a twice-married man and father of grown children. Hearing Rachel's father's voice, cheerful until he had a chance to see who'd come to invade his peace, in the midst of his wife's accusing tirade, was humiliating.

Maeve slipped to his side and put her hand in his. He squeezed, grateful for her. Yes, for her, he would get through this ordeal. Once he was free from this familial nightmare, he might be able to relax and appreciate their concern.

"We have visitors," Mrs. Michels called.

"Oh, who?" An elderly man in loose-fitting jeans and thin white tee shirt walked in, a gimpy stride causing him to lurch from side to side. He did a double take when he saw Gervas standing hand-in-hand with Maeve and removed his cap. Gervas let go. The old man squinted, then looked at his wife.

Gervas stepped forward. "Sir, my name is Gervas Friedemann. I am Maeve's father."

The man affected a blank look, and cocked his head.

Maeve hissed. "Grandpa, this is Gervas, my father," she said a couple of notes higher than his. "He's come from Germany where he's a college professor."

Mr. Michels sat on a chair. "Why's he here?"

"They're looking for something of Rachel's," Mrs. Michels said.

"A ring that belongs to Da-Gervas," Maeve said. "And I wanted you to meet."

Gervas looked at her swiftly, hoping he hadn't imagined her near slip calling him "dad."

She didn't meet his eyes. "Mom took it from him. It belongs to his family, and is priceless, thousands of years old."

"And when did this supposed theft occur, son?" Mr. Michels asked.

"Twenty-three years ago. Sir." Gervas put his hands

behind his back and clasped his wrists.

Mr. Michels looked from him to Maeve and back again, his left eye twitching behind the glasses lens. "Payback?"

Gervas squirmed. "Perhaps."

"And now you need it? What, fallen on hard times?"

"Gramps! It's not like that." Maeve crossed the room to plunge down on her knees next to him. She took his gnarled hands. "It's really important that Gervas get it back. Do you remember anything about this? Did Mom ever say what she did with it, or tell you about it?"

His eyes behind the heavy glasses misted when he stared at his granddaughter. "No. Right, Ma? Rachel never said anything to me about any ring. You?"

"No," Mrs. Michels said in a quiet voice.

"So, you finally show up, after all these years?" Mr. Michels said loudly.

"I had no knowledge of Maeve," Gervas said. "Things would have been very different if Rachel had told me." He folded his arms and stared at the picture the two of them made, Maeve on the floor near the man who could have been his father-in-law. Should have been.

"This ring is important, then, eh? How did you find our Maeve?"

"I found him, Gramps." Maeve twisted so she was sitting fully on the floor. As long as her grandmother stood, so would Gervas. "He was looking for Mom over the internet, and I answered, but only after my friend Melissa…"

Here she blushed, and Gervas's suspicion that the friend had been the instigator was confirmed.

"Said he had eyes like mine. She'd never seen eyes the same color and we should meet."

"What does your mother say?" Mr. Michels asked.

"We haven't talked to her. Yet." Maeve sat back with a pout.

"I met with her," Gervas said. "At her office."

"She didn't tell you about this ring, then?" Mr. Michels flashed a saw-toothed grin.

"We did not discuss the ring," Gervas replied.

"Anyway," Maeve said in a bright voice and hopped to her feet, dancing. "Oo, my foot's asleep. Anyway, we're looking for Mom, too. She started vacation a week early. Did you hear from her?"

"Why, no." Mrs. Michels developed more soft worry wrinkles along her forehead. "She didn't call here, did she?"

"Nope. You try her cell phone?"

"Yes, and she's not at home, either." Maeve tapped her foot on the floor. "There. The feeling's coming back. We really should go. I want to track her down before we lose her. Time's wasting."

"Thank you for your kind hospitality," Gervas said to Rachel's parents. "I wish we had met under different circumstances."

"Me too." Mr. Michels rose and reached out a hand. "You be good to our little girl, here."

"Gramps!"

Gervas nodded again and started after Maeve who had nearly reached the door. He stopped and turned back. "Excuse me, please, perhaps you could tell me…" He swallowed. "I wrote to Rachel, and telephoned, many years ago. Were you the ones, perhaps, who returned my letters?"

"No, we wouldn't have done that."

The swift response came from Mrs. Michels, while Mr. Michels looked puzzled. "Would our Rachel have done that?" he asked.

"She said she did not." Gervas was relieved that these weren't the people who had tried—and succeeded—in keeping them apart. He nodded once more and took Maeve's shoulders, turned her, and walked out with her.

"Oh, wow, I can't believe I forgot to ask them about the letters," she said. "Good thing you did. Do you believe them?"

"Of course."

"So, who do you think did it? Aunt Ann?"

He shook his head as they walked down two flights of steps and out into the summer heat. "I do not believe so."

"But you have a suspect?"

He smiled at her enthusiasm. "I do."

She sighed. "Which you don't seem eager to share."

"Not yet."

Maeve unlocked her car. "Okay, then, let's go to Aunt Ann and Uncle Mark's. Maybe they know where Mom is."

"Perhaps you should telephone first?" He raised his brows at her, then waited.

"Yes, yes." She removed the cell phone from her purse.

As he listened to the call, he was glad to postpone more awkwardness today, though he needed to meet with Rachel's brother-in-law to discuss his troubles.

Maeve slapped the phone back into her purse. "Uncle Mark says to wait until later. He's taking Aunt Ann to the doctor in the morning."

"I hope her illness is nothing serious."

"Me too. Speaking of illness, I want to hear more about Katrine. Since I have no idea where to look for Mom next and she might just be shopping or something and not looking at her phone, let's get out and go for a walk. Maybe we'll see some eagles."

"You're not too warm?"

"Oh, no. I'm not. Are you all right?"

Her concern touched him. "Yes. Let's go. Show me your eagles. We will put this hunt for your mother on—how do you say? The rear fire?"

"Back burner."

"Yes. For the moment."

18

Rachel sat at Ann's tile-topped kitchen table the next morning, nursing a mug of hot black coffee. Mark stood nearby, flipping through the morning paper. Ann wasn't ready to get up yet, he'd told her earlier. Nothing tripped off the house alarm last night, and Rachel had eventually slept, dreaming of dark vans in her rearview mirror that never came closer or got farther behind while she drove and drove and drove toward a red speck in the distance that stayed the same size.

"You get in touch with Colleen?" she asked Mark.

"Yes. I called a little while ago. She understands, and hopes Ann feels better but plans to come if Ann is okay. I'll call her later to confirm."

"Good."

Rachel took the back seat for the ride to the doctor's office. Ann was unsmiling but quiet, ungraciously allowing Mark his peace of mind appointment. She munched on some saltine crackers. They'd made their short grocery list last night before bed. Rachel added a few extra things this morning in anticipation of Colleen and the baby's visit. She was excited to spend time with them, and refused to think anything the doctor said would change their surprise. Hopefully it would cheer them all up. Maybe Ann had just developed some kind of irritable stomach problem or had an ulcer, and with some medication, her trouble would clear up. Rachel remembered the months of misery when she'd been expecting Maeve, and Peggy held her head more than twice at the toilet bowl.

Ach, Maeve. Rachel had forgotten to call her daughter.

One more thing to add to the mental to-do list.

Mark drove up to the clinic overhang and opened the door for Ann. Rachel got out, waved, climbed into the driver's seat and drove off. She couldn't help checking her mirrors more than she usually did, and drove aimlessly for ten minutes, circling the block of the grocery store before pulling in and parking. She stood at the door of the car, watching, before going into the store. Rachel made her selections quickly and efficiently, fresh greens and other produce, ripe bananas, soup and other canned goods, bread, a red and while marbled cut of beef, not wanting to keep Mark and Ann waiting no matter what they'd told her. The appointment couldn't be that long unless they were really backed up.

After leaving the checkout line with her bags, Rachel hesitated in the entry of the store while other customers whooshed by with loaded carts, mothers with tots, elderly couples squabbling, day laborers stopping to get lunch to take to work. She moved out, taking her time to look left and right and studying the area around Mark's car. Would someone be waiting for her? Was that dark van in the parking slot over there…*Stop it.*

She would not live in fear, especially since she was on vacation. No one would know she was driving Mark's new Audi. She'd almost gotten through a public outing without Scott showing up. Rachel shivered and drove the cart in a fury to the car, unloaded and squealed back to the clinic.

She'd gotten an insulated bag for the meat, though in this heat that wouldn't protect it long. She decided to run in and see how things were going. Hopefully they were waiting. No, there they were, sitting in the waiting area. Hadn't they even gone in yet?

Rachel drew nearer. Ann, even paler than usual, huddled

in the chair, eyes blank. Mark, though, made Rachel nervous. He looked as though he couldn't decide whether to be scared or angry.

She approached hesitantly. "Hi, guys. Looks like a backlog?"

Ann shook her head.

"We've been in," Mark said, stiff-jawed. "We're just waiting for someone to do some tests."

"Oh." Rachel perched nearby on a turquoise and rust-patterned chair with a thin cushion. Ann and Mark made a bubble of stillness in the low-ceilinged room. The place wasn't quiet, what with receptionists making and taking calls, and nurses asking for their next patients. "Um, so, the doctor thinks…?" She didn't want to pry, but she also couldn't stand not saying anything.

"She wants to do some blood work," Ann mumbled.

"How'd the shopping excursion go?" Mark made a visible effort to relax. He leaned back, put his arm around Ann, and then raised a brow at Rachel. "No problems?"

"None." Rachel shook her head, looking curiously at Ann.

Her name was called. Rachel watched Mark help her to her feet, then start to follow until she brushed him off. "Just hang out. With Rach, okay? It'll take a second, that's all. Then we can go."

She walked away with the staff worker.

"So." Rachel needed to ask. Of course her sister was her business. "Are you guys okay? What's going on?"

Mark wiped his face and closed his eyes, opened them again. "Well, it's not just menopause." He tried to grin. "Hormones." His grin cracked. "She wouldn't say exactly what she was testing for. Yet. A routine blood draw for now before she orders more tests."

"Menopause? Ann's not that old."

"Yeah, well." Mark shrugged.

"Older women."

He twisted his lips, then hunched forward again, face in his hands.

Neither mentioned other possible diagnoses.

Ann reappeared, slipping her mustard-colored over shirt around a bandaged arm. "They took enough for a transfusion," she griped. She stopped short and put her hands on her hips. "Goodness gracious. You are both about as cheery-looking as a tax audit." She rubbed her stomach. "Now I'm hungry. How about we stop for a strawberry shake on the way home, or will your meat spoil?"

Mark jumped up. "I think we can manage that, right, Rachel?"

"Absolutely!" She tossed the keys in the air and caught them, one-handed. "Long as I get to drive."

<>

Mark slurped the last of his shake, then blabbed his secret while they were still a block away from the house. "I have a surprise, Ann, as long as you're feeling up to it. Colleen and the baby are coming today, and Ritchie's joining us on Thursday night."

"Is this the big secret? I'm not contagious, you know."

Rachel looked at them in the rearview mirror. They watched each other.

"I thought you'd like to see them," Mark said.

"Aw, you know I would." Ann heaved a sigh. "Push the button for the garage door opener, will you, Rach?"

"Right." Rachel drove in. They all grabbed the bags from the trunk. Mark playfully gave Ann one filled with the two loaves of artisan bread Rachel bought. She batted his arm. "I'm

not that feeble."

"Just getting old," Mark teased back.

"Huh. Just you wait. It all goes downhill at forty, doesn't it, Rachel?"

"As long as it's with you, babe." Mark leaned down to kiss Ann.

"Get a room." Rachel brushed past them to take the groceries to the kitchen. Unpacking, thoughts of what it might be like, to be married, kept her watching her sister and brother-in-law. She had wanted to be married, once. To have someone to come home to, someone to love Maeve, watch TV, and hang out with on weekends. To see another adult face across the dinner table. To fight with, even. After Gervas, though, she just couldn't imagine anyone else to be with, and then there was Maeve. Scott had seemed nice, fairly normal, at least at first. Was Rachel really ready to share her life? Look how well she'd done on two dates with him. Then he went all stalker. Or had he? Rachel looked at Mark, wondering again what he and Scott had talked about yesterday. No way would she ask again.

Ann's voice broke into Rachel's reverie. "So, what do you think?"

"Uh, about what?" Rachel bit her lip.

"Put the roast in the slow cooker for tonight? Is that what you planned?"

"Right! Yes, with the mushrooms, and some sherry. I saw this yummy-sounding recipe on Great Chefs."

"I love that show!"

Mark's phone buzzed. He put down the can of spinach to check it. "Sorry, gals, I have to take some calls. Work, you know. Not everyone can take extra vacation." He ducked under Rachel's swat.

"Go ahead," Ann said. "Run away."

Ann put her arm around Rachel's waist. "Oh, Rach, I wish…"

"It's okay. I have pretty much everything else I've ever wanted. I've been blessed. One day, maybe Maeve will get married and have children. In that order."

Ann laughed softly. "She's a good woman, you know. You did well."

"With your help. And Mom and Dad's."

"Hey, I wonder if we can coax them over here while Colleen and the baby are here."

"Just mention it, then try to stop them." Rachel moved away and slid the last of the canned goods in Ann's pantry. "And I have to check in with Maeve. I didn't tell her that I started vacation early. I hope she isn't worried. It's getting close to lunch time. I think I'll try her at work."

"Sure. Say hello from me."

"Will do." Rachel went up to her room, sat on the bed, and took out her phone. She'd also have to make time with Mark later to find out if he'd heard any more from the police. She wasn't terribly surprised to get Maeve's invitation to leave a message, which she did. "I'm staying with Ann and Mark for a couple of days. I just started vacation a little early. Talk to you later."

Back in the kitchen, she and Ann planned out some meals and activities for the next couple of days. If Ann noticed she mentioned only crowded public places out in the open, like the zoo and the arboretum instead of the Children's Museum, to visit, she didn't comment.

"David's too young for the museum anyway," she said.

<>

Colleen arrived late in the afternoon, after Rachel and Ann lazed away in the heat of the day, catching up on

magazines and gossip. Mark had stayed holed up in his downstairs office, coming out only once to check the mail.

"Hi, Rachel, it's nice to see you, too. I'm glad you're here," Colleen said. She was a sweet girl, a good foil for the more volatile Ritchie. Colleen had a backbone, but was more even tempered. She taught school, too, and would be going back soon.

"You have daycare all arranged?" Rachel asked as Ann unbuckled and lifted the baby from his car seat.

"Well, my mother is going to help out with that a couple of days a week," Colleen said softly.

Rachel wondered how Ann felt about it and watched her coo at the smiley baby. David was six months old now, and sturdy. He had dark wisps for hair and one tooth that he showed off constantly. He put his fingers on Ann's chin and patted.

"That's right," Colleen said. "Gentle."

Ann's shoulders stiffened just a bit, then relaxed, thankfully. Rachel hoped she would stop telling everyone to quit treating her like she might break. Love should be accepted and appreciated while it was there, because who knew how long it lasted.

"I'm so glad she agreed. You know I'm available in an emergency."

"Of course."

"So, then what?" Rachel asked. "Daycare the other days?"

"Right," Colleen said. "It'll save us a lot. Something smells wonderful."

"A roast," Ann said. "We bought a baby swing for the boy, here."

"Thank you, that's so sweet. We're starting to try some solid foods."

Mark came back down after carting their cases upstairs. "How long you staying?"

"Ha," Ann said, making David dance. "He doesn't know how many outfits you go through in a day, does he?"

"Right." Mark cleared his throat and rubbed his hands together. "So, Rachel, wanna come help me a sec?"

Rachel narrowed her eyes. "Sure." She heaved herself off the carpeted floor where she'd sat next to Ann and Colleen. Seemed like chairs no longer mattered when a baby came to visit. She looked back to see David edging himself like a bumblebee toward the cabriole-legged coffee table and their abandoned magazines. She grinned and followed Mark out to the garage. "What's up? I ding your car or something?"

"No." He chuckled. "I just wanted to tell you that my, uh, source, confirmed some information Scott Warfield gave me the other day."

His eyes turned serious and he touched Rachel's shoulder. The sound of a car passing echoed in the open-door garage. She glanced at the street, almost expected to see the red Fiat, and shivered. She straightened. "Okay. What?"

"There's an organization, mostly working in the underground, that wants to see the European Union fail."

Rachel grabbed her elbows. "Yeah, so? I'm not surprised. No one wants to have another superpower rise up. And what does that have to do with Scott? Or trying to run me off the road?"

"Scott's involved with the group. He wouldn't give me any specific names but he did supply me with two cyber operations they carried out, and some other information that backs him up, like fueling strikes in Europe and leaking misinformation about the world monetary fund. A website and some reports about banking interruptions agree with what he said."

"Why hasn't the government intervened? Why haven't we heard about this? I should go call work, tell HR to terminate his contract." She turned to head back inside, to her phone.

"Wait!"

Rachel stopped.

"He already gave notice. What you need to know is that the group originates in Germany, and the Friedemanns, or at least Manheim Friedemann, is reportedly one of the leaders."

She shook her head. "Gervas's brother? He's in the government. But that doesn't mean Gervas is…" A lot of time had passed. The Friedemanns had been wealthy, well-to-do. If that family fortune was threatened by the success of the Union, or because Germany agreed to help out the other members of the Union who were in financial trouble and watching the euro slowly devalue to nothing, what would they do to keep their money? She grimaced. "I don't know, Mark. This is all so…so outrageous. Are you sure? I just can't accept that the Gervas Friedemann I knew and, um, worked with—that he would be capable of such things. And what does all this have to do with me?"

Mark cocked an ear at the door to the kitchen. Voices. Ann and Colleen must be in there. He beckoned her to follow him out to the yard. He lowered his voice as they stood in front of a flowering crab tree he and Ann planted last year when they'd moved in. "These people followed Gervas, Warfield told me. Apparently Manheim needs to keep stalling an important vote in the German parliament, and he's being blackmailed about some big theft from Nazi times if he doesn't return the items. Apparently his vote is crucial to the outcome of Germany splitting from the Union."

Sinking. Rachel felt as though the grass had softened

under her heels and began to swallow her in slow motion. Her hands had grown cold and she rubbed them together.

"Do you know anything about this?" Mark asked. "Warfield seems to think so, because apparently he knew Gervas had been to see you. At your office?"

"How-how does he know that?"

"He told me he saw Gervas. Apparently the people following Gervas believe you're involved somehow." Mark glanced up at the sound of squealing tires in the distance. A police cruiser drove slowly past the house and Mark nodded subtly. Then he took Rachel's arm and led her back inside. Rachel started to breathe shallowly, afraid of throwing up or jumping out of her shoes, and desperately wanted to get in the Audi and drive, smoking hot, for someplace…anywhere…

"Maeve!" She stopped before Mark could open the door to the kitchen. "Wait! I think…I think he's seen Maeve, too. How much danger is there? Is she in danger? What can we do? I tried to call her before, but she didn't answer. Oh, my. We have to find her!"

Mark watched her, his eyes quiet and calm. Then he put his arms around her and drew her close. "Shh. Yes. We know." His voice was a warm whisper in her ear. "They were here. Gervas told me a little about the situation. That's why I believe Warfield. Maeve called me yesterday, looking for you, but I put her off."

His arms tightened when Rachel, fury growing, started to pull away.

"It's in our best interest to assess the situation, make some plans," he said quietly.

"Just how long do you think we can afford to *assess* the situation, Counselor? They already tried to k-kill me."

"They wanted to stop you, Warfield said, and talk to you."

"That's not what it felt like."

"He intervened."

"Is she safe? Is Gervas?"

"I hired some people I know to watch them. Discretely. I left a message for Maeve to come here tonight. With him."

"But, did you talk to her? Why didn't she answer me?" Rachel jerked away. "Maybe she did! I left my phone upstairs."

Mark touched her arm. "Don't say anything about any of this yet, please? I don't want Ann upset."

Rachel inhaled deeply, trying to calm herself. "Sure. I don't know what to say, anyway." She scrunched her brows. "Wait. Did I hear you say you say Maeve and Gervas were here? Together? Last week? Before I met with him." She stamped her foot. "Oh, I could kill him myself! He didn't say anything about that." She inhaled deeply and slowly in an attempt to control her breathing. "Though I didn't give him much chance. But you!" She pointed at Mark. "You should have told me. At least Ann, my own sister, could have…could have told me." Tears gathered and she sniffed furiously.

The door opened. "What's going on out here?" Ann asked. "And close that door—you're letting the heat in. What do you think? Air conditioning grows on trees? C'mon, we're getting ready to eat." She disappeared after hitting the overhead control to close the outer door.

"He and Maeve will come here later," Mark said.

"It'll be good to see her—them—with other people around," Rachel groused. "I can't murder either of them in front of witnesses. Is she all right? About…him?"

"Yes," Mark told her and led the way to the door.

Back inside, Colleen finished placing napkins at the place settings while David patted and pulled on dangling toys on the arm of the swing. Ann, wrapped in a floral apron, made gravy.

"You must be feeling better," Mark said and stood behind her, leaning down to rest his chin on her shoulder.

Pangs of regret over the past wrenched Rachel's heart of sync for a few beats. Ann had to be okay. Maeve had to be okay. The Friedemanns could rot. Then again, she'd better get a grip before Gervas, the skunk, showed up. She wouldn't be a good role model if she had a temper tantrum in front of the baby.

A good meal, light conversation centered on memories of raising their children. Ann ate lightly, something Rachel noted while they loaded the dishwasher later. "You're not nauseated at my cooking?"

"Not this time."

"Catch this, you two," Colleen called from the living room. "The news is on. Some guy who's visiting Madison is talking about world economy, but guess who I see in the background."

Now Rachel felt her gorge rise and swallowed several times.

"Be right there!" Ann called back as she studied Rachel. "You all right?"

"Yeah, sure," Rachel said.

"You're missing it!" Colleen called. "Maeve is right there. I'm sure it's her."

Rachel trailed behind, in time to hear, "This is Bree Thompson, reporting live from Capitol Square. Back to you, Donna."

Talking heads in the studio went on to comment. "Weren't we fortunate to have such a distinguished visitor give an opinion on the current state of affairs in Europe?"

"We'll have to see if we can get him to come in and sit down with us," the partner said. "Doctor Gervas Friedemann, visiting from Germany. The professor was part of a popular exchange program at Mendota College several years ago. His textbook is still being used."

"Isn't that your college, Rachel?" Colleen asked. "Do you know him?"

Rachel noted Ann putting a hand over her mouth. Mark was not in the room. "Yes, I met him," Rachel said.

David pulled on the leg of the coffee table in front of Rachel. Such innocence. Maeve had been like that sweet child, once. Rachel reined in bubbling fury. What was her daughter doing in public, taunting the terrorists like that? Had Gervas no shame? No concern at all for Maeve's safety?

Mark came into the room then, carrying the portable handset of the house phone. He stopped in the doorway, glancing from one to the other. "What's going on?"

Ann hit the off button on the remote control. "We were just watching the news."

He advanced, held out the phone. "Call for you. The doctor."

She looked at it and paled. Rachel's heart ached for her and chanted a silent prayer, "Please, God, please God."

Colleen came over, picked up the baby, and took him out of the room. Rachel probably should have followed, but she couldn't move, buried as she was under the weight of secrets.

"Hello?"

Ann's tremulous voice carried on muffled shockwaves.

"The results are back? You want me and Mark to…no? Then, what?"

Mark gripped Ann's waist. He was so close he had to have heard the conversation, Rachel thought.

It looked like Rachel was right when both of them started crying.

"Thank you. Yes, I'll do that," Ann said and pushed the off button. She raised her arms and slid them around Mark's neck. "How could this have happened?"

Rachel got up, unsure whether to join the huddle, or leave and find Colleen.

"We were so careful," Mark said in shaky voice.

Rachel cocked her head. Careful? She watched Ann pull her husband's face close. "It'll be all right," she crooned.

"No, it's too dangerous."

Rachel took two steps closer to them. "Oh, Ann. What can I do?"

Ann turned a tear-stained face in her direction, laying her cheek on Mark's shoulder. "Help me shop for maternity clothes, I guess."

19

Gervas twitched his lips as Maeve pushed the button on her remote control to shut off her television.

"Wow, that was surreal," she said.

He echoed the sentiment inwardly. They were at her apartment that evening, and watched the news station that featured the brief interview.

"Some luck that reporter happened to catch us in the square today during lunch." Maeve pulled her leg up and curled it under her as she turned to face him. "Are you okay with this?"

He chuckled. "Well, I believe my agent would say any publicity is good."

"I'm sorry to have had to leave you all day while I'm at work."

"No, no. You cannot feel that way. All this upheaval. My presence should not interrupt your life. You must take care to do well and not jeopardize this prize employment, yes?"

She plucked at a spot on her navy slacks. "At least we got to meet over my break time and I happened to have to be in the big city. Speaking of food, I'm hungry."

Gervas rose too. "Now it is time to partake of the meal I have prepared. I am not much of a cook." He shrugged. "But your Pig-lee Veeg-lee has a good deli."

Maeve laughed.

His daughter had returned to her office that morning. Since she'd had a client meeting in Madison, she suggested meeting for lunch, which he was happy to do though it meant a cab ride. They'd simply been walking in the area after eating when the reporter approached them, microphone in hand, cameraman lurking.

"I didn't realize they had me in the background while they were talking to you," Maeve said. "I've never seen myself on TV before. No wonder they say the camera makes you look fat."

Gervas chuckled. "It is all self-perception," he told her. "You are not fat. Where are your table utensils?"

Over the reheated chicken dinner, Maeve told him that her mother had telephoned and left a message about starting vacation early. She added margarine to her dry dinner roll and dipped it in gravy as well. Gervas swallowed and tried not to frown.

"Just like Peggy said." Maeve drank from her glass. "And she's at Aunt Ann and Uncle Mark's. Mark wants us to come later."

A shiver stayed Gervas's hand, holding the fork with its stabbed piece of fowl. He set the fork down and folded his hands on his lap. The look of panic in Rachel's eyes at the end of their last encounter haunted him. He had never wanted to make her afraid. But after all these years? What could upset her? "Not now."

"He seemed like he really wanted us to come. But I can call, ask if we can stop in sometime after work, tomorrow, right? We have to talk to Mom, get her to hand over the ring, right?"

Gervas was never easy around English vernacular, no matter how often he heard it. "To ask her to 'hand it over' she would have to admit to taking it in the first place."

"You said today, to that reporter, that the Union might fall apart any minute. We don't have time to pussyfoot around the issue." Maeve waved her fork and dug into the soft carrot coins that came with the meal.

"You exaggerate. I merely said the Union was in danger of destabilization due to the weak economy."

"But you told me about the other part. You know, how you're being blackmailed? Did you talk to your brother today? What's going on now in the government?"

"I have lost the connection with his telephone," Gervas said. "Our last conversation was cut off." The strange warning flashed again in his mind. "Do not trust…" The van. Was that what Manheim meant? What authority could handle such an incident? He looked at his daughter across the table, eating with enthusiasm, innocent and naïve. Perhaps he needed to see Rachel's brother-in-law again, even tonight, though he said he planned to leave Madison for another city for a short while. Gervas didn't have to worry about Rachel. There were enough troubles to plague him at the moment. Perhaps he could invite Mark for a quiet conversation and arrange to see Rachel later.

He cleared his throat and forked more of the chicken. "I have tried several times and cannot reach him. I should look into the matter, yes, of fixing the connection, or getting a new cellular telephone company? How would you advise me?"

The topic took Maeve off in another direction and he happily listened to her expound on the various and many different cellular services. With making arrangements for Katrine to come for her treatment, perhaps he should invest in another service, one for the States for both of them. He needed to attempt one more time to contact Manheim, ask him to clarify his warning and tell him about the mysterious follower. But how would the person know to follow Maeve's vehicle? Surely no one else knew about their relationship. It must be a matter of them being seen together—like this business interview today.

A fierce need to protect his new-found daughter made his heartbeat stutter. What could he do to protect her without alarming her?

They were loading the dishwashing machine when Maeve took a call. She frowned at the screen. "Uncle Mark."

Gervas listened to her side of the conversation, relieved, when she said, "Okay, well, I hope it's nothing…all right, I'll wait…no…sure. In a couple of days. Mom will call? Again? Yeah, all right. Bye.

"Mark says we shouldn't come tonight after all. But he didn't sound right. And he wants to talk to you sometime."

"Oh?" Gervas felt like he was hanging in the event horizon, trying not to get sucked into the black hole of this family. Though when he compared Rachel's family drama to that of his own filled with blackmail, secret votes, a psychotic ex-wife, and the terrible illness Katrine suffered, he thought it might not be so bad to let go of the edge and fall in.

But for Katrine, who didn't deserve to die.

"I must make some calls to Germany," he told Maeve.

"It's two o'clock in the morning there. Who you gonna call?"

"Er, you are correct." He looked at her fondly, inwardly chastising himself for not thinking of the change. A sign of aging, perhaps. Or stress. He pushed aside the feeling of vulnerability and agreed to watch a program on television.

"Mom and I usually get together a couple of times a week," Maeve told him during a commercial.

"You have not done that recently," Gervas replied.

"It's funny. I'm grown up, independent, yet I don't want to lose the apron strings." He watched her twine her fingers.

"Apron strings? You mean, ties, correct?"

"Correct." Maeve looked up from her lap where she rested her hands. "Do you wish your children—your other children, that is—still lived with you?"

Fondness, regret, sorrow flowed through him. Gervas shook his head. "No. It is not good for them. Although Katrine, of course, must have someone with her always. Perhaps now that her mother is no longer able to care for her she will spend more time…" His voice cracked and he cleared his throat.

The television program droned quietly in the background. Maeve leaned over from her seat on the sofa and set her hand on his. "It will be all right," she said softly, her shining eyes on his. "University Hospital is well known for its care. She'll be in good hands."

"Yes, I believe so."

Maeve moved back and held up the remote control device. "Do you want to see any more? I have work to do before bed."

"No, thank you. I, too, should do some research."

His daughter stood and stretched comfortably. "I'll check with Mark tomorrow, but we can go see them later." Her countenance changed to slightly worried anticipation. "It's okay if you're home alone again tomorrow? I don't think I can get away like I did today."

She was really asking him to wait, to not try to see Rachel on his own. He forced a slight smile and refrained from sharing his worries about her. Coincidence, surely—the van incident. "I will be fine. I want to visit the hospital and finalize Katrine's visit. Perhaps arrange for a telephone."

"You should wait on the phone thing. It can be crazy trying to figure out the American companies with all the fees and garbage. I'll help you."

He conceded, glad also to make sure he was with her in public in case perceived danger became a reality. "Point taken. I would welcome your help. But don't you have friends you'd rather spend time with?"

Her glowing smile was his reward.

"I can go out with them anytime. I'd rather hang out with you now that you're…now that you're here."

"I am agreeable. As long as I get to meet your boyfriend and give my approval."

"Ha!" Maeve gave an impish grin, tossed her hair and retreated to her room.

Gervas mourned the unspoken sense of loss, and promised himself again he would do what he could to make it up to her. The lost years he could not replace, but he could offer new memories. He went to the guestroom Maeve allowed him to use, thankful they had no adjoining wall that could potentially allow disturbing noise or private conversation to pass through.

He sat on the chair next to the bed and opened his computer, setting it on the small tray, TV tray, she called it, and booted up. If only Rachel would allow him to explain and ask for forgiveness, he felt the gaping hole in his spirit would begin to mend. They would have to meet.

With his wife ill, did Mark still plan to go on his business trip? Perhaps with Rachel staying there, he could safely leave.

Gervas did not know how much longer he should remain in the States, though it was true he wanted to prepare for Katrine's arrival and participation in the medical trial. In the morning he would call both her and the doctors again. He needed to check in with his agent who'd left three messages, and get in touch with the university. His class would begin next month.

Once his e-mail program was open, he returned two new messages from the university and assured his agent he was still alive and yes, working on the manuscript for the new book. He was completing the syllabus for the class when his phone buzzed.

Apparently the middle of the night was not a problem to call from Germany. Gervas checked the name on the screen, hoping it was not Manheim. No, not his brother, but Konrad Meissen, Katrine's physician. Gervas took a deep breath in an attempt to calm the shivers of worry that made his hands shake and answered.

<>

Rachel wasn't as shocked as Mark appeared to be. She thought Ann was the only thing holding him up as he leaned on her shoulder. Ann really did have that glow people talk about when referring to pregnant women. Pregnant? Ann was almost forty-eight years old, not twenty-eight! Who gets knocked up when she's almost fifty?

Colleen, holding a sleepy David, hovered in the doorway. "Bad?" she mouthed at Rachel.

"No." Rachel glanced at Ann, who nodded. "Come in."

Mark, who was quite a bit taller than Ann, had folded over her. He moved so his forehead rested on her shoulder, then pulled himself straight and wiped his face.

"Why don't you go wash up?" Ann suggested with a swipe at a tear on his cheek and a gentle smile. He took a deep breath and without looking at anyone else, left the room silently.

Ann reached for Colleen and Rachel in a group hug. "We're going to have a baby," she told Colleen. Rachel felt her quiver. "That is, if I can carry one."

"Oh, Ann." Colleen stepped back and patted David's back. The little one's eyes were closed. "Are you? I mean, you're—"

"Not a young chick, that's for sure," Rachel cut in. "Can I put him to bed?" She reached for the baby, hoping Colleen would agree. Rachel needed to hold that little bundle, something solid and real, and she needed to leave the room for fear of blubbering over, shrieking at Ann for allowing this to happen at all, let alone so soon after her stroke.

Colleen transferred David to Rachel's shoulder. She cuddled the warm baby and tiptoed out. Passing Mark on the way to the stairs, she was doubly glad to have her arms full. The need to hit her brother-in-law, or at the least scream, was so huge she didn't know what she might have done without the distraction.

They stopped and stared, or glared on her part, at each other. Mark swallowed. "I called Maeve and asked her to wait, not to come tonight."

Rachel nodded and moved by him to the steps. The best idea he'd had in the last twenty minutes. Colleen had dressed David for sleeping in a blue and white pinstriped fleece, but Rachel wasn't ready to lay him down. She stood beside the crib and swayed, remembering Maeve and the feelings of helplessness and hurt, delight mixed with fear and anger; the perplexing joy her baby brought and the despair of never seeing Gervas again. Gervas had tried to reach her, he'd said, not knowing about the baby. To say what? That he was sorry? That he wanted to see her whenever he breezed through the States? Would she have told him about the baby?

He might have sent money. Thinking that hurt worse than cutting ties.

"Rach." Ann stood silhouetted in the door, dark against the backlit hall.

Rachel twitched with surprise and settled David in the

crib, pulling a light blanket across his little tummy.

"Aren't you going to say anything?" Ann whispered.

You idiot! What are you thinking?! was the first thing that came to mind. Rachel settled for the second. "I love you." She walked over to hug Ann. "And I can't stand the thought of watching you suffer."

Ann led the way to the room Rachel was using and turned to face her once inside. "Um, maybe I didn't say this right. It's a baby, not cancer."

Rachel felt the tears and wiped them. "I heard you. Women die, even now. And you're almost fifty. What are the chances of having a normal pregnancy? All the—"

"Thanks," Ann said, cutting her off. She sighed, looked at her reflection in the mirror over the bureau and smoothed a hair at her temple. "It's not like I planned this. I probably won't end up, you know, having the baby anyway. Remember how it was before Ritchie."

And after. Yes, Rachel recalled the devastating miscarriages. "I'm sorry. Of course I'm excited. I guess." She went over to hug her sister, gently, from the side, and rested her cheek on Ann's shoulder. "Mark looked train-wrecked."

Ann breathed out. "Yeah. He'll be all right. I left him explaining to our dear Colleen why he wouldn't want a baby with me."

"Oh, no." Rachel pictured Colleen, who was on the naïve side, with her china doll eyes and gentle voice, trying to discuss the matter logically with Counselor Mark Roth. She shook with withheld giggles.

"Mark said he was going to get a vas…a vasectomy tomorrow," Ann choked out. "And Colleen…she…she says, 'Why? Don't you want any…more…more babies?'"

Rachel let her laughter out.

"That's when I had to leave," Ann said.

Rachel hugged her closer. "You do know how serious this is, right?" she whispered.

"Yes," Ann whispered back. "Doctor Granger is sending me to a high risk specialist who's at University Hospital. They work with the specialists at the baby hospital. They're very good. If anyone can get me—us—through this, they will."

"Okay. You have lots of good hands to hold, you know."

"I know." Ann wiggled and Rachel backed away. "Mark called and told Maeve and Gervas to wait, not come tonight."

Rachel couldn't help the twitch at the sound of Gervas's name. "You have something to tell me, sis?" She stared at Ann, who went pink and looked away.

"It wasn't my place," she said evenly.

"How can you—" Rachel lowered her voice, "say that? She's my daughter. You shouldn't keep secrets like that."

"Only for a couple of days. Mark was worried. He told me that Gervas asked him some questions about international law."

I'll bet he did. "That's not Mark's field."

"No, but there are people he can ask. Rachel, what's this all about? Does it have something to do with whatever you had yesterday? In your pocket? And why the police keep circling my house?"

20

Rachel allowed herself to be pulled away from the delicate topic of her sister's pregnancy. Hiding the ring seemed pointless now. She walked to the bureau, opened the top drawer, and grasped the velvet bag. Turning and not meeting Ann's eyes, she thrust the bag in her direction. "Here. This is what Gervas is after. I'm sure."

Ann took the bag and shook out the ring on to her palm. "Oh."

"Disappointed?" Rachel asked. "It's not much, I know. It's not even very big."

"But it belonged to him, and you needed to keep something else, besides Maeve, something to remind you of him."

"You don't have to get all analytical," Rachel groused.

"It's beautiful in its simplicity," Ann said. She held it up by the bottom. "The stone in this twisting design isn't cut but sort of polished. It's red?"

Rachel walked closer to study the ring. She'd never really spent much time reflecting on it after she'd taken it. She'd hidden it away, trying not to allow guilt to consume her, like a naughty child who refused to admit fault, or an insane person who justified every action, no matter how crippling to society. "Right—a ruby, just chipped into a sphere. Set in pure gold, of course. This ring was designed before jewelers learned how to create facets in gemstones."

"Wh-what?"

Rachel saved the ring from hitting the carpet when Ann's

hand started to shake.

"Good heavens," Ann said. "I was thinking that it looked like something I saw in a museum, but, really?"

Rachel slipped the ring back into the bag and cinched it tight. "He used to wear it, you know. It's not loud and flashy, but it is unique. Part of a set from antiquity. Etruscan."

"Antiquity? Etruscan?" Ann sat on the bed.

"Are you okay?"

"No wonder. But why does he want it now? Surely he didn't just wake up one day and think, 'Ah ha! I know where my ring's been all these years. I'll just go to the States, find Rachel Michels, and ask for it back.'"

Rachel sniffed, sighed. "I…when he came…" She stood and paced back to the bureau and tucked the bag in the drawer again. "I guess I was so overwhelmed I didn't really give him a chance to explain." She blinked rapidly in an attempt to stem tears but gladly fit into her sister's welcoming embrace.

"I understand," Ann said. "You love him."

"I can't! I can't be just another of his groupies." She took a breath and wiped her eyes, yet stayed huddled against Ann.

"He wants to see you. I've got your back."

"Yeah. Like always. Tomorrow's too soon."

"I don't know," Ann whispered. "Seems like the world is about to fall apart, from what he said on the news. Who knows? This little ring might be the secret to save us."

"Ha." Rachel leaned back to look at Ann. "I think it's more likely the next generation is going to help us." She touched Ann's stomach. "Who knows? You might be growing that special person right now."

Ann quirked her mouth. "I doubt it. Anyway, what's Etruscan?"

Rachel laughed. "You're slipping off your pedestal, big

sister. I thought you knew everything."

"Right now I only know that you're troubled and I want to help. Gervas seemed like a nice man. He was sincere. I felt it."

"Maybe." Rachel pulled away. "He'd better not hurt Maeve." The memory of last Sunday's surprise visit from her daughter made sense. She smacked her forehead. "Of course!"

"What?"

"That's what Maeve was doing. Sneaky. He's got her trying to do his dirty work." Anger surged down to her toes, which she curled in the carpet. "Oh, I could kill him!"

"What?"

Rachel glanced at Ann. "Maeve stopped in on Sunday, but didn't want to come to church—"

"I didn't go, either."

"And when I asked what she wanted, she said she was just going to look for something, but she wouldn't tell me what." Rachel sat to tie on her sneakers.

"What are you doing?"

"I'm not about to call every hotel in town to find out where that creep is staying, but I can—"

"He's at Maeve's place."

The news only fueled Rachel's ire. She ground her teeth.

"Wait!" Ann called from behind when Rachel stormed out. "I'm coming with you."

Mark met them at the bottom of the stairs. "Now what?"

"Give me your keys," Rachel said and held out her hand.

Mark looked past her to Ann. "What's going on?"

"She wants to see Gervas."

"And Maeve," Rachel added.

"I'm going with her," Ann said.

Mark folded his arms. "It's late. It's Tuesday night.

Ritchie's coming on Thursday. I've had enough drama for the day. Seriously, none of my courtroom trials have had this much ridiculous activity." He shoved his hands in his pockets and looked down while slumping against the wall. "I can't handle any more tonight. And you of all people, Rachel. After all that's going on, I would think you would have more sense. You know very well no one's going anywhere right now. Let's not make hasty decisions. Sleep on it."

"Save all the platitudes, Counselor." Rachel whipped back up the steps and almost slammed her bedroom door before remembering the sleeping baby. Mark was right, as much as she hated to admit it. Risking Ann's safety with those goons out there was stupid. She paced back and forth twelve times, stripped and took a long, hot bath before sliding into bed with a book she knew she wouldn't read.

At 12:03 her door opened and closed.

"Ann?"

Ann hugged herself, then crawled into bed. Rachel moved over to make room. "Never much of a sleeper, were you?"

Rachel's sister ducked her chin and pulled up the blanket. "I was sleeping fairly well, after the stroke and all. But, tonight." She rolled over. "Mark took something, so he's snoring. I can't take any other meds. Obviously. There's just so much to think about."

"Yeah."

"Rachel, you need to tell me what's going on. I have to know what to expect. How to defend myself. And the baby. I never want to be that helpless and vulnerable again after we found out about Gene."

"I guess." Tormented by promises and memories of what Ann had gone through while her first husband had been missing and her mother-in-law held the purse strings, Rachel let go and mentally apologized to Mark. "Yesterday, some weird things happened."

Ann rolled back. Rachel squeezed her sister's hand while she composed her thoughts. Nothing was going to make sense no matter how she put it. "My former lover came to see me and I freaked out so I was told by my assistant to take an extra week of vacation, even though I'm technically in charge of my department and I'm starting to really hate my job. I found out the guy I was crushing on belongs to a terrorist organization intent on the downfall of the European Union and my daughter discovered the father I tried to keep her from her whole life. Everyone lied to me, and then some creeps in black vans tried to kill me on the highway. And, ouch, let go of my hand."

Ann released her nail-gouging grip. "Sorry."

"I wouldn't be surprised if Mom and Dad knew about this."

Silence.

"Do they, Ann?"

"I don't know. They'd probably come and take custody of you if they did." Ann reached over and turned on the bedside lamp. She plucked up the book Rachel had been reading.

"What?"

Ann grinned. "Just wondering what dreams I'd woken you from, and if this book had triggered them."

"That's a ridiculously sappy romance about a couple of vets."

"I see." Ann leaned her head against the crook of the elbow and studied Rachel's face. "Vans? Ancient jewelry and the downfall of Europe? What has your Gervas been up to? And you think he's trying to induct Maeve into this terrorist organization? That's why the police are around? Looking for

Gervas?"

"No, no, no. Gervas is…he's…he couldn't. No, it's his brother. The one who's a member of the German parliament. Scott told Mark he was part of an underground organization Manheim founded that's trying to keep the European Union from succeeding. If they create enough chaos, the Union will fracture and war will result. You can see some of what's happening with the euro—you know, how some of the countries in the Union can't get their money regulated, and they're in desperate financial condition?"

"I read about Greece going bankrupt. And Ireland demanding help. Is that it?"

"I think so."

"But what would they hope to gain if Europe goes bankrupt? We'll just bail them out, like we always do."

"No one country can do that. It's too big. And if I understand it right, it's not just the money. Can you imagine how vulnerable the rest of Europe would be? How chaotic?"

Ann shivered. "Just like the late thirties, all over again. I think I get it. Some delusional being will step in with a plan. Gervas involved you? You were chased? Is that why you don't have your car? What happened? Mark should have told me."

"Don't be mad. You've just been so sick. We would have told you."

"I don't like being kept in the dark."

"Neither do I," Rachel said, using her "you've been naughty" voice.

Ann snorted. "All right, then. Go on."

"I think Scott was following me after I left work yesterday morning. He met up with me at a gas station. I sort of flipped and left quickly. I was on my way here, out on the beltline, when all of a sudden two vans came along on either side of me.

I tried to drive ahead, but then I got a flat, and neither of the vans would let me move off to the side of the road, or exit. I was riding on the rim, sparks flying like crazy and I had to do something. Of course there were no cops around. I stomped on the brake, then Scott came racing in and cut off one of the vans so I could exit. I limped into a garage, called Mark, reported it to the cops, and you know the rest."

"Oh, dear Lord. You could have been killed."

Now that she was reliving the scenario, Rachel admitted how terrified she'd been. It had been a joke at first, like someone says she was almost killed when some inattentive driver cut her off. This had been real and intentional. She swallowed several times and let the adrenalin rush roar through her.

"The police?" Ann asked after a couple of minutes. "Did they find out who they were? And why they were chasing you?"

"I don't think so. But Mark asked them to watch the house."

"Fat lot of good that will do. That's why Mark put off his trip. Trying to be a hero."

"Yeah. He is, you know. Not like, well, you know. Him."

"Gervas."

"Yeah." Rachel took some cleansing breaths.

"At least he tried to keep in touch, all that time ago. And he's here now."

"But not because… Only because he wants the ring back."

"I don't know. Do you think he knew about Maeve before he came over?"

"No."

"What do you think Maeve did when she found out?"

Rachel owned that hurt, let it funnel in and curled her

fists. "I'm more concerned about why they didn't come to me, what they hoped to accomplish by keeping the news secret. Maybe I'm wrong and they've known each other for years."

Ann uncurled Rachel's hands and squeezed. "That's not the way it seemed when they were here. He said he had only just found out about her, and that he'd never meant to hurt anyone. Honey, it was Maeve who wanted to keep the secret for a while, at least until she got a chance to know him before they told you. He and Mark went outside to talk before they left. I don't know what about."

"Maybe Gervas wanted to ask him about returning missing international property, or something."

"Hmm? You mean, all the treasure the Nazis took during World War Two? And, missing?"

Rachel squirmed. "Stolen. I stole it. There, okay?"

Ann giggled. "Righteous Rachel."

"Yeah, yeah. Anyway, Gervas must have told Maeve, got her to help him get it back."

"If anything, Maeve's the one who thinks she's helping by trying to find it first before asking. Love that girl, but we…anyway, do you think the ring actually has anything to do with that other business—vans, you said? I can't believe the police aren't on the case, have you in protective custody, or something." She sat up. "Oh! What about Colleen and the baby? Are we in danger? We should—"

"Shh!" She tugged Ann's arm. "Calm down. We're perfectly safe. No one would get away with any acts of terrorism in the US. It's been ten years since 9/11. There are too many government safeguards in place."

"Hmm." Ann snuggled back in again. "I hope you're right."

"Besides, we have your hero to protect us."

"Mark is pretty special. I have surely been blessed."

Rachel stayed quiet until Ann's breathing made her think her sister had fallen asleep. Thoughts of Gervas, the tone of his voice and the weariness in it echoing, making her heart continue to thaw despite her best efforts at keeping herself immune to the effect he'd always had on her.

"Rach?"

Apparently Ann hadn't succumbed to slumber yet. "Yes?"

"Do you ever wish you'd found someone else? Gotten married and had more kids?"

"I couldn't."

"Couldn't wish or couldn't fall in love again?"

"Couldn't be that vulnerable again," Rachel whispered.

"Oh, Rachel," Ann whispered back. "If it's any comfort, when I saw him look at Maeve, I could tell he had that father's love for a daughter. He was disappointed that he'd missed so much of her life."

"His choice."

"Maybe not entirely."

"He did say he'd tried to contact me." Rachel sighed and let it drop.

"What are you going to say to him tomorrow?"

"You mean, tonight?" Rachel looked at the clock. One a.m. Now she'd never get to sleep, worrying about talking to him. "I'm not sure."

"I'm looking forward to seeing Colleen's reaction to meeting him."

"He can act all suave and sincere in public. He's good at that."

"Colleen has this sense about people," Ann said. "She'll tell us."

"Go to sleep, Ann. You need to rest for two, now."

Ann yawned. "Right. You get your beauty sleep."

"Ha."

<>

Gervas watched the tight grip Maeve had on her steering wheel the next evening as they drove into Madison. She must be nervous about seeing her mother. So was he, to tell the truth.

"She'll be mad," Maeve said, as if she'd read this thoughts.

"She's had some time to think about it." Gervas had tried to contact Rachel by telephone twice during the day, in between working on his manuscript and taking a walk through the neighborhood. Humidity had lessened and the day had been pleasant. It seemed most people were away during the work week and he'd met only a young mother pushing a child in a pram. Rachel had not responded to his calls or messages, eerily reminding him of the early days after he'd left her alone, and unknown to him at the time, expecting their child.

Other media people who had seen the news report had called also. He'd done two radio interviews and handed off two other requests for speaking engagements to his agent. Manheim had remained as unreachable as Rachel. At least he'd not seen suspicious vehicles in the area.

"I hope Aunt Ann's appointment with the doctor went okay," Maeve said. "Maybe she just has an ulcer or something."

"Perhaps."

"Here we are." Maeve shut off the engine in front of Ann and Mark's home. Two other vehicles were already in the driveway. "Oh, good. That's Colleen's car. She's married to my cousin Ritchie."

"Ah. More family."

"Come on. You'll love her. She's so sweet. And their baby, David, is adorable."

Gervas followed. As he walked, he prepared himself mentally and emotionally for this meeting, much the same as he did before giving an address to a vast audience. He breathed deeply and focused on his topic. His topic? He had no real agenda. Even the importance of the ring and warding off that traitorous blackmailer had faded since learning of Maeve and getting to know her family.

Manheim was up to some trick. Gervas had sometimes called him Loki, after the Norse god, during their childhood. Gervas knew his brother's vote was crucial, but he also knew that Manheim had placed too much importance on this one item…on the furor caused if Regenbogen dared expose the family for lack of discovering their neighbor's fate and attempting to return items held in safekeeping during the Reich. No one spoke of those times, though everyone knew they could not be so easily put aside. Manheim's last garbled news of questionable provenance of the items was puzzling at best.

"Come on!" Maeve stood at the front door with Mark.

At least these thoughts had kept Gervas from a rare attack of nerves which had threatened earlier. Maeve was smiling.

Rachel was not.

21

Gervas once again allowed Maeve to pull him by the arm. "Come in! Now, don't be all mad, Mom. I just…well, I deserved some time to get to know him first. See? It's all right."

Dark rings beneath Rachel's eyes were exaggerated by the use of cosmetics. Her face was pale, though not washed-out. She looked more like her sister, Ann, now. Fragile. In need of protection. Or comfort. He locked eyes with her, the dark blue mesmerizing. He'd forgotten that. Or had he?

"There he is!" Maeve squealed, breaking the spell. "Come to me, little David buddy."

He watched her take the baby from her mother. Ann appeared at Rachel's side and the tall husband, Mark, looked over their heads. The women were lovely, not exactly alike, of course. Both wore khaki-colored short pants women like for summer wear, and blouses of complementary colors. Ann set her hand on Rachel's arm and whispered something. Then Ann and Mark walked away. Gervas waited, patient now in a way he couldn't have been when he'd been younger and much less wise.

Maeve stepped through the door and closed it behind her. Rachel rubbed her arms as if she was cold, though the temperature was still pleasant and warm in the early evening. The sun had slowly moved west but hovered yet. Lingering scents of rose and musky lavender surrounded them. A dog barking nearby and a mourning dove made this neighborhood cozy. He stood still, letting her come.

"I apologize for my behavior on Monday," she said. Her

voice was modulated with little inflection.

"No need, though accepted of course. I never wanted you to be afraid. Apparently my methods of searching for you were…how is it? Over the top?"

"Yes."

He took note of the silver threads in her hair and remembered the times he set his chin on her crown when he held her. A perfect fit. "Rachel, please."

She closed her eyes.

"Let us talk. As old friends, perhaps?"

"Friends with a past." Rachel looked beyond him, across the lawn. She put her hands in her pockets, took them out, twisted them, and then grabbed her elbows.

"Shall we walk?" he asked and nodded toward a paved path that wound out of sight behind Ann and Mark's home.

"Yes." She set an energetic pace. He let her work off some of the tension they both obviously felt. Skaters and dog-walkers and bicyclists steered around them.

"Maeve is a treasure," he said at length, when she finally slowed. "May we sit on that bench?"

In the silence after they settled a foot apart, Gervas considered what to tell her. "You have done well. Had I been aware I would never have left you to raise her alone."

"Why did you stay away?" She still clutched her arms and stared ahead.

"I was perhaps mistaken in my thought at the time that you would accept a man like me…hampered as I was by an unstable marriage and lifestyle of travel. Of constant turmoil."

"You said, and I quote, 'I am tangled in a web of my own choosing.'"

"So I was." He nodded, wishing she would look at him, and touched she'd recalled his words. Of course they could have been less profound. "Rachel." At last she turned her eyes on him again. "I was not a good person. Even now, I recognize that I am not a good person. Older, a little wiser, disappointing and disappointed." He knew he sounded melodramatic.

Rachel raised one eyebrow. "When did you learn about Maeve?"

"When she forced me to look at her a few days ago. I was in the airport about to fly home and she made me see my features in her face."

"Why are you here? In the States? What do you want?"

Gervas reached to touch a lock of her hair with his forefinger. She allowed it, staring back at him. "So much alike, mother and daughter. Questions. Yes, I will answer. I came to find you. A desperate hope that you had kept the bauble, the ring I'd worn once, flaunting a tie to antiquity as if I had the right to do so."

Rachel broke eye contact. "If you knew I had it all this time, why didn't you ask for it back when you first missed it?"

"I tried to stay in contact with you. By telephone, by letter. I explained, or tried to. The calls were refused, the letters returned. I wrote to you at your residence in Madison. Not to the house you have now."

"My house? You've been to my…never mind." She set her hands on either side of her hips and leaned forward. "I've been thinking about that. My parents didn't know about you, so it doesn't make sense for them to not even let me see letters. I stayed with them before I moved in with Peggy."

"Your vigilant friend."

"Too vigilant." Rachel sighed softly and searched his face.

Such a sad smile she wore, full of regret. He longed to change her mood.

"It was her. She would have…would do something like

that, thinking she was protecting me."

He nodded. "Yes, it makes sense. When Maeve explained that you shared an apartment while she was young, I considered the possibility. Ms. Atwater shows great animosity toward me even now. I did not at first understand why."

At last Rachel smiled. "How rude of her to treat a famous person as you with so little civility."

A laugh burst from him. "Exactly!" He was delighted by her changing temperament. Dare he hope she would let him back in her life, at least as the father of her child?

"I have your ring," she said, splashing ice water over them. "It seemed your desperation led our daughter to lie to me about wanting to find it. Shall I assume you put her up to it?"

"No, no, no." He held out his hands. "You must let me explain."

Rachel rose and began to walk again, but not toward her sister's house. He followed. All he'd been doing since he came to the States was follow. "Rachel, consider the circumstances," he said to her back. A young boy riding a bicycle made him dance out of the way. "I had only learned of her. Our daughter. I had no idea how to treat her. Perhaps I was wrong. Rachel, stop, please."

She came to an abrupt halt and stepped off the path, keeping her back turned. "She wanted the chance to learn our story from my side. To decide whether I could be trusted."

"Can you?"

"Won't you let me show you?"

She slipped her hand into her pocket and reached back, all without looking at him. "Here. Take it."

Gervas stared at her palm where the ring lay. In it he saw betrayal, generations of it in all situations. He stepped close to her, took her hand and curled her fingers over it. He slid his arm around her and set his chin on her head. "Let me tell you why I came to find it. Your trust is important to me as well. Then, together, we will decide what to do."

Rachel turned her cheek to lay against him as she had done long ago, when he'd had no right to hold her. "Okay."

He had taken something precious from her back then and left her with the pain and joy of raising a child. Not without support, but without him.

Without him…a curious tingle made his fingers tremble.

Selfish, he had always been. He would never deny that. But now he wondered what that looked like to others. Had he hurt Katrine with his absence? Max? Surely Julianne, during their very brief marriage had been wounded by his emotional and physical absences, but she was an adult and could take care of herself. He'd never had to carry that kind of responsibility— of being there—in his other relationships with adults. The closest he'd come to feeling needed was with Katrine, and Max.

But Rachel had never been like Sylvie, Julianne, and the other faceless and nameless women who'd been a dalliance. Selfish, spoiled at the ease to which whatever he'd wanted had been available. Rachel's face came to him often over the years, usually when he was unprepared to push aside the memory. Her responses came silently to his ears only during student seminars. What would she have thought of his latest chapter? How would she have advised the next book tour? Why did he carry the imprint of her voice, the feel of her mouth, the expression in the depth of her eyes after so many years? Their relationship had been shorter than his second marriage, yet he understood now that Rachel was the only woman who'd truly held his heart.

Gervas touched his chin to Rachel's temple and tightened his grip.

He couldn't expect her to trust him, but he needed to try. Now that he held her, he couldn't imagine letting go again. Together was right. He would start by trusting her and told her of his brother's garbled message.

<>

"Okay" came out of Rachel's mouth as if it was the only response to Gervas's comment. She wondered again what she was getting herself into as they strolled back to Ann's house, her arm clutching his as if she would fall off the face of the earth without it.

"Wait a minute." Rachel slowed, the "trust" word he'd used clicking on another track. "Manheim said something, you said…he told you not to trust….who? or what?"

"I don't know. The connection was unstable and lost soon afterward. I cannot reestablish it." He squeezed her hand. "Although your resourceful daughter promised to help me purchase a new telephone."

"Our daughter. I don't like any of this," Rachel whispered. Should she tell him now or later about the incident on the freeway?

"Neither do I." He stopped and raised her knuckles to his lips. "Except for this."

Feeling herself flush, she ducked her head. "Gervas. Slow down."

A young man in running shorts passed them, leading a boxer with bugged eyes and lolling tongue. They moved out of the way together and kept on walking, slowly. She let him wrap her hand through his arm, blinked away the feel of the kiss, and refocused on his story of political espionage he shared in a quiet, too calm voice.

"This is not the outline of a new book? You've not switched to fiction?"

"I have not. I assure you, when I hear these details I struggle with disbelief. However, I must reach Manheim again soon. I cannot talk to anyone else."

Ann's house was in sight. Soon they would join the others, and Ann would know. She would see how weak Rachel was, how she'd simply melted into Gervas like he'd never left. What was she doing? How could she have allowed this? She tried to remove her hand from Gervas's grip, but his answering clutch evaporated all desire to detach herself. Trust? He wanted her to trust him, he said. "Maeve knows how much of this? Enough to try to find the ring for you?"

"I did not ask her to find the ring," Gervas replied.

"What were you doing at my house?"

"Maeve stopped in. I was with her and she invited me to enter."

There was more to it, but Rachel wouldn't push yet. She wanted to know one more thing before they got back. "How…how did Maeve act? When she knew…when you told her? About us?"

"When I admitted that I was her father?" He slowed and inhaled deeply. "She had realized the truth before I did."

"Melissa."

"I believe so." Gervas halted when they left the path and stepped onto the sidewalk leading to Ann's. "She had many questions. I answered as truthfully as I could."

"I was so angry for so long. I didn't think you cared, and then I didn't want you to know. I was afraid you'd take her away. Or pay me off quietly, or something." Rachel felt bared and bleeding after her admission. She looked only as high as his mouth to see he chewed on his lower lip.

"I do not know what I would have done," he said. "My marriage to Sylvie was always…vitriolic at best before we ended it. I must admit that I had several affairs."

Rachel sniffed. "You married someone else."

"Yes. Briefly. A mistake for both of us. My memories of you were not…overwritten."

Rachel hitched a breath. She cocked her head. What had he meant? His arms had felt natural around her and she could have stayed with him rubbing his face against hers, leaving his never-forgotten musky scent. His heartbeat galloped beneath her cheek and she held her smile at her effect.

"Mom?" Rachel turned at the sound of Maeve's voice. The girl stood barefoot on the concrete, David on her hip. The picture made her sigh at the memory of herself at about that age, with a child of her own. What would she do to make sure Maeve never went through the same trauma?

Gervas took her elbow and led her on. "We appear unscathed, yes?"

Maeve giggled. "Yes. So, did you…?" She cleared her throat.

Rachel wasn't ready to hear her own voice, afraid of what might come out.

"I believe we have made much progress toward clearing the air, as you say," Gervas said in place of the vacuum.

"I was worried," Maeve said as she shifted the baby in her arms.

"Allow me." Gervas took David who lifted his hand to pat Gervas's chin.

Nothing would stifle Rachel's oncoming tears. She mumbled "excuse me" and quickly moved past them into the house, rushing to the powder room before she met anyone else.

Broken bits of her life rattled as she ran, tumbling inside her. She felt like a toy being shaken in frustration when it refused to light up. Tears released most of the pent-up angst she'd carried since she knew he'd come looking for her. He had made a choice, he'd told her, all those years ago. And again, now. He asked for a chance. He told her he trusted her and depended on her to help him know what to do about the blackmailer.

Rachel ran water in the sink and flushed her eyes. She wouldn't deny that she had longed for him, dreamed of him, even when she knew he'd never come back. Even last week when she'd been angry and afraid. She'd deluded herself she could attempt a relationship with another man. She leaned over the sink, avoiding her reflection. "Not just any man, Rachel," she whispered. A mental image of seeing a red car in her rearview mirror, speeding up to cut off that black van made her lip quiver. A piece of the foggy puzzle fit into place. Scott Warfield admitted to being a member of a faction determined to create chaos and split the European Union. Gervas's brother was being blackmailed to vote against bailing from the Union so they wouldn't have to help members facing economic ruin, and in so doing, jeopardize their own infrastructure.

She whirled and faced the door. If he was being blackmailed to vote against, that must mean he hadn't wanted to vote to save the member countries in the first place—that he wanted to take Germany out of the Union. Rachel patted her pocket. She had the heirloom the blackmailer wanted. Who else knew? Why was Scott even at Mendota? Was he trying to organize a faction there too? Rachel was a fool to trust anyone. For a minute she thought she might vomit, and swallowed away the sensation.

That made her think of Ann. Rachel thrust her fears of everything else aside for the moment. She practiced a few smiles, pinched her cheeks, and left to find the others.

She tracked voices to the living room and stood out of sight, listening.

"Seems that as soon as I knew why I was feeling so sick, I got much better," Ann was saying.

"I'm so excited for you, Aunt Ann," Maeve said. "I can hardly believe it. I'll have another aunt or uncle who's a year younger than a nephew."

General chuckles sounded.

"I hope so," Ann said softly.

Rachel sauntered in at that point. Ann sat in a chair close to the door, the others ranging on the other pieces of furniture around the room. Gervas and Maeve were in the soft maroon love seat. Mark perched alone on the matching sofa while Colleen rocked the baby in an oversized stuffed chair with stylized peacock feathers decorating the upholstery.

"Hello, all," Rachel said and sat on the arm of her sister's chair, though she knew Ann disliked it. She squeezed a one-armed hug around Ann and smiled at the returned greetings. "I'm glad you're doing better."

"And you?" Ann asked.

"Hungry, actually. I'm sorry we stayed out so long."

Colleen rose gracefully and without giving Mark an option, settled David in his arms. "I'm on it! Dinner in a few."

Rachel exchanged a smirk with Ann, who then lovingly watched her husband hold the sleeping baby. "Practice," Ann mouthed. They moved toward the kitchen, followed by Maeve and Gervas.

Colleen took pity on Mark and put the baby to bed before they ate. During rounds of "please pass the potatoes" conversation flowed around the work of the younger generation. Since Maeve had been absent for many days,

Rachel was happy to hear about her job and new advertising client.

Mark stayed quiet, eating picky fashion, staring at Ann or Maeve or Gervas in turn. Rachel wondered what, besides his own pending fatherhood, was on his mind. He did seem to be studying Gervas and his treatment of Maeve—something she could hardly stop doing, either.

They talked about the television reporter who'd interviewed Gervas, laughing and sharing their opinion of the experience. Rachel smiled and picked up her water glass, leaned back and fell in love with motherhood all over again. The jealousy and resentment she'd enjoyed for most of her life was gone and she finally understood serenity without its weight.

"I had no idea the camera had me in the background," Maeve said. "I never would've stood there, gawking like a teenager in front of the newest boy band."

Gervas wiped his mouth. "You made appropriate facial expressions," he said. "I even believed how dire the state of the world has become."

Ann chuckled, then turned pale. Rachel hoped her sister wouldn't be sick, but realized it was a lost battle when Ann hopped up and left. Mark picked up his dinner knife and tested the edge with his thumb before raising his eyes to Rachel.

Rachel hadn't realized how pervasive the silence had become until she spoke loud. "She knows about the vans chasing me yesterday."

Rare anger sparked in Mark's eyes. "Why? Why did you have to tell her?" He set the knife down much too precisely. "This isn't some spy game. She cannot be put under any more strain. Especially not now." He pushed back and got to his feet. "It's time we had a talk, Gervas."

Tossing her napkin next to her plate, Rachel matched

glares with her brother-in-law. "This needs to be an open discussion, Mark. We can't keep tiptoeing around. It won't go away if we ignore it."

The sudden spurt of a siren outside on the street made Rachel jump. She reached for Maeve's hand before noticing her daughter and Gervas sending each other some kind of telepathy? "What's going on?"

"Vans chasing you, Mom?"

Gervas's phone also chose that moment to stun them with some reggae measure. "At last." Rachel took a deep breath as Mark headed for the front door and Gervas, already frowning, checked his screen.

Uh, oh. Rachel realized she had failed to mention that teensy-weensy little action sequence on the beltline the other day.

Ann returned, hovering, as if she needed to herd them all in an emergency change of direction. "Let's move to the living room for coffee and dessert."

Gervas stood. "Excuse me. I must hear of this…chasing. But I must first accept this call from the embassy."

22

Gervas said nothing when Mark followed him into the hall while the others went the opposite direction, passing into the living room. Gervas forced himself to remain calm in light of hearing about Rachel being chased, a fact she'd chosen not to share with him, and instead pondered this call. What was this about? The ambassador from Germany, Karl Schelling, held a PhD from Harvard besides having studied law at Freiburg, his own university, and was a brilliant politician. He was not particularly jocular, though not ill-humored during their past occasions to meet, mostly at social or diplomatic functions.

Stopping just inside the room near the front door, the one with the glass doors, Gervas stood and held the phone while he waited for the receptionist to make the connection. Schelling came on the line abruptly, as usual.

"Professor Friedemann. Thank you for answering my call. I wish to discuss your television interview which was brought to my attention earlier by Deutsches Generalkonsulat Chicago."

Gervas pressed his lips together and tried to commandeer his whirling thoughts. Perhaps he'd erred giving the brief comments on television and cautious neutrality would be best. "Ambassador Schelling."

"No pleasantries, my friend?" The ambassador chuckled dryly. He spoke in English, less accented than Gervas's. When in the States… "The Consular General apparently does more than hand out German language certificates and renew passports. He also watches television. Now, you are invited to

DANK Haus in Chicago to speak on the topic of the looming crisis in Europe as you adroitly put it. You will receive an invitation shortly with directions, and are expected promptly at four p. m. tomorrow. Naturally you will stay on topic, that is, of the obvious struggle to maintain our monetary policy within the Union. The plan to work on coordinating our common fiscal policy."

"Of course, Ambassador. Thank you."

The ambassador barely paused. "You will then report to Washington DC where the German Language Club will sponsor another discussion before which you and I will rehearse talking points."

What else could he say? "Very good, Ambassador. There are extenuating—"

"Madam Chancellor has asked me to remind you of the importance of presenting the correct facts. She recognizes your expertise in the field of socio-economics and requests your counsel in the Bundestag. The Federal Minister of Economic Cooperation and Development has need of some, ah, perspective. You will please return home to offer your, shall we say, unique viewpoint."

The ambassador was particularly obtuse, almost as if he knew someone was listening, much like Mark, and needed to make sure no privileged information leaked. Gervas sincerely doubted that his brother, the Federal minister of Economic Cooperation and Development, desired any perspective and most certainly not from him. Unless he returned with ancient artifact in hand to appease Regenbogen. What would Rachel think he should do? "I am honored, Ambassador. I must also tell you that I am making arrangements to bring to the States my…a family member for specialized…" Aware Mark had not given him any privacy, Gervas turned and lowered his voice, "medical care."

"How can we be of assistance?" the ambassador asked.

"Perhaps we can discuss the matter further," Gervas said in a louder voice, "after I arrive."

"Your flight information and lodging arrangements will be sent to your e-mail address."

Without even a farewell, the ambassador disconnected. A voice near his shoulder intruded.

"You are really a piece of work, aren't you, Friedemann?"

Gervas faced Mark's accusation. The vernacular "piece of work" he understood, though he still asked, "To what are you referring?"

"You just got here. Found your daughter. Made her believe you wanted to be a father to her after all these years. Got Rachel eating out of your hand. Again. And then you up and leave? You pig."

Gervas studied Rachel's brother-in-law. This version of Mark Roth was not the easy-going yet sharp attorney of a few days earlier. This man was obviously struggling, in distress. Gervas overlooked the insult. "I am not leaving permanently. I would never do that. I could not do so now." He kept his hands at his sides and studied a nearby photograph on the wall. Rachel and Ann's parents. "It seems I made a, a stir with my comments on television. I must make amends to my government and help my brother."

"You have what you came for, in other words. The ring you can return to your brother to stop the blackmailer."

"I wonder the wisdom of that action now. Nevertheless, I want Rachel to come with me."

"Huh."

"It is convenient she has vacation. Consider, if you will, that my proposal to keep her in my company, my care, will also remove her from being chased by vehicles on the road? Is it true? That must not happen." Black vans had followed Maeve. Dare Gervas tell this angry man? "Perhaps then Maeve will stay with you when she is not at her place of employment?"

Mark rubbed his hand over his face. Maeve slipped inside the room to grasp her uncle's elbow.

"Maeve is perfectly capable of taking care of herself," she said. "However, I will concede that since my parents," she smirked, "need some time to catch up, I will make the great sacrifice of coming here after work while they are out of town. I can pitch in here, love up David and all." She winked at Gervas, who was once again astounded at her acuity. He still needed to make her perceive the danger.

Mark stared at her, then set his eyes on him. "Something else?"

Maeve tugged his chin back in her direction and spoke softly and firmly. "I didn't know about Mom being chased. No one bothered to tell me. However, a black van tailed the two of us on Monday when we were driving from her office to the house to check on her."

"Nothing happened," Gervas added. "We weren't certain of being followed at the time."

"Oh, I think by the third time I'd circled the block and the van was still behind us, we were positive."

Mark set his hands on his hips and asked like he already knew the answer, "And the police said what?"

"Oh, come on, Uncle Mark."

"Maybe you should go with him and your mom."

Maeve pursed her lips. "After all you did to help me get this job? You really want a nanny for your new baby that bad? Cuz that's all the work I'll ever be able to get if I get fired. That won't do your rep any good, either, you know, after you vouched for me to help me get the job.”

Gervas watched this exchange through narrowed eyes. Of course Maeve was correct. Timing. He’d been a victim of bad timing his whole life. First with Sylvie, then Rachel. The son he’d raised as his own—Max. Maeve’s employment schedule.

“I can, however,” Maeve said, “work from home mostly. I have everything I need on my computer, and you have great WiFi, and the client’s in Madison anyway. I haven’t seen any black vans around here. I have seen, however, several police drive-bys and a rather conservative Buick parked at random places with conservative people around and in it on the cul-de-sac.”

Mark nodded at her.

Gervas had not noticed those things. He glanced at Maeve who answered his unasked question.

“Uncle Mark’s rich. Like independently wealthy, maybe as rich as you, so he can hire...*people*...for security purposes. Why they live here in some little house in a *neighborhood* instead of on some sweet country estate, I don’t understand.” She rolled her eyes at Mark.

“I’m not buying you a pony, kid. Get over it.” Mark swatted her bottom and strode away, calling over his shoulder, “We still have to talk.”

Gervas swiveled back to see his daughter’s eyes filling with tears. She sniffed. “I’m okay with you going, you know, if Mom’s with you.” She wiped her eyes. “I just want to know what’s going on. Will you call me every day?”

He wrapped her up tight and spoke into her hair. “Twice a day.”

“So where are you going, when will you be back, and what about Katrine?”

<>

Rachel knew something drastic was up when Gervas and Maeve strolled into the living room where Ann had set up a coffee tray and cookies.

"Guess what, Mom?" Maeve giggled and dove toward her. "I hope your passport's up to date."

"My passport?" She turned toward Gervas.

"Da-Gervas is taking you to Germany with him!"

"I beg your pardon?" Since she couldn't raise her eyebrows any farther, she pushed herself to her feet, even though she was working up to a full-fledged tremble with vying anger, excitement, and terror.

"How exciting, Aunt Rachel," Colleen said from her position in the rocking chair where she fed David under a nursing cover.

"Beats Door County," Ann said.

Rachel shifted her attention to Ann. "Sounds like a plot."

Ann shrugged. "I had nothing to do with it."

"Maeve?" Rachel folded her arms.

"Huh, unh." Her daughter shook her head. "If I was in on it, though, you bet I'd be coming too." Maeve helped herself to a delicate gold-rimmed cup and poured coffee.

Rachel wanted to go with Gervas and hated herself for struggling to find an excuse to say of course she wouldn't drop everything and run away with a man…who had shown up out of the blue after leaving her decades earlier, alone and pregnant. She slowly focused on his hopeful, but gentle encouraging expression. He'd been like that all those years ago in lectures and discussion groups, urging her to come up with an appropriate answer. She lov-liked the way the years had mellowed him, with his goatee grizzled gray and the long character lines folded around his mouth. Half-glasses perched atop his receding hairline.

"Mom? Passport?"

"Hmm?" Rachel broke contact, catching Ann's wink while she swung back to Maeve. "Renewed two years ago. Up to date."

Mark appeared in the doorway, leaning in with hands spread to either side of the frame, as if he could hold everything together. "I was just checking the CDC site. There's no reports of the H1N1 flu recurring. Have you—"

"Yes, of course I've been vaccinated," Rachel said. "Don't worry. I'll quarantine myself at home before I visit you and Ann."

Colleen patted David's back. "Sounds like you're all set, then."

Rachel snorted. She hadn't put up even a token argument. Gervas came closer. "I must speak in Chicago tomorrow, then go to Washington before Berlin. I would very much like your company at DANK Haus."

"Dank house?" Colleen asked, wrinkling her nose.

Gervas smiled. "The German American Cultural Center. It seems the Counsel General there saw the interview and tattled? Yes? To Ambassador Schelling."

"Counsel General?" Ann asked. "What is that? I don't think I've heard about that before." She waved her hand at the sofa. "Please, won't you sit and tell us more?"

Rachel followed and sat next to him, close enough to feel him, far enough to keep her senses. As it was she couldn't concentrate on much more than the tone of his voice as he explained about the different sites where the German Embassy spread out in the US—eight other Consulates General to help both German and US citizens breach the cultural barriers. Whether work, study, or travel, the countries were doing their best to overcome international differences. She had been to three of them, accompanying Gervas on lecture tours sponsored by Mendota and Freiburg. Chicago was wonderful. Maybe they could go to the European Jazz Meets Chicago weekend. She'd loved that. What time of year was it held?

"Yes," Gervas was answering something Colleen asked. "I teach one course yet on the development and flow of world modern monetary systems to keep my sixty-year-old mind active. It is a somewhat basic course yet the discussion can be lively. I must keep up with the times."

"I bet," Maeve said. "Especially with the euro. I mean, how is that really all going to work out? With every country having a different way of figuring out what something's worth. Sure, there's a gold standard and all, but, well, look at Ireland. They're going down for the count. And Greece? Really? Who's going to help them? All they have going is tourism."

Rachel grinned. Maeve had the same passion as she had, back in the day.

Gervas leaned forward, resting his elbows on his knees and studied the girl before looking down. His classic thinking pose Rachel remembered well. Had she been a girl still under his spell, she would have flown to find a notebook and pen to take notes.

"My country was known at the end of the last century as the sick man of Europe. It is no secret. A decade later we are the foundation of the European Union, the wealthiest and strongest of them all. What changed?"

He looked up from his hunched position, not exactly inviting response at this point but engaging all of them as he gave each of them brief attention. "In 2003 our former Chancellor, Gerhard Schroder, and his coalition party, much like getting the Republicans and the Libertarians together here in the US, passed a series of reforms, the most prominent of which gave business incentives and unemployment incentives that drastically reduced the unemployment rate. It was of course, not the cure, but a stimulus. Salary rates rose and stabilized due to rolling part time work into full time work. Business grew slower than expected, but because more people had the means to do so, they spent money, unlike Greece, as Maeve pointed out, which, sadly, has little manufacturing base. Too much immigration—perhaps seeking a better climate? Those who cannot afford to pay for artificial heat choose to buy food instead, if they can live in a warmer climate. Thus, the economy has become mostly service based."

He smiled at their daughter, who grinned and rocked back to hug her knees as she sat on the floor near Colleen.

"Yeah, the way we're going. I get it. Like, what do you want on your burger?" Maeve said, tongue in cheek.

"In fact, Germany enjoys a great mutual business partnership with many factories and businesses in the US. Many are transportation. Daimler. BMW."

"Volkswagen," Colleen said.

"Yes. It is a vast list," Gervas said. "Contrast that with the other twenty-seven member nations in the European Union who still have extensive restrictions on work and trade. For instance, the top foreign businesses in Greece with American ties are food and pharmaceuticals. Non-EU workers must have a permit before they can begin to work. So when foreigners, such as those from the only two countries behind Greece in economic stability, Albania and Bulgaria, enter Greece looking for work and do not find it, how are they to live in a country whose government has no funds to provide assistance, or stimulus, or contract for manufacturing and trade, such as we have in Germany? Germany cannot take care of every member of the Union."

Rachel watched Mark slowly edge into the room. He looked as though he'd like to participate in the conversation but wasn't ready to make that nice yet with the enemy.

"How, Dad?"

Rachel raised her brows at the address and looked at Gervas. When had she started referring to him in such intimate terms? Moreover, what else had she missed between father and daughter?

"How is Germany going to work it out?" Maeve said. "There must be some way of figuring out how to stabilize the economy. It's been over a decade now since the euro came out. I mean, even after the Civil War the US economy worked its way back on track in ten years or so."

"Only through violence, vigilantism, force of governance," Gervas responded. He sat up and caught Rachel's eye. She noted his brief weak grin and flicker of gaze upon Maeve.

"After your centennial election, President Hayes withdrew Federal control of the South."

"It never really worked," Mark said quietly. "Even now. Oh, things are much better."

"I see what you mean, Dad," Maeve said.

The quietness must have provoked the baby to babble.

Ann laughed and pushed to her feet. "On that cheerful note, I'll get started cleaning up in the kitchen."

"I'll help." Maeve rose in one fluid movement. Colleen stood as well and with a sympathetic smile for Rachel, followed the others.

Alone with Gervas, close to him, Rachel searched for but couldn't find any traces of her trepidation. True, Maeve hadn't always shown the best judgment, but on wanting a relationship with Gervas, Rachel agreed. "Dad, huh?"

Gervas blushed. "I…" He swallowed and ducked his head.

"She's been calling you that all along?"

"Just tonight."

Rachel changed the subject. "Are you in much trouble with the government? Was it because of your remarks on the local news? What did the ambassador say?"

Gervas answered with a turn of lips and light touch on her cheek. "I do not believe I am in hot water," he said. "But Madam Chancellor wishes my counsel, and I feel obligated to attend her." He turned so he faced her and took her hands, hope softening his expression. "Rachel, will you travel with me? I find that I have sorely missed your wisdom in times like these. For now, will you let me be your companion? I ask nothing else, expect nothing else."

Rachel took a deep breath trying to make sure her mouth stayed behind her brain. She would have been upstairs packing if he hadn't been holding…no, kissing her…knuckles. Ahhh. "I would like to be your traveling companion." She watched the top of his head where he leaned over her hands. The essence of their relationship had changed and developed naturally between them. Neither of them needed any complications.

He raised his face to hers. "A week, I think. Will that work for you? Your Atwater person said you did not have to return until the middle of August."

"True."

Gervas's face came closer.

"Gervas. We're seeing your brother?"

He stopped. "The chancellor asked me to assist."

"Will he…I mean, he'll want the ring back. Right?"

Placing her hand against his heart and holding it there,

Gervas settled them against the back of the couch. He put his other arm around her. "Let's assess the situation first. I hope your brother-in-law can provide some advice?"

"Probably. Do you really think I was chased down because the proverbial 'they' know I have your ring? Why now? In all honestly, I'm a little scared."

"Manheim will know what to do. I do not understand why we have lost contact. I think the ambassador will help. We'll see him tomorrow night in Washington, after the talk in Chicago. It has been arranged." He shifted a little. "Rachel, you must share your recent adventure with me. What is this of chasing men on the highway?"

Bubbles of laughter come from her gut. "It's the other way around, mister." She briefly explained about the vans, the flat tire, and getting off the beltline to find a mechanic. Leaving out the part about Scott seemed the right thing at this point. "I wasn't hurt. I didn't think they wanted to do more than scare me."

Leaving out the Scott to the rescue part might not work. No, she didn't want Gervas to know how stupid she'd been.

"But why me?" Rachel asked. "I can't imagine how anyone would associate me with…well, you. Your situation, your brother? Is that it? The factions in Europe able to intimidate even innocent nobodies here in America in order to…proceed with their agenda? And, if that's it, that anyone associated with you could be in trouble, what about Maeve?"

Gervas hesitated before she felt him tighten his grip. "I am not certain. I wonder if my cell phone's GPS is being monitored. That would make sense. I will destroy it and get another, in any case."

He touched his chin against her temple. "Your brother-in-law is aware of certain aspects of the situation. It was necessary to inform him and he has hired guards."

"That's why he wanted me here, and not alone in my house."

"He will take care of our daughter. I believe him. But we are playing no child's game. My brother's warning is coming true. You must promise to do nothing rash, and do as I tell you on this trip. Can you?"

"I can."

She hoped.

Gervas held her hand to his lips. "I have a thought about the ring."

23

An hour later, Rachel was glad to see Ann seated next to Mark in his home office, where he'd agreed to meet them. Rachel approved of Gervas's plan and hoped Mark would help.

Mark took a deep breath after greeting them. "I apologize for my earlier rudeness, my outburst, Gervas. I regret the things I said."

Surprised, Rachel studied Gervas, who again blushed.

"Forgiven and forgotten," Gervas replied. "If I may?"

What? Rachel widened her eyes and glanced at Ann, who shrugged. Rachel would definitely have to get to the bottom of this. Nuts. Now she missed Gervas's request. She tuned back in.

"I think that would be wise," Mark said. "I prefer to use my bank safety deposit box to store the ring, however, rather than our home or office safe. If you agree?"

In another surprise move that nearly floored Rachel, Gervas turned to ask her, "What do you say, Rachel?"

"I-I thank Mark and agree that keeping the ring in another place is better than here or in his office." She warmed at Gervas's smile of approval.

At a rap on the office door, Mark called, "Come in."

Maeve escorted a man Rachel didn't recognize who was dressed in dark slacks and dark windbreaker. He was average in every other way, so much so that Rachel couldn't even describe him after she blinked. Brownish hair close to his head, a little taller than Maeve, not thin or heavy, regular nose.

"Maeve?" Mark said.

"I want to stay."

Mark looked at Gervas before Rachel, which prickled her mother sense.

"What's this about," Rachel asked.

"Close the door," Mark said. "We believe Gervas is being tracked, and the obvious culprit is his cell phone."

Gervas removed his cell phone from his pocket and handed it to Mark, who turned it over in his hands, then handed it to the stranger.

"That's how they figured I might be involved?" Rachel asked. "Because they followed you to my office and home." It fit.

Gervas squeezed her hand.

"Can we reroute your calls to a new phone until we get this business sorted out?" Mark asked.

"Maeve was going to help me get a new phone and service anyway," Gervas replied.

"Yes, this weekend." Rachel noted a defiant note in her daughter's reply, coming from a straight face that meant she was nervous. "This is no game," Gervas had told Rachel earlier. That same mother instinct said something had happened to Maeve and Gervas too.

"Your callers will not be aware of this arrangement," Mark said. "We will get you a new phone and set up the transfer system."

"So I won't have a new number? There are people I would need to inform if change is necessary."

"Not yet," Mark said. He nodded at the man, who quietly left.

Rachel went light-headed as she realized she was holding her breath. She blinked rapidly to shake off the sensation of watching some spy thriller.

"What about my computer?" Gervas asked. "It has my e-mails and information about the trip, flight arrangements and so forth."

"You didn't take it into Rachel's office, did you?" Mark asked.

"No."

"I think it's safe, then. When do you have to be in Chicago?"

"Four o'clock," Gervas said. "That much I know. I…we need to meet with the Consular General, have an early meal and discuss the talk, if we follow the usual protocol. It is short notice so I hope we have a good audience."

"You'll stay the night?" Mark asked.

Gervas shook his head. "I haven't had time to check the itinerary, but I have a ticket for a late flight to Washington."

Rachel hoped it was an itinerary for two, and held an inward giggle at the thought. She really was losing it. But she wasn't about to go traipsing after Gervas while he traveled first class and she was forced to take a later flight all alone or get stuck in a hotel room somewhere by herself while she didn't speak the language. "Uh—"

"Don't worry," Gervas said, squeezing her hand again. "We are traveling together. You will stay within my sight at all times."

Except at night, Rachel amended silently.

"Except for sleeping arrangements," Gervas said, as if reading her mind.

Ann laughed softly, receiving a pursed-mouth look from Mark and Rachel's best scowl, which only made her laugh out loud.

Rachel sighed.

"Your expenses are covered, Rachel," Gervas said.

"What will happen when your brother finds out you didn't bring the ring," Ann asked.

Good point, though Rachel and Gervas had discussed it when they'd determined earlier to ask for Mark's help.

"Since I am returning to Germany because of a request from the chancellor, and have not been able to stay in contact with Manheim, I can safely explain that my search for the artifact did not go as planned."

"Right on, Dad," Maeve murmured.

"What aren't you telling me, Maeve?" Rachel asked. "I know something happened."

Rachel didn't take her eyes off Maeve while her daughter frowned toward Gervas. "It seems your black van followed us around the neighborhood for a while," she said reluctantly. "I think Scott Warfield chased them away."

"Excuse me?" Nothing could hold Rachel in her seat. "Scott?" Of course he was involved. She took two steps toward her daughter before she rounded on Gervas. "You know about Scott and his little band of terrorists?"

The blank look in his eyes before his expression turned puzzled answered Rachel. Gervas furrowed his brow. "This man who wants to be your suitor?" He looked at Maeve.

Uh, oh. Rachel cocked her head at Mark. "You didn't tell him?"

Mark rolled back in his plump leather desk chair and crossed his legs. "It's not like I've had time."

Another rap on the door invited an "enter" from Mark. The same man brought in a laptop computer, which he set on the desk, and left again. Rachel noted Colleen hovering in the hall and felt sorry for her. Ann rose and went out, closing the door behind her.

Gervas, in jerky motion, picked up the computer.

"Yours?" Rachel said.

"From my house," Maeve said. "I gave that guy directions and my key."

Gervas plucked a key from the front pocket of the laptop case and tossed it at her, still silent, which Rachel knew meant he was furious.

"Let's print out your itinerary and other information about the trip," Mark said. "I'll have a car and driver take you down to Chicago tomorrow, after stopping at the bank."

Gervas again looked at Rachel, a touching confirmation that he had softened over the years, becoming more respectful and less arrogant. She nodded in agreement. "What should I do with the ring?" She plucked the velvet bag from her pocket and held it out.

"You've had it here all along?" Mark didn't seem surprised, just annoyed. "I can put it in the safe for tonight." He paused. "Later."

After we've left the room so we don't see where you keep the safe. Rachel smiled. "One other thing," she said. "I didn't bring my passport with me. I'll need to go home to pack properly."

Gervas came to stand directly behind her and put his hands on her shoulders. "You may also need formal attire."

"In that case, I'll have to raid Ann's closet too."

<>

Gervas didn't dare put his arms around Rachel in front of Mark. At least the man had calmed down considerably and decided to provide security, something he would repay. He would also have to arrange private security for him and Rachel while in Germany. Perhaps on the flight. But not the service the family had retained in the past. The embassy in Washington DC should be safe enough for them, so perhaps the ambassador would advise him about the matter.

How was that man Warfield involved? He had been at Rachel's house immediately after the van had left its pursuit. Rachel obviously knew something he did not. He felt his ire rising again at being kept apart from vital information.

"Rachel, perhaps you wouldn't mind if I spoke to your brother-in-law privately? I promise I will tell you all the boring details of trying to arrange for protection on the flights and in Berlin later."

She stiffened under his hands. He'd had to risk annoying her, but it couldn't be helped.

"Okay." Rachel twisted, placed a brief kiss on his cheek, offered a subtle, silent message that she expected a report later, and walked out.

Gervas strode to the desk and his laptop, which he opened and booted up. He needed to talk himself through the familiar process in order to keep calm. Press that button to turn on the power. Enter the password. Open the e-mail program. Click on the message from the Embassy. Process the information.

Mark turned on his wireless printer.

While the documents flowed through the printer, Gervas found his voice. "There are some details of which I am unaware, apparently."

"I've had my own issues to deal with," Mark replied. "I'm not sorry that my family concerns came first."

"I would do the same," Gervas conceded.

"Scott Warfield became involved with that group, Americans call it ONUS, while he was in army intelligence."

Gervas dropped into a chair and put his hand on his chest, rubbing the area of his fluttering heart. Perhaps he'd misunderstood. "Onus? Responsibility for what?"

"Don't dissemble here with me," Mark said. "I can see

that you understand the implications. They're out to preserve German culture and the economy. Twentieth century heritage. A little scary, don't you think? Surely you, the expert in societies, knew about this?"

"Rumors," he whispered and cleared his throat. "Always the idealism of those who need to feel powerful, to demand control, have kept alive such perversion. Others who vow never to let it happen again, a rise of the Reich, work against such hoodlums. No one takes them seriously."

Mark clutched the paper he held. "Think on this, then. Is it coincidence that Warfield happened to take an IT job where your former lover has worked for years? I doubt it. That's bringing terrorism to American soil. Threatening my loved ones in order to destroy European unity. What do we have to do with it? Nothing! I will not allow your family to destroy mine. Whatever it takes—"

"My family?" Gervas sat up. "Destroy yours? To what are you referring? We have nothing to do with this group."

Mark punched some keys on his computer and turned the screen so Gervas could see. "You don't honestly expect me to believe that you don't know your brother is one of the founders of the group dedicated to the failure of the European Union? To create chaos so the rise of a super power to challenge the US so the Islamic state will be welcomed? Why did you come to me with some sob story about your brother being blackmailed over an artifact you assumed Rachel had taken decades ago?"

Gervas looked at the articles, but could not yet accept Mark's assessment of Manheim and the terror group. Rumors and innuendos circled amongst their acquaintances. Gervas had discussed the possibilities of such an organization with colleagues and student groups, but proof such a group existed had never been found.

"But doesn't it make sense?" Mark argued. "Lack of proof does not mean the group cannot exist. Look at all these incidents." He'd waved at the computer screen which showed a grainy video clip of a mob holding signs. Gervais couldn't tell for certain, but it looked like Istanbul. Bah, the Turks could argue a bell from a camel without much thought. Which was the problem. Trade, bartering at an advantage, was what too many cultures thrived on. There was nothing anyone could do to set a standard pricing index across societies, even those mixed in the same neighborhoods.

Gervas read the report of strikes, a bombing, a shipment of commodities gone missing, an assassination of a minor official in other news wire services. "Why point out these particular episodes?"

Mark remained grim.

"You must have gotten information from someone. Warfield, perhaps? He seems like a person who must have attention."

<>

"I like Gervas, Aunt Rachel," Colleen said.

The women were up in Ann's bedroom. The baby was down for the evening and they were looking for suitable formal wear in Ann's closet for Rachel to take with her. Ann tossed a black beaded number on the bed, followed by a blue silk formal gown and a creamy-colored thing with ivory buttons down the back.

Rachel picked it up. "This looks like a wedding dress."

"It's not." Ann's voice was muffled. "Oh, here." She emerged with a black cocktail dress and matching jacket. "It might be warmish for outside, but those places are always cold indoors."

"You must go to a lot parties," Colleen said. She sat on the bed and fingered the blue dress.

"I had to when Gene and I were married," Ann said. "Business. Mark has to attend some dinner parties too, some award ceremonies and the like. I hoped we could do some entertaining too, after I got better."

"Hoped?" Rachel looked up from where she held the black dress against her, checking the reflection in Ann's mirror. "You are better. You hardly even need the cane."

Ann just patted her stomach.

Rachel went back to admiring the dress. "This isn't the Middle Ages, sister. You don't have to hide your condition."

"You know I'll help with anything, Ann," Colleen said.

Sometimes Colleen's sweetness made Rachel want to smack her for sounding too naïve, too brown-nosey, though Colleen's personality was something to strive for. Much like Rachel's hero, Melanie Wilkes. "Mealy-mouthed Melanie," Scarlett O-Hara called her sister-in-law. Being a church-going believer was so hard sometimes when Rachel wanted to let her snide side rip.

"Doesn't Mark mind that you kept Gene's clothes?" Colleen asked.

"These aren't, well, mostly aren't, from that time," Ann said. "And no, why would he mind?"

"Ritchie would hate it if I had kept something from another man."

"Hmm."

Ann was still inside her huge closet. "Shoes?"

Rachel set the black dress aside. "I think I'm good. How many outfits do you think I need? I have plenty of stuff from work that should be all right."

"Maybe one more dress." She came out with a long mauve

outfit under a clear dust cover. "The fit should be okay." It was smooth over the bodice and flared a little at the sleeves and skirt.

"I guess I'd need shoes with that one."

"It's beautiful. You'll look great in that, Aunt Rachel."

"Thank you, darling." Rachel held that one up in front of her as well. "So, does Ritchie still connect with his dad?"

"We sent him a birthday card, but we don't know if Linda let him see it. He still gets upset sometimes, if he remembers his old life, Linda says."

"At least he's getting good care," Ann said. "Whew. I need to sit a minute."

Rachel went to get a glass of water from the bathroom for her. "Here. It's still hard to believe everything that happened with him. Gene, I mean. That mother of his was something else."

Ann sipped then held the glass on her lap. "She was punished enough, I think, in the way she died. She never liked me, and it was unconscionable to keep the fact she knew Gene was alive and his whereabouts from me all those years, but in a strange way, I understand." Ann looked at Colleen with affection. "I'd never do something like that of course." She patted her daughter-in-law's hand.

"Absolute power," Colleen said. "I don't believe you could ever lie like that, not to keep such a family secret."

Rachel grinned. "So, you said you liked Gervas?"

"Oh, yes." Colleen transferred her sincere expression from Ann to Rachel. "There's something sad about him. Like his friends had a party and no one invited him."

"Perhaps." Rachel looked away. Yes, yes, that was it, precisely. And her fault. Making amends could start with being more gracious about Maeve's desire to know her father. The fact that Maeve knew she'd fly off the deep end hurt, even though it was true. She'd apologize to them both before she left. Maeve was in the kitchen, doing some work on her computer. This trip with Gervas, then…who knew what would happen?

Rachel had that prickling sensation and turned back to find both Ann and Colleen watching her. Smirking. "Oh, you!"

24

The SUV might have looked like any normal expensive car from the outside, dark colored, of course, windows lightly tinted. Gervas was fascinated by the array of dials and screens and data on the dashboard. Mark assured Gervas and Rachel the vehicle was secure, as was a similar one following, both driven by members of the security team Mark no longer hid. After depositing the ring in Mark's bank safe deposit box, the three of them sat in the back, comfortable in body, if not so much in each other's presence. A drive to Chicago took only a short time, which they passed by discussing what Rachel could expect tonight at DANK Haus and in Washington DC, where they would not spend the night but travel to Berlin immediately after the talk.

"I am sorry to offer you a night on an aircraft," Gervas said. "Although perhaps you can nap in a room at the embassy."

"It's such short notice," Rachel said. "And you said they have a pretty good audience already? For both talks?"

"It's an important subject," Gervas replied.

Mark was on his laptop but looked up.

They'd argued last night over the damages to the economy, the burgeoning mistrust of member countries.

"What would my brother stand to gain by siding with terrorists?" Gervas had said. "He has always been worried about family honor and reputation. It has been his singular focus since our father died."

Mark had said nothing more. Gervas had gone to sleep,

uneasy, mulling over the wisdom of taking Rachel. In the end, he knew he didn't want to let her out of his sight, not that he could personally protect her if Mark's theories were true, but at least they would be together.

The light of day hadn't offered any new revelations, and so the three of them, plus the guards, were on their way to Chicago. Gervas was still suspicious of the failed communication during that last conversation. Anticipation of seeing his brother the day after tomorrow made his stomach churn. Rachel squeezed his hand and he smiled at her, glad for the distraction.

Mark went back to typing away on his laptop.

"Who else will you see in Germany?" Rachel asked quietly. "Or will you be in meetings every minute?"

Gervas was quick to reassure her. "I won't neglect you," he said. "Not willingly. I have adjusted our arrangements in Berlin to stay at a guest house not far from parliament. Mark knows." He earned a small smile from Rachel's brother-in-law, still tapping the keys on the other side of her.

"You won't be staying with your brother?"

"No." He rubbed his thumb across her knuckles. "Manheim has small quarters in Berlin. Our family home, south of Berlin and close to Freiburg, is occupied now by my son, Max, who takes care of his mother and sister." Gervas spoke around the subject delicately, not wanting to make her feel left out. "Of course he will welcome you, but perhaps we will plan that in a future visit. There is much to show you. I do not expect many meetings to which you are not invited. Yes, some, but if you care to visit parliament with me, it can be arranged."

She looked at their clasped hands. He wasn't sure what she thought and wondered again if wanting her with him was a mistake.

"I look forward to being in your country," she said eventually. She glanced at Mark and back to him. "Maybe later, on the plane, you can tell me about Max. And his sister."

"Of course."

They shared quiet conversation for the remaining time, Mark occasionally joining in. He told her of the updates to DANK Haus since she'd been there last. He also practiced a little of his speech on them both, and answered questions Rachel and Mark asked about the world economy, using his new cell phone to research responses from the latest reports.

Rachel watched the lights of DC fade as they flew east, over the ocean. She closed the window panel and leaned back in the seat. First class. She hadn't flown a whole lot in her life, and never in the front of the plane. She could recline the seat without bothering the person behind her and an attendant had stowed her carry-on bag for her. She pulled the light blanket across her lap and lay back, turning toward Gervas. He had his eyes closed. He must be exhausted after the past two days of speaking, smiling, shaking hands, answering questions. Even she was tired simply after absorbing so much attention and she'd been on the periphery.

He'd offered her melatonin, but she didn't take it. Missing a night, or going on two hours of sleep once in a while never bothered her. They'd be seven hours ahead, not even a full shift, and she figured she could handle the time difference, adjust to the change easily enough for the rest of their stay.

In the quiet before reaching their destination, she wondered about his home, a couple of hours away from Berlin. People in smaller countries tended to think hours were more like days of travel, unlike people in Wisconsin who thought nothing of a trip between Madison and Milwaukee, or Milwaukee and Chicago. She wished they could make time to go there. Seeing the house and that of their neighbor would put the Friedemanns into a perspective she'd never get anywhere else. Then again, she wanted to stay far away from his former wife. And how could she possibly look his children in the eye?

Rachel watched his eyelids twitch and his fingers tremble briefly. Was he worried now, nervous, even? He hadn't broken from character during the speeches, or the semi-private discussion with the ambassador, Karl Schelling, in Washington. She'd been awed to be invited to sit with them and squirmed at the slap on his wrist the ambassador gave Gervas for speaking about economic problems on television without going through proper channels. She heard it again, in Schelling's academic lecture voice, "The recession which began last year continues to damage world economy. Yes, those are public facts. When you speak as an authority, you must do so responsibly. In the past you have shown remarkable insights, enough to sway public opinion. You must manage this gift to encourage, not discourage."

Gervas had agreed, looked properly chastised, and they had not spoken of it since. In fact, they'd had no time until now to be private. Rachel smiled. Not even now. They weren't alone at all.

The sound of Gervas thanking the flight attendant and the scent of warmed, bleachy and damp towels made her blink into consciousness. Sunlight streamed into the cabin from other windows. Gervas had mercifully left theirs closed. Rachel inhaled deeply and came more awake at the feel of the warm cloth along her temple.

"It's nearly three p.m., Berlin time," Gervas told her. "Are you hungry? Best to eat lightly now." He nodded at another attendant who came over, smiling, and took their order for tea and a small meal of rice and steamed vegetables.

"We'll be landing in an hour, sir, madam," the attendant said. "May I take away your cups and blankets?"

Rachel excused herself to the lavatory, and found their meals waiting when she returned. "How long have you been awake?"

"Half an hour," Gervas responded.

"You look a lot better than I do," Rachel grumped.

He chuckled and stirred her tea. "You will always be the Rachel of my misspent middle age. Now that I am old, I wish I had been much wiser then." Gervas scooped his rice with a piece of crunchy pale green asparagus. "Mm, just right. Try yours." He gestured with his empty fork. "Sleep allowed me to work on my problems unencumbered by the distractions of subliminal feelings. I have a renewed sense of purpose." He set his fork down and studied her. Rachel felt her cheeks warm and looked away.

"Do not do that, please," he said. "You inspire me. Your response to the ambassador was the most comfort I'd known since the last time we were together, just us."

"Oh, I hope I didn't embarrass you." Rachel huddled into herself and reached for the mug of tea. "I just wanted him to know how much influence—positive influence—you've had on the students who take courses based on your book."

"Never could you embarrass me. Thank you for your support." His eyes were warm and Rachel couldn't help turning her lips upward to echo his mood. "So." He turned to finish the last bites of his food. "The ambassador's message from Manheim about his communication woes was meant to reassure me. I have come to the conclusion, however, that your astute brother-in-law is correct in his belief about my brother."

Rachel glanced around. This part of the plane was small, not cramped certainly, but the twenty or so seats in first class weren't far apart, either. "Do you really want to talk about that here?"

Gervas frowned and followed her look. "Of course. You are wise as usual." He took her hand. "Let us speak of our week instead."

Rachel listened while he described the places he wanted to show her when they were not offering advice to Manheim and the other ministers. She even looked forward to meeting the dynamic Madam Chancellor and thought of asking Gervas to teach her a proper salutation in German.

"Tell me about your family," she said into their quiet.

He looked at her, cocked his head, and questioned her with his eyes. "You know my parents are deceased. I have one brother, Manheim, the Federal Minister for Economic Cooperation and Development. He and his wife have no children. He is four years older than me. We are not very close, as you suspect. My first wife, Sylvie..." He looked away from her. "We...we have—"

She watched him swallow and felt pain emanating from something he couldn't say. Maybe someday he'd tell her all of it. Hopefully his children wouldn't judge her...hate her...blame her. "That's all right, Gervas. We can wait."

"Nein, nein. My son, Max, he is thirty, a good boy. Man. He is an engineer. My daughter Katrine, twenty-seven. Katrine is—has—she will be coming to Madison for a while."

"Oh? To study?" Rachel cut in, wondering why he was so distressed. "I hope she and Maeve will get to know each other. Does she speak English? I really should learn more German."

"I can help you with that," he said and began to hold up

various objects near them and say their names, which she repeated. When they ran out of immediate vocabulary, Rachel clutched his hand.

"What is troubling you?" he asked.

"I'm worried about Ann. I can't understand how she allowed herself to get pregnant." At his rumbling laugh, she lifted her head from his shoulder. "Oh, stop it. I know how…I guess. It's just that she's not doing very well, health-wise. I'm afraid for her."

"She is under very good medical care, is she not?"

"Yes, but bad things can still happen."

"I know." He drew her near again and kissed the top of her head. "We must trust in her physicians."

"And God."

"Yes."

She closed her eyes until the Lufthansa flight stopped in Frankfurt, with barely enough time to get through customs and to the next gate and the last leg of the trip.

The small jet landed at Tegel Airport with a skid and a rumble of brakes. After disembarking and passing security, they were approached by a somberly dressed bearded man in dark slacks and gray button up shirt. The man showed Gervas papers and, very briefly, some sort of ID. Gervas nodded and led her to a silver Daimler. Along the way, the back of Rachel's neck prickled. A dark blond man came off the plane right after them, staying within sight even when they'd been separated for a few moments going through security. He hailed a car which pulled out directly after them.

"Gervas," she whispered, earning a look in the rearview mirror from their driver. She lowered her voice even more. "I think we're being followed."

"The car behind us?"

She looked into his eyes. "Blond man."

His eyes crinkled. "Good, yes. I hired him. His partner picked him up for their detail here." He patted her hand in a way that made her feel not childish, but cherished. "Mark and I did not want to worry you, though I assured him you would catch on."

Rachel pursed her mouth. "Not very quickly, obviously. Though now that I think about it, someone's been with us the past two days."

The dark-eyed driver looked back at her again in the rearview mirror. Instead of feeling spooked, she felt safe, and thankful. She nodded back slightly when he winked. He refocused on the road, changing lanes every once in a while for no apparent reason. She shuddered, remembering being chased not that long ago, and felt Gervas's hand tighten around hers.

"It is not far to the hotel," he said. "I will arrange a private tour for you of the Reichstag, the Parliament building, tomorrow while I meet with my brother."

"Let me guess. I won't be alone much, will I?"

"Just a precaution. I will introduce you. Phillip and Viktor Scholz. Phillip is currently driving. Viktor occupies the passenger seat."

Rachel smiled. "I'm happy to know you both."

Viktor stuck his long, thin hand back to shake hers. "We watch out for you," he said in rudimentary English.

"Hans Belter, the other member of the team behind us, the blond man, and Gustav Hartmann, are the others. They come highly recommended." Gervas spoke a few German sentences to Phillip, who apparently agreed. Viktor spoke on a cell phone.

"The others will meet us at the hotel. Phillip will take us to see some sites now. We will not leave the car today. You are tired from the travels, yes?"

He must have seen her droopy eyes. Rachel smiled and sat up straighter, but agreed she was tired. "Car trips do that to me."

"I remember," he said and put his arm around her. She told him she was happy there were so many trees in the city, the wide roads under skies dark blue through the tinted windows. And so many cars around them, like a cushion.

"Here is very famous Victory Column," Viktor said over the seat.

They were driving fast with the traffic, entering a multi-lane roundabout. Rachel slid harder against Gervas. "Sorry."

"I'm not." He hugged her.

"I hate these things. They make me feel like I'm going to fly out of the car."

"Centrifugal force," he murmured in her ear. "It's a virtual sensation of being pushed to the outside while spinning. Do not worry. I will keep you safe. You will never fly out of the car while you are with me."

The Brandenburg Gate was awe-inspiring. The next thing Rachel knew Gervas was helping her out of the car.

Before she could remark on the graffiti marring the stonework of the lovey old Mark *Appartements* on Wilhelmstrasse not far from the busy river Spree where Gervas had booked rooms, Hans, the blond man, strode up to them. He grabbed Rachel's elbow, hustled her into another car idling against the curb behind them and slammed the door.

25

"**E**xcuse, please, madam, my apologies. New rooms. Please to wait fur…for…furzer instructions. Thank you," Hans said from beside Rachel in the backseat of the vehicle.

Viktor gave a small wave from the driver's seat. "Please to put on safety belt," he told her as he sped from the curb.

Rachel released a small squeak, the remnant of a scream. She was too shaky to buckle up, so Hans apologized some more, reached around, and managed to fasten the belt without touching her. He grinned when she gathered the courage to look at him.

"Why isn't Ger—Professor Friedemann—wi-with us?" Rachel asked.

"We drive you new hotel," was all she could get out of Hans.

<>

Gervas watched the Daimler speed off with Rachel and regretted the manner in which Hans and Phillip had chosen to handle the situation of discovering listening devices in the rooms of the private apartment building. He regretted even further that he had chosen to make the reservations from a computer at the embassy in Washington, which meant he was responsible for this glitch. "I think it's time I met with the minister," he told Gustav, who nodded and ushered him back into the car. "Europahaus, *danke*. Stresemannstrasse."

Gervas had not visited his brother's Berlin office of the Economic Cooperation and Development, the BMZ. The main department headquarters were yet in Bonn, but many of the eight hundred department staff worked in embassies and offices all around the world. A barb poked his conscience. *All around the world.* If any business anywhere made a perfect framework for potentially nefarious acts, this one certainly did. He shuddered and looked toward the door. After submitting to security, he saw Manheim standing against a column, waiting, with his hands behind his back.

Impeccably dressed as always, Manheim's face remained impassive during their restrained greeting. They shook hands, per Manheim's choice, instead of the more intimate usual manner of air brushing cheeks. Manheim's grip was cold though firm. The only callouses he wore were from twiddling a Montblanc pen and carrying a briefcase.

"Welcome, brother," Manheim said. "Madam Chancellor informed me of your arrival."

Gervas needed a light touch with this revelation. "As I was informed of the request through Ambassador Shilling two days ago. I have been traveling since."

"My office." Manheim led the way, sauntering, nodding and returning quiet greetings to others they passed, many on the way home for the evening. Behind him, Gervas noted the way he twisted his left hand around his right wrist, a nervous habit he'd developed when their father lay dying, still issuing directives.

Once in the large department where nearly a hundred people took calls and tapped on computers and watched the rise and fall of currency, Manheim told his personal secretary to leave them undisturbed unless a vital issue came up. Another Minister was expected shortly and then she could leave. He closed the door to his office and pressed a button on a small device the size of an air freshener. A quiet shushing sound issued from it.

"Sit," he told Gervas who was still focused on the device. "That?" Manheim shrugged and grew a sour expression. "Since that bad business last November when the Americans had the poor taste to hire that young man with loose lips, questionable ethics, and a penchant for drama—"

"Snowden?"

"Ja. We all must take care." Manheim sat behind an enormous desk with a blinking phone and notes taped all over the glass top. "The Minister of Digital Infrastructure has been kept busy," he said in his dry way. "So." He steepled his fingers and crossed his ankle over his knee. "Shortly we will be joined by Helmet Kellner, the Minister for Special Tasks, but first we must speak."

"What happened to our line of communication?" Gervas asked. "Why could you not answer your phone or return my calls? Your last message was garbled. I have been worried."

Manheim cut his eyes toward the noise machine.

"What did you mean," Gervas persisted, "about not trusting? Not trust who?"

Manheim blinked. "Regenbogen, of course."

Liar. "Why would I not trust him? Had he gone to America to search for me? He has never contacted me directly." Gervas pursed his lips, searching for his next words. "There have been some disturbing incidents for my—me—while in Wisconsin. I have been followed deliberately, by strangers."

"Do you have it?" Manheim asked, ignoring Gervas's comment.

A bolt of anger flashed behind Gervas's eyes. He sat back and eyed Manheim, who continued to tap a pen he'd picked up. "It?"

"We must put this blackmail matter to rest quickly and

quietly, brother. You found the woman, yes?"

Gervas looked at him. "Of what are you speaking?"

"Such an important mission for you. Naturally I made sure help was available should you need it."

"Help? I tried not to believe it was you who sent vehicles to chase down innocent victims. Since when does putting people in danger constitute help?"

Manheim studied the pen, clicked it twice and then set it on the desk. "You do not seem to understand the seriousness of the situation. Time is slipping through our fingers. We took an opportunity."

"We? Your opportunity failed."

Gervas's brother hunched over the desk. "A mistake by a misguided *assoziieren*, an associate. Time, brother, is up, as they say in America."

"The ring was not the only reason I visited Madison."

Manheim expelled an impatient breath. "Your daughter is well, I trust?"

Gervas narrowed his eyes at Manheim's raised brow and slight smirk. He slapped the wooden arm of the blue upholstered chair in which he sat across the desk's vast expanse. How dare Manheim mock his family? "Katrine is gravely ill."

"I am sorrowed to hear. Where is the ring?"

A cheery voice outside the door alerted them to Kellner's impending entrance.

"Gervas!"

"It is in my—our—possession," he hissed. "Mine and Rachel's. It is safe. In America. In a place neither you nor your men can touch."

A knock sounded from the other side of the door.

"You will pay," Manheim uttered in a low voice. Louder,

he said, "Enter!"

<>

On shaky legs, Rachel followed Hans and her luggage down a short red and black carpeted hallway with tasteful sconces and inset doors. They'd entered an impressive small hotel several blocks from the original place they'd planned to stay, Hans hustling her past the reception desk and into an elevator which he'd opened with a keycard. Rachel had been too frazzled at the time to think about the odd lurching of the elevator car that made her stomach rise instead of sink. Someone must have arranged for rooms. The porter set down a case near one door in the hall. He opened a door nearby and set her suitcase inside. Since seeing the enormous chandelier in the lobby and the uniform the porter wore, Rachel thought she was prepared for the presumed elegance of the room.

She was not. She took a few steps into a space larger than her living room at home, decorated with heavy dark and antique furniture. An elegant striped taupe sofa and two cozy chairs grouped around a fireplace with a marble mantle. A dining room set was placed in front of heavy, closed drapes on a carpet that probably came right from Istanbul and cost as much as her car. Soft lighting came from recesses in the ceiling. Vaguely she heard Hans tip and thank the porter in German, or at least she thought so.

Hans left the door open. "Frau, *bitte*. Please to look? Bed-room *hier*. Bath-room *hier*. Rest. Herr Professor returns for meal." He held up eight fingers.

Rachel nodded tiredly.

"He is…" English apparently exhausted, Hans pointed to a door in the wall opposite the bedroom and bathroom.

"I understand," she told him. "Danke."

Hans cocked his head, sympathy in his gray eyes. He

bowed and left her room.

Rachel turned in a circle, then headed for the bedroom. Tears of uncertainty blurred the curtained four-poster. She caught a glimpse of another fireplace before crawling onto the huge bed, sinking into the duvet, and curling up with the bolster pillow. Surely this was not Gervas's normal lifestyle? She couldn't believe it. It wasn't real. She might acknowledge she had never stopped loving him, but that didn't mean she had to accept this lifestyle. Was that menthol in the pillow? Rachel sat up and blinked.

She patted the duvet. This bed was amazing. For a queen in a castle. Did the fireplace work? Of course it was summer, so she didn't need it for heat.

Where was Gervas? Had he known before about changing hotels? He'd looked surprised, and sad, when she'd looked at him as Hans rushed away. How long until eight—if Hans could be trusted. She looked for a telephone. Who would she call, anyway?

Get a grip. Rachel Michels, you are not a conspiracist. Go take a shower. Two days of traveling made her feel yucky. She went to get her case and wheeled it into the bedroom. At least Hans hadn't come in here. That would have been weird. Did he live in Berlin? Have a family?

She picked clean things to wear and approached the bathroom. The pocket doors were etched, beveled glass with brass inset pulls for handles. She gingerly pulled one, peeked and closed her eyes. And took deep breaths. More luxury meant for the rich and famous.

Yeah. She'd be perfectly content to camp out here for the week.

Rachel went into the blue and gilt tiled room with a deep spa tub and walk in shower. Yep. Toilet *and* bidet. Double sink.

Buttons on a counter top that looked like an intercom. No—for music. Lotions, oils, soaps, shampoos, toothpaste. Lots of thick navy blue towels. A chair and small round glass table. Maeve would adore this. Rachel could take some photos, call her later.

She rubbed her arms. Maybe hanging out with Gervas and the whole spy and chase thing wouldn't be so bad after all if she could have a piece of this once in a while. But only once every five years. Rachel took a whiff of the moisturizer she test-rubbed between her fingers. Maybe every two years.

She and Maeve had watched movies with rooms like this visited by astronomically rich characters who were always sad.

Shower first. Sad later.

Shocked to see the time when she was done pretending to belong to the elite upper class, Rachel scurried to unpack her few outfits. Seven thirty. What should she wear? Where they were going for supper, Hans hadn't said. She eyed the glossy dining table, surprised to be hungry. Maybe they were eating in. Under the adrenalin rush and the refreshing shower, tiredness would lay her out soon. Seven forty. Would he be on time, or was eight a rough estimate? The walls were sound-proofed, or else Gervas was not in his room next door. Deciding against formal wear, Rachel put on slacks and top and sandals. She tiptoed to the adjoining door and twisted the handle. It turned and she stepped back, feeling her heart race. Knock first.

As Rachel reached her fist toward the door to rap, it opened inward. Pulled by an invisible force she managed to regain her balance before falling into Gervas's arms. He smiled at her. There were bags under his eyes, offsetting the crinkle lines at the corners. His glasses perched atop his head and he still wore the same clothes. Rachel caught motion behind him.

Hans.

Gervas turned his head and spoke quietly to Hans, who bobbed his head, spared her a glance and walked away. She heard the door click before Gervas took her hand and held it to his check.

"You must have been so frightened. Believe me, that was not planned. You are all right now?"

Rachel couldn't open her mouth but pressed her trembling lips together. With a rumbling groan, Gervas drew her close. She lay her head on his shoulder, breathing in deeply the days-old scent she remembered from their travels years ago. His hands soothed her back as she wrestled with the urge to cry.

He whispered in her ear in German and it didn't matter she couldn't understand. If she couldn't know his promises, she couldn't know if he broke them. He changed to English.

"You will never be able to trust me again. I understand. I love you but expect nothing in return. I have never earned this right—"

"Gervas, no—"

"Please," he whispered. His hand moved from her shoulder to her throat, caressing and sliding through her hair to her ear. "Wait. You must hear this. I am ashamed for my family. I no longer believe I can protect you." He leaned back and looked into her eyes. "Circumstances dictate I confess everything."

So close Rachel could see the faint redness rimming his eyelids. She touched his cheek and pressed her lips to his. He deepened it for three seconds before pulling back and taking a ragged breath.

"Rachel, Rachel, what are doing to me? I can never ask you to share my shame once you are aware of the depth of it."

Much to her everlasting embarrassment amid this tension and confusion—what did he mean, never ask her?—her stomach growled. Gervas chuckled, kissed her cheek, and then framed her face to look at her with shimmering eyes. "We are hungry and tired. Let us not speak or make decisions in this state. Would you mind eating here? You can call room service and order a meal for us while I clean up?"

Rachel flushed and looked down. "Yes. What would you like?"

"Anything you order will please me." He let her go and stepped backward into his room.

Before he closed the door, she mumbled, "Um, do I go to the desk? Or use my cell phone to order?"

Gervas smiled slowly and led her to an end table next to the sofa. He brushed the base of an antique lamp. The base was open on one side, but out of Rachel's line of sight. She sighed. "You upper crust are too much for me. I expect the telephone is in the same place in the bedroom?"

"Yes. A menu is in the drawer underneath, I believe. And this is a rare luxury for me, Rachel. I have stayed here only once before, with my daughter Katrine, on her twentieth birthday." He smiled. "Upstairs. It was not so very different from this." He kissed her once again before leaving quietly.

Sauerbraten seemed safe enough, besides one of the few items she recognized on the menu which was thoughtfully printed in English and German. While she waited she calculated the time back home and risked a one p.m. call to Maeve to give a brief update. "You wouldn't believe the amazing room I'm staying in." They exchanged bits of nonsense. Ann was fine. David was so much fun. They said good bye and hung up.

Rachel went to pull the curtain aside at the window, only

to be met by a brick wall. She hadn't realized they were so close to another building. Of course, she'd been upset at the time. She let the drape fall back into place and paced.

What had happened to make Gervas so upset? He'd obviously seen his brother—earlier than planned. Gervas's words to her, his love for her, kept pounding in rhythm with her pulse. He couldn't ask her to share his shame. Ask her to share? What did he mean? Love conquered all, didn't it? It was not hard to love this older, wiser version of Gervas. In his late thirties he'd been vibrant, passionate about so many things Rachel couldn't help be swept up in it. She hadn't taken the time to try to get to know him, only about him. She heard what he'd shared back then, but she hadn't wanted to know anything that would potentially tarnish the image of him she'd made up, one who'd been wronged and deserved better.

This time, she'd give him the gift of listening to him. And if he couldn't ask her to share his life, that didn't mean she couldn't ask him.

A knock indicated room service, and shortly after the table was arranged, Gervas walked through the connecting door, dressed less formally than usual in a Henley shirt and dark jeans, mingling a whiff of sweet clean soap with the spicy sauce of the meat. Rachel's stomach growled again. She was beyond tired at this point, kept awake on hunger pains, and would probably toss and turn when she finally got to bed. By the time she adjusted to the European schedule, they'd be home again. Unless Gervas had made other plans. He looked calmer, but refused to discuss his meeting and thoughts while they ate.

Later, after the porter had returned and cleaned up, over a glass of mild wine Gervas said would help them sleep, they sat on the sofa in Rachel's room. The lights were low and

Rachel forced her eyes to stay open by holding the cool glass and taking sips.

"I had wished to spare you," Gervas said. "I admit jealousy when Maeve first informed me of your suitor, Scott Warfield. When I learned unsavory news about him, I did not share it out of fear you would dismiss it and me." Gervas set his glass down and leaned forward, over his knees, clasping his hands. "Your brother-in-law first brought this to my attention, but I did not want to accept the implication."

"You mean about Scott being involved in a group that's trying to break up the EU? Scott admitted it to Mark after he…well, he was the one who cut off the goons who were chasing me."

Gervas turned his head. "Somehow I am not surprised you knew. Yet still you chose to accompany me." He removed his glasses, put them on the end table and took her hand. "I should stop worrying and let you protect me."

"I'd like to." Without letting go of his hand, Rachel set her glass of wine down. "Earlier, you said—"

"Wait." He leaned forward to touch her lips, lingered a moment, then looked away. "Perhaps you know the other part? About Manheim?"

At her hesitation and shiver, he went on. "Mark found evidence that my brother was involved with this group. I could not accept it. At first. I met with Manheim today. Again, I apologize for the subterfuge. I never meant to frighten or hurt you."

"It's all right. I trust you."

His smile made her toes tingle. "I am not sure that is wise, but I must accept your faith in me or I may not survive."

"Gervas—"

"There is more, of course. I did not want to believe, but

now I have little choice. Manheim's very office, the ministerial department he was appointed to, is a perfect secret place to manipulate world events. He has workers in many countries around the world. He has access to the World Bank, and the finances of the economies of every country who receives loans. He has connections to money, goods, news, and people who will do anything for money." Gervas stressed the last point, and squeezed Rachel's hands.

"Why are you still alive?" she whispered, cold, now, and more awake than she'd ever been. Or maybe she was dreaming.

"Viktor is Interpol. These are safe rooms on a floor below the surface that technically does not exist in this hotel. We will be escorted to the Parliament building tomorrow for my meeting and your tour." He pulled her close again and sat back. She struggled.

"Wait? We're…underground?"

He nodded, eyes on hers.

"But. Oh." She'd been so frazzled she hadn't realized they'd gone down instead of up. "That explains the weird feeling in my stomach on the elevator and the brick wall in the window."

At his wrinkled brow, she said, "Just look through the window over by the table later." She relaxed against his shoulder.

Putting his lips to her temple, he said quietly, "I had promised you a week of sightseeing, I know, but in light of the current situation, we must be circumspect."

"I agree," she said, unable to speak loudly. "What will happen? How long do we have?" She raised her face to kiss him.

"It is not so melodramatic." He accepted one kiss, then pushed her gently away. "We must not let our fears or the decisions of others control us, or excuse potentially regretful actions."

"Maeve?" Rachel took a breath, disappointed, frustrated, yet relieved.

"I do not regret our daughter. Not one iota. I regret only the circumstances surrounding her birth and upbringing." He paused, looked away and back. "And now, of course. Betrayal by my brother. This situation puts you in danger."

Appeased, she snuggled against him. "But what will happen? They're obviously looking to hunt you down, now that you know. Does Manheim know that you…know?" The conversation was getting ridiculous. "Is it safe for you to go to see the chancellor?"

Gervas's chest heaved some beneath her cheek. Let him laugh.

"While there is some potential threat, Manheim by now has received multiple messages from Interpol, the chancellor's office, the World Bank, and others, subtly letting him know he is under suspicion. It is hoped he will keep this quiet. But I must warn you, our situation is not some crime drama, where the criminal will be caught and tried in an hour-long television program."

Rachel heard his voice catch on the word "criminal." "Was this really about the ring?"

"Manheim demanded its return today, but we did not discuss it further. Hans attempted to find Regenbogen while I was in the meeting, but the fellow has apparently left the country."

"Why does your brother want it? Is it still true that he's being blackmailed? What about the vote to split Germany from the EU?" She yawned, and covered her mouth late.

Gervas began to stroke her shoulder blade. "As I look

back, I am guilty of listening only to my brother and not trying to prove his claims of blackmail or the upheaval in parliament. Why should I have?"

"You believed him. He's your brother. World events seemed to back him up."

"We have never been that close. Perhaps he had a buyer, or was in league with Regenbogen somehow to claim the items. I chose to use finding the ring perhaps for another reason, a personal one."

"To look for me." Rachel smiled and no longer tried to keep her eyes open.

26

In the morning, at eleven fifteen, Gervas met with the chancellor, a very quiet Minister of the Interior named Franz Dimmer, and Kellner, Minister of Special Tasks, whom he'd met yesterday in Manheim's office. Gervas tried to control his outrage at what he heard by sitting very still. Manheim was not in attendance in the private conference room at the Parliament building.

"There has been no formal call for a vote of no confidence," Kellner said in an impatient tone. "There has been no need for such a thing, nor is anyone ready to take immediate office, according to article sixty-seven, which, as you know, states the Bundestag must elect a new chancellor immediately. No one has been forced out of office since Schmidt." Kellner stopped for a breath.

Gervas had a gut feeling there was someone prepared to take office should article sixty-seven of Basic Law ever be invoked, but shook it off. After his meeting with Manheim yesterday, Gervas realized how little he had understood his brother's motives for gathering prospective supportive votes in parliament. Manheim must have a prospective candidate to back if he was prepared to oust the current chancellor.

"Not that we have heard of a vote." Madam Chancellor shifted in her seat to cross her legs and rest back in the chair. "Of course there are always rumors, planted in the media. Usually by other nations." She folded her hands on her lap and stabbed him with a glare. "But let us hear first your perspective on the current state of social economics of our great experiment—the European Union. Because of your unique perspective on the development of economics across the social order, we have called upon you to advise the cabinet regarding the long-term structure of the financial stability of the euro in our Union members. A summit on the debt crisis is pending in about ten weeks in Brussels to discuss a plan to recapitalize weak banking institutions in the Eurozone. I have it on good authority that Sarkozy is working on some plan with China's president."

"Hu Jintao," Gervas murmured. "Interesting."

"What advice can you offer, then, hmm, for stability?"

The chancellor's scowl slashed two lines on either side of her generous lips.

"I expected to advise parliament," Gervas said.

"Circumstances have changed. I will take any relevant ideas to them."

Gervas leaned forward, hands on his knees. "Very well. My advice is to boost the bailout fund." He swallowed and looked her in the eye. "One trillion euros. Slash Greece's debt substantially. Force Berlusconi to agree to…guidance. Italy must take some responsibility."

"I see."

Kellner sputtered. "One trillion euros. Ridiculous. Better to force Greece and Italy out of the union."

The chancellor grinned evilly. "Is this what you and your brother talked about, Professor? Breaking up the Union?"

"No. We only met briefly before Minister Kellner arrived. Mostly about family matters."

Madam Chancellor abruptly set both feet on the floor. "Thank you. I will consider your advice before and during the summit."

She hunched forward to pick up some papers and tapped

the bundle to align the pages. "We can be frank with the professor." She looked at Gervas with assessing brown eyes. "I am preparing to dismiss certain ministers of my cabinet. I am pained and disappointed to do so, and naturally you will not share this information with anyone."

She cut a glance at Kellner. He cleared his throat and spoke.

"A report from Minister Friedemann contained certain irregularities with that of Minister Schleice of the Department of Finances. Since Madam Chancellor does not interfere with the departments, the Vice Chancellor was asked to study the matter. About that time more rumors of a no-confidence vote surfaced, ones without substance."

"I trust," Madam Chancellor said with a direct stare at Gervas, "you understand the delicacy of the situation. It is coincidence that you are close family to Minister Friedemann."

She looked beyond Gervas's temple. He was aware of Dimmer rising, felt the draft of the door opening and closing, and his heartbeat fluttered in response. He swallowed.

"We prefer to keep the matter quiet," she said. "You have been out of the country, your communications monitored. These men would like to ask you some questions."

Gervas's heart raced and he began to sweat. His hands trembled. Betrayed on all sides? But he had done nothing wrong. "Madam Chancellor." He willed his voice to remain steady. "What is this about?"

The chancellor pressed a button on her intercom. "Dodie, please bring kaffee. For six. Danke."

Dimmer spoke for the first time. "Because the situation has taken an international aspect, the *Landespolizei* has taken the liberty of aligning with the *Bundeskriminalamt*, Interpol National Central Bureau."

"Under the Department of the Interior, as appropriate," Kellner added.

Madam Chancellor nodded for the interrogation to begin.

Two men dressed soberly in business casual gray and black pulled up chairs that had been aligned to the side wall. One had a pen and paper, the other a recording device with a small microphone he placed on the chancellor's desk. The sandy-haired man with the pen asked, "How much do you know about the organization known familiarly as Onus?"

At one thirty in the afternoon, Rachel sat with her hands locked around a lukewarm cup of tea at a pretty little patio table with an umbrella. Under her feet were patterned circular stones. Fluffy yellow and cone-shaped orange flowers nestled in between green hedges around the courtyard to create a sense of privacy. She didn't feel like trying to figure out if she knew any of the names of the plants. She'd been alone for a half hour, hungry, waiting for Gervas and headed from concerned to anxious.

The tour of the building had been pleasant, though she didn't remember much of it since she was so busy mentally looking over her shoulder. Even now she knew there were at least two cameras covering her. Rachel lifted the cup to her lips, but lowered it at the sight of a blurred figure approaching from the other side of the glass doors. At last.

"Gervas. I was beginning to worry." The cameras kept her from hugging him. He seemed burdened, skin slightly putty-colored, as if he'd been inside too long.

He kissed her cheek. "Rachel," he whispered near her ear, tickling her.

"Are you all right?" She inadvertently glanced at one of the discreet rooftop camera lenses.

He acknowledged her concern with a squeeze of her arm. "Yes, of course, I am fine. I am so sorry for my delay. Did you enjoy the tour?"

His voice was chatty, light-hearted, and she followed his lead. "Oh, yes. I didn't realize how hard it would be to move capitals from Berlin to Bonn and back again. This is such a lovely building, too, so unique. The guide made a really big deal of the dome. To think the new one is only twelve years old. The garden up there is amazing."

She let him take her arm and stroll back to the door, though that was the last thing she wanted—to go back inside.

"We shall take lunch, yes?" Gervas asked. "At the restaurant on the roof?"

"I-if you like."

He stopped just inside, before the elevator. "You are tired, perhaps? Or would you rather take a walk?"

Rachel looked left and right. She stepped close to him. "Are you truly all right? Do you need to stay here for more— more meetings?"

He took both her hands. "I do not have to stay. Would a stroll be better? We can buy food elsewhere."

Rachel put on her patience and took his subtle hint about waiting to talk until they were out of the building. "Will we be safe?" she whispered as the elevator doors swooshed closed.

Gervas put his right arm around her waist. "Yes, I believe so. And I have no doubt Viktor is close."

As predicted, Viktor, in a casual white shirt and jeans, a cocky little gray plaid fedora and dark glasses, stayed two paces in front of them. How he knew where they were headed, Rachel could not imagine. Possibly Gervas was following him. Viktor had an earbud in one ear, with a wire to his front shirt pocket. In this, he looked little different than many on the streets who were attached to some type of electronic device.

The blur and occasional bump of people on the sidewalk made Rachel stick like static to Gervas. They weren't moving all that fast, but she struggled to regulate her breathing. She'd never been so nervous and sweat formed at her temples. Gervas slowed and raised a hand. A car pulled alongside and she fought a shriek. "I think it best to return to the hotel," he said.

Viktor opened the back door of the familiar Daimler. Rachel scooted in. Hans, in the front passenger side, handed her a chilled mineral water. "Frau."

Touched, Rachel could not stem the tear that spilled over. "Thank you. And I'm sorry."

Gervas tucked her close. "It is I who must apologize for taxing you. Nothing has gone as I expected." He leaned back as they pulled into traffic. "Drink slowly. I have come to a decision I hope you will like."

"Tell me."

"Would you like to meet Katrine, my first daughter?"

Stunned by the change in direction, Rachel blinked. "I'd love to."

He hugged her tighter and laid his chin on top of her head. "Good. I'll arrange for her to come."

Rachel reclined on the sofa of her room at the hotel, directed there by Gervas, after they'd shared a meal. She was pleasantly muzzy-headed with tiredness, and very glad to be underground and under protection. Something to tell her grandchildren about, she thought as she listened to Gervas on the telephone. She drifted into plans of future holidays with little ones, baking cookies and playing in the snow, when she vaguely heard the click of a telephone being replaced in the receiver. The sofa end depressed when Gervas sat. She nearly moaned when he began to rub her feet.

"I remember so many things," he said, "about you, about us. Memories return like faded photographs being touched up, growing stronger every moment we are together."

"I loved traveling with you," Rachel said. "Making arrangements, then standing at the back, watching you work your charm on the audience. Like earlier in the week in Chicago and DC."

"I knew I could count on you. You made everything sync in perfection. I never worried whether the sound equipment would fail or whether we'd arrive on time with suitable copies of books."

"And a pen with ink." She laughed.

"Yes, and always that. I was never so panicked at the first signing when I realized my pen was empty. Like an angel, you slipped to my side and handed me five more."

Rachel continued in her mind, the trips between classes, arranging for rooms, interviews, the staging areas, all the big things that shed light on the current topic, its expert, and the sponsoring entity—Mendota College. The things he didn't know, like discovering his preferences for food, and an hour of privacy in the middle of day; even the type of pen he liked best. She'd made that happen.

"Those pens, they were my favorite type, gliding. I always use them now."

She closed her eyes, hoping the dim light hid the heated flush of her cheeks.

He rested his hands along the tops of her feet. "I was never served canned pineapple after that first dinner when you were there."

"So long ago, Gervas. I would like to know, please, about

your meeting today, if you can tell me more. And about Katrine."

"You recall also my dislike to discussing business over food." He sighed. "Very well."

Rachel pulled herself away and curled, sitting, to show she was paying attention.

"I am afraid I received a taste of your fright this morning when Madam Chancellor called in two Interpol officers. I was…unprepared."

"You thought they were coming to arrest you?" What would Rachel have done if he'd been taken into custody and she was left alone in a foreign country? She immediately chastised herself. Of course she would have done whatever she could to free him.

"Perhaps I should not have been surprised. However, the nature of the meeting did not go as presented to me." He gave a little smile and one-shouldered shrug. "There was little advice to give. Only to take."

"Was your brother there?"

"No. I must, of course, be circumspect in this report. It is not a matter of trust."

Rachel raised her hands in surrender. "Only international security. Don't worry, I don't want to know."

He smirked. "Suffice it to say, I told them what I knew." He took off his glasses and rubbed his eyes. "I am sorry that the name Warfield came up."

"I'm not. If he's part of this operation, he should get what he deserves."

Gervas stayed quiet, seemingly looking through some window in his soul Rachel was not privy to. She took his hand. "Gervas?"

"Hmm? Yes." He sighed. "So I have thought lately about

what I, too, deserve. My family is a long line of deceivers, from when we first came to Freiburg on the heels of Bonaparte. My ancestors claimed Catholicism. But we have never been greatly faithful."

Rachel waited, wondering where he was headed.

"Despite your brother-in-law's distrust of me and my motives, he did something I cannot dislodge from my heart."

"What was that?"

"The night before we came here, when we made travel arrangements, he prayed." He shook his head in self-deprecation. "I will not claim to have had a religious experience. Nonetheless, I was touched." Gervas looked at Rachel, holding her with his expression. "Even though little has gone according to plan, we are still safe. I am no longer responsible for my brother's miscreant ways, and I do not have to feel guilty about his choices."

"But you do about other things."

"I always will. There is nothing I can do to completely remove those feelings."

He was right, but Rachel was not the person to counsel him on that. "So you think your brother will be arrested?"

"Perhaps in time. The case is mounting."

"You're sad."

"I wish I had spent more—how is it?—quality time with Manheim. We haf always been so different."

"Siblings don't always turn out to be best friends. Ann and I fought a lot. We were very different too. She was the smart, beautiful one who had a well-heeled lifestyle. Even when her husband went missing, I thought she had it all, though I felt sorry for Ritchie, her son. But I learned she was also good at keeping secrets. I never knew her mother-in-law was forcing her to live almost in poverty, humiliating her by making her ask for every penny, even though she worked for her husband's company." Rachel squeezed Gervas's hand. "We can't make ourselves feel bad for the secrets the people we love keep from us."

"The 'what if' game again, Rachel?" He squeezed back, set her hand aside and rose. "Like this window of yours, eh?" Crossing the room, he went to pull the drape aside to reveal the false window. "All illusion. Yes, I have finally seen that, and only now begun to comprehend."

He clasped his hands behind his back and strolled around the room. Rachel watched until he crossed beyond her line of sight.

"Due to the delicacy of the situation and the possible…complications, I have been asked to postpone my teaching assignment for the upcoming semester."

"Oh, no." Rachel inhaled his hurt. "So they canceled the class? What will you do?"

He circled the sofa and came to stand in front of her. "At first I was stunned and disappointed, naturally. I had done much work in preparation. Then I realized the advantage such a situation will present." His smile gradually turned wicked and he reached down to pull her up against him. "I cannot think of a better place to hide than in a small city in America, while international politics play out."

"A small city that has big ties to Freiburg?"

He'd been about to kiss her but pulled back. "Ah." He swooped close again. "How about a very small village some kilometers from the big city with ties to Freiburg?"

"Cottage Grove?" Rachel met his lips and wound her arms behind his shoulders.

He was the one to pull back, breathless, some seconds later. He tapped her on the cheek but didn't let her go far. "I have a plan, but it involves some risk."

"Doesn't everything? What is it?"

"We must all speak of it together. Maeve, Katrine, you and I."

"Katrine? She's involved?"

"Yes." Gervas moved away, walked to the small refrigerator and poured them each a drink; the diet cola she liked and a sparkling water for himself. He placed them on the coffee table and they both sat again. "It is a ninety-minute flight from Freiburg to Berlin. Hans has gone to escort her. There are some other complications I need to make known to you."

Before she could ask what he would tell Katrine about their relationship, his phone chimed with an incoming text.

"Excuse me." Gervas pulled out the phone and checked the screen. "Good. Katrine has packed and is on her way with Hans. She should be here tonight."

Another chime sounded. He thumbed the screen and frowned. "Your brother-in-law." He looked up, face ashen. "He says their home was broken into last night."

"Are they all right?"

"I believe so—"

A door crashed in Gervas's suite, which they heard through the open connecting door.

"Herr Professor! Frau Michels."

Gervas strode to meet Viktor at the interconnecting door. Didn't those guys ever sleep? Rachel was losing that safe feeling very quickly.

Gervas half-ran back to her. "Pack quickly, please. I will answer questions later."

After sending his bag with Viktor, Gervas crossed the room quickly to Rachel. She would be unhappy, again, at the arrangements, but her safety was tantamount. Later, on the journey, he could berate himself for wanting to bring her along on this ridiculous trip to Berlin.

She was standing at her case, full but unzipped, on the bed, her left hand on her chin, eyes wild.

"Rachel, are you ready? I cannot express deeply enough my regret."

"How bad is it?" She blinked out of her hesitation, though worry lines he hated to see crossed her forehead. He chose to ignore her question for the moment.

"Anything else?" He indicated the bag, and at the shake of her head, pulled the zip and took it from the bed. "Come." This time he was one leading, though he wished under better circumstances. They hustled into the hall, then the elevator. Once there, he leaned closely and kissed her forehead and spoke softly into her ear. "It's Warfield. He has remained at large, and has wounded one officer during an attempt to arrest him. He sent messages to my computer, and yours. It is believed he is on his way to Europe."

"What kind—"

"Sh. Wait." The frustration vibrated from her, but even now he couldn't risk her speaking. With Warfield's understanding of technology, he didn't even trust the cell phones they had been given and insisted she leave hers in the room, as he had left his. One of the security people would take care of the instruments.

The doors opened quietly and he took her arm. Should they move slowly? Or quickly? He looked around as soon as they emerged, saw Viktor, and decided to walk with purpose but without drawing attention. Warfield might be coming to Germany, but he was only one small part of Onus. News of Manheim's deception and involvement had already spread.

"Fairly serious," Gervas told Rachel once in the car, answering her question from the elevator. "Viktor said they'd intercepted three messages scheduling riots in Greece and Poland, and one assassination attempt in Africa. They thwarted a flashmob at Ataturk Airport in Athens, and quelled a run on the banks in France. The analysts are doing what they can to keep the stock market relatively stable for now."

"What about Katrine?"

"She will meet you at the airport," he told her, touched that was her first question. "It must be this way for now." He set his mouth and looked out the window. When he felt her cool hand touch his, he allowed himself the comfort of flipping his palm to twine fingers.

Their parting at the airport was spirit-crushing.

"When am I seeing you again?" she asked.

"Soon." He meant it, as he watched Hans lead her away.

"I've never been to Switzerland," was the last thing he heard her say. He had little time to talk to Katrine, try and explain more, prepare her for meeting Rachel, as Phillip held her at EuroAirport, Basel-Mulhouse-Freiburg, about an hour from her home. At least they would have each other on the way to the States.

"Herr Professor, this way." Viktor beckoned.

Back in the car, Gervas accepted the copies of Die Welt, and Junge Welt, daily newspapers. "So soon?" He clicked his tongue at the garish headline, "Antique Claimant Fraud." "Who in the department would have released this information?" No wonder the Roths' home had been burgled.

"The investigation has been underway some weeks already," Viktor reminded Gervas. "This is old news."

Gervas caught his toothy grin in the rearview mirror. "So it is." He continued to read the article outlining an elaborate plan concocted by an obscure relation to the Regenbogens who'd been living in Idaho, United States. The young man had changed his name from Reitmann—a grainy photograph showed the application—and began the restitution process. He'd managed to be granted secure title to the house and real property in Germany, and had been busy gathering information and locating Regenbogen's documented antiques.

The former Reitmann had a number of circumstances in his favor, as the US State Department policy on Property Restitution in Central and Eastern Europe was created to simplify reclamation. Gervas was mulling over the possibilities of using some of the points of the document reprinted in the article, "Privatization programs should include protections for claimants," "When restitution of property is not possible, adequate compensation should be paid," and admiring the ingenuity of the man's gall when he heard a clink.

The window near Gervas's right cheek popped in a spider web. An adrenalin rush sent a stream of energy through his trunk and he reached to unbuckle his safety belt as Viktor's head slammed into the restraint in front of him. The front passenger side window shattered completely and Viktor's howl made Gervas quake. There was no time to assess the damage of flying glass, however, as the new driver, a man whose name Gervas did not know, slumped over the wheel. Gervas tried not to think about the man's warm, squishy hands and accelerator foot as he thrust himself between the seats and grabbed the wheel in an attempt to gain control of the automobile. They lurched against a rusty green truck with a grinding sound that made him clench his teeth.

Cars on either side had slowed, thank the heavens. His hair whipped around his head with the force of the wind through the broken window. He had to blink often to see as the sun had fallen low in the sky. Burned rubber, oil, and fuel assailed him, making his nose run. He tried to settle into a more convenient position atop the driver whom he hoped was not a corpse. An emergency vehicle with flashing lights careened up behind them. To trust? "Viktor! Slow down or not?"

"I can't see! What color is it?"

Gervas risked taking his eyes from the road in front of him for a second to check behind. "White. A green stripe."

"Yes, yes, move off."

"Are you all right?"

"My eyes," he moaned.

Praying the shooter had gone on, Gervas kicked aside the driver's foot and slowed.

<>

With no phone, no desire to page through magazines in the back pocket of the airplane seat in front of her, and too jumpy to try to find a relaxing music station, Rachel stared at the monitor showing the plane's progress south. Hans had passed her off to a female Interpol officer, Mona, who sat across the aisle on the small airplane. The seat next to Rachel was empty, for which she was grateful. The officer had opened a magazine, but never turned the page the whole flight. Instead she alternated swiveling her head and listening or staring intently over the passenger seats. Twice she walked the length of the cabin, strolling as if unconcerned. Rachel sat with her hands clenched on her lap, her feet planted straight beneath her and the seatbelt tight. She shook her head at the attendant's offer of a beverage and made her lips turn up when he nudged the airsick bag up higher in the seat pocket.

How was she ever going to talk about this trip? People at home were going to ask what she saw, where she went, what she and Gervas did, and she had nothing to tell them about the mere twenty-four hours she's been in Germany. Thinking of that, she was annoyed with Scott in a new way. She would have loved at least another night in that bed. And a swim in the tub. The plane shuddered and dipped slightly. Turbulence. Yep. The attendant came by again, and this time she accepted a miniature bottle of water.

Upon landing, Rachel did as she'd been instructed. The other passengers disembarked, the attendants walked the plane, and then Mona ushered her out into the terminal and immediately into a waiting airport open cab car which zipped them to the security checkpoint. Mona took care of the passports, giving hers at the right moments, and breezing them toward the correct departure gate. Colors and echoing sounds and scents both spicy and sweaty, swirled in a miasma.

"Now ve cross into Svitzerland, ma'am," Mona told her.

"So this is the third country I've set foot in today?" Rachel was still unnerved, but stepped out of it to enjoy this moment. "We arrived in France, and now this is the line?" Okay, this was something to tell the people back home. An airport straddling two countries, serving three.

"Und here we greet Phillip, ja?" Mona shook hands, nodded her short strawberry blond head, uttered "goot luck," and disappeared.

"Frau Michels. Goot jhourney, yes?"

"Yes, Phillip. It's nice to see you again."

"I present Fraulein Katrine Friedemann."

Rachel was disappointed he didn't click his heels at the introduction. She beamed and stepped forward, excited and anxious to meet Gervas's older daughter. What did the girl—woman—know about her? She and Gervas had never had a chance to—

"Miz Michels." A frail blonde unfolded herself from the seat behind Phillip and rose.

The woman smiled back, anxious eyes imitating Rachel's feelings.

Rachel knew her expression of happiness had slipped a bit and forced the shine back into it. Her initial thought was how this poor girl had been cheated. There was obviously something wrong with her health, and she sincerely hoped her illness wasn't news to Gervas.

"I am ha-happy to meet yu," Katrine said.

The girl's voice was so ugly it made Rachel take a breath and grasp all the self-control she could manage to keep a pleasant smile on her face. Katrine wore a moss green scarf looped at her throat so Rachel couldn't tell if the harsh rasp was permanent from a wound or the result of a case of temporary laryngitis.

Rachel took her hand, which was chilly. Rachel wanted to tuck it between her own to share her warmth. "Katrine. I am very pleased to meet you."

Phillip had gone to the desk and now returned. "Fiff-teen minutes to early boarding," he announced, and then stood guard while the two of them lowered themselves to sit. Large windows overlooked runways. A SWISS jet was attached to a boarding ramp close by. Rachel tried various conversation openings, but having no idea the extent of Katrine's English, felt tongue-tied beyond "Do you travel much?" and "Have you been to the States before?"

"Father told me liddle bit," Katrine whispered, holding up her fingers about two inches apart. "Uff meeting again wid you." She pursed her lips. "Forgiff my voice. Operation. I practice English." She pulled out a pad of paper and pen. "Write better."

Rachel nodded cautiously. Operation? But, more importantly, "again?" She and Gervas? What had he told the girl? Rachel took the comment at face value for now. "I am happy to practice with you, Katrine."

Katrine smiled widely. "Yes. Goot. Danke." She wrote "Thank you."

"You are welcome. It's a long flight."

"Yes. Many hours. Ve haf a meal?"

"That's right. I wonder what it will be?" Rachel enounced each word as if she'd been teaching Maeve, as a toddler, to speak.

"I hope not wienerschnitzle."

Rachel chuckled along with the young lady's gurgling laugh. They'd get along with a mix of writing and talking. Questions could come at the appropriate moments. "Do you know if your father will fly with us?"

"Fly?"

"Come along on this plane?"

She frowned and queried Phillip in German. He replied briefly, then checked the screen on his phone. He made a sudden fist around it and spoke some more.

"Nein. Father meets us at Ouiskon-sin."

"Oh." Maybe that was a good thing. It would give her and Katrine time to spend time with each other. Rachel had plenty of dreams about a future that included Gervas no matter what their relationship became, and it was always nice if all the players at least liked each other. How should she ask about Katrine's health?

Phillip interrupted her train of thought. "Ladeez, it is time."

On board, business class no less, Phillip seemed in a rush. "Please to meet Wilhelm Bosch, new…uh…new guide, yes? To the Schtats. I must leaf yu now. To check mein bruder."

Rachel had been assessing Bosch before she caught the last. "Your brother? You don't mean Viktor? But he was with Gervas."

"Ja. They are safe now. *Auf wiedersehen.*"

"Wait!"

Katrine touched Rachel's arm, holding her phone in her other hand. "There was accident. Father will call later. He is AOK."

<>

Gervas stood at the accident scene which had temporarily shut down the road. Men in fireproof suits moved about, making sure glass and fuel was cleared away. The driver's body bag lay zipped nearby. Gervas clutched Viktor's hand reaching out from the cocoon of the gurney blankets while waiting to be loaded into the ambulance. Blood trickled from numerous cuts along his face and neck. White gauze swathed his head to cover his eyes.

Diesel stink eddied in the twilight. "Viktor, my deepest gratitude, friend." Gervas snuffled. He watched Viktor swallow and understood his fear. He squeezed the man's hand and stepped back when the medics loaded the gurney into the ambulance and sped off. A tow truck hauled away the Daimler, from which he'd extracted his luggage. Three men stood arguing on the outskirts of the site. One black-haired and bearded man, dressed in threadbare slacks and sandals, pointed at the green truck, now crumpled at the edge of the road.

Officers began opening lanes of traffic. Gervas stood for a moment at the door of a police vehicle, thankful for his life and that he'd not had Rachel or Katrine with him. At the station he gave more interviews, signed papers, and twiddled his thumbs. He thought about borrowing a phone to call Katrine, but realized they were in the air. He could send a message. Better wait.

Finally, Hans Belter arrived.

"Thank you for coming again. I'm sorry about what happened to Viktor," Gervas told him. "I hope he will keep his sight."

"We know the risks."

Hans took him to the airport, this time in an official armored car borrowed from the embassy. Although he was embarrassed by the ostentatious vehicle, the motorcycle escort and the whole need for it, his main objective was to get back to the States and meet Rachel and Katrine. He'd never gotten a chance to explain about Katrine's illness. By now it must have been obvious to Rachel he'd withheld this information, though not on purpose.

They arrived in plenty of time to make the flight and boarded early with a preferred traveler pass. He followed the instructions of the attendant, buckled up automatically and listened to the captain's little speech though he couldn't have repeated any of it.

In the air he began to shake with delayed reaction from the shooting and car chase.

"Is normal," Hans told him. "To be expected. You have no health problems? No heart trouble?"

"Neither."

After a quick consultation with an attendant, Gervas was

handed two small white pills.

Gervas swallowed the pills with some tonic water and fell asleep.

<>

Rachel, Katrine, and Wilhelm changed planes twice. The layovers were not lengthy, and they passed through customs in Chicago without trouble. Katrine was walked through a different line than Rachel, though both were long. Rachel passed the time guessing where her fellow Americans had been to visit and watching the luggage juggling act they all performed. She had yet to find out exactly what was wrong with Katrine. Manners prevented her from asking outright, and in any case she wasn't sure the girl's English was strong enough to explain. Rachel told Katrine about the college and her work there in Student Services. Katrine had been at a loss to explain what she did for work, and slept heavily after the meal.

At O'Hare, Wilhelm and Katrine cleared their line before Rachel. Wilhelm made a call while they stood waiting, before taking the airport tram to catch a flight to Madison. Katrine's eyes were wide and sparkling with excitement, though her cheeks were pale.

"Are you feeling all right, Katrine?" Rachel asked her quietly.

At her puzzled frown, Rachel tried again. "You are well right now? Healthy?" Rachel winced when she realized how she'd asked the question. "I mean, right now?"

"Tired? Ja?" She struggled for more words. "Very much travel." Katrine raised her head and gestured at the new waiting area. "Exciting. Is small trip next?"

"Yes, it's a short airplane ride."

While Katrine visited the restroom, Rachel called Ann.

"Well, hi there, sister of mine," Ann answered, after

Rachel explained dialing from a pay phone. "You lost your phone?"

"No. Well, sort of. Anyway, I'm in Chicago—"

"What? Never mind, go on."

"There was…" Now Rachel wished she'd spent more time thinking of what to say. "Things didn't quite work out the way we hoped. Gervas's, um, meetings, are finished for now, so we—I came back." Seeing Katrine saunter toward the waiting area lounge, Rachel dropped her voice and hurried. "Gervas's class was canceled, so he's meeting us at home."

"Us? Why are you whisper—"

"I have his daughter Katrine with me. We'll be in Madison in a couple of hours. I'll call you then." Rachel thought she heard an excited squeal in the background of Ann's house and hoped it was just the baby, David, as she hung up. Putting on a smile for Katrine, Rachel strolled to meet her. "We should be able to board soon."

"Goot. I cannot call mein father," she said. "He say we have none…" she mimicked holding a phone to her ear.

"We'll update the provider from Maeve's phone," Rachel said.

"Ja." Katrine smiled with a hint of nerves. "Danke."

Wilhelm strode up to them. "Come. We can board now. I have spoken to Herr Professor. He meets us in Madison. Two hours and a half."

When they landed in Madison, Wilhelm collected their luggage and piled it on a cart.

Rachel turned to head out the door when she heard that familiar squeal from earlier on the phone. "Maeve?"

"Mom, hi!"

Rachel's daughter scurried past her with wide open arms. For Katrine.

Gervas's daughter dropped her purse, squealed back and met Maeve with an exuberant hug.

Rachel lowered her brows and frowned. Apparently Gervas forgot to tell her that not only was his daughter ill, she had also somehow become acquainted with Maeve. When had that happened? And why hadn't Katrine mentioned it?

Wilhelm passed her, pushing the cart. "This way, ma'am."

28

Rachel sat in silence next to Wilhelm who reluctantly allowed Katrine to ride in Maeve's car. "Drive slowly, please. Ve follow." Wilhelm would stay with them until Herr Professor arrived at the Roth house, he explained with a grim "you better not cost me my job, young lady" look at Maeve.

Right. Any of them might still be a target as long as the ring was presumed in her and Gervas's possession, Scott was on the loose, and Manheim so eager to commit fratricide. No, Gervas hadn't told her about Manheim in so many words, but she could read behind what little he shared after their meeting. She probably should be more afraid but she was too numb. Gervas would tell her such daydreaming would get her killed. What about the break-in at Ann and Mark's? She still hadn't heard details.

She was tired, that was certain. Delusional. Missing Gervas. What had held him back from traveling with her, anyhow? Maybe he had second thoughts about renewing their relationship.

Rachel sat beside Wilhelm in the front and eyed Maeve's taillights. Phillip said he was concerned about his brother. Katrine had said something about her father being AOK after an accident. The constant no one telling her things was getting old.

"Wilhelm, do you know what kind of accident the professor and Viktor had?"

He glanced out of the corner of his eye, apparently reluctant to take his attention from Maeve's bumper. "I beleef they vere run off the road."

Rachel gasped. "On purpose? And Viktor was hurt. Do you know how badly? Was anyone else hurt? Who would do that?"

Wilhelm's lips pressed together and his hands clenched around the wheel. "I could not say, madam."

Of course he couldn't. Or wouldn't. Rachel folded her arms and stared to her right. They were not far from Ann's neighborhood. Would anything feel normal again? Ever since Gervas had showed up her life had flipped. If he hadn't come back, she'd be…what? Dating an international terrorist? Every red car they passed made her jumpy.

Scott was still at large. "Wilhelm, do you know if Mr. Warfield made it to Europe?"

"I haf not been informed."

She had liked Viktor. Wilhelm—not so much. He wasn't as warm and fuzzy. Rachel hoped Viktor had not been hurt badly and worked on taking calming breaths to quell the worry until they followed Maeve's car into Ann's driveway.

Rachel's senses went into overtime as she got out of the car. An athletic man in navy blue shorts and a tee shirt ran slowly along the walking path, a German shepherd heeling. An unmarked squad, the license plate the only giveaway, was parked on the curb two houses over. A man with a military haircut was talking on a handheld device. The man with dog reappeared.

Ahead of her, Maeve and Katrine chatted in some kind of hybridization of German and English, and occasionally exchanged scribbled notes. When had Maeve learned German? Probably since meeting her father. She had not seemed put off by Katrine's voice. Did Maeve know more about the operation that had damaged the girl's vocal chords?

When Wilhelm unlocked the rear gate, Rachel reached for her bags. Mark opened the front door and approached, hands in the pockets of his jeans.

"Hi, good to see you. Sorry your trip was cut short. How was the flight back?"

"Mostly uneventful." Rachel glanced again at the girls.

Mark took a bag from Wilhelm.

"Oh, right, Mark, this is Wilhelm…um—"

"Bosch," Wilhelm supplied. He shook Mark's hand.

"We spoke earlier." Mark nodded. "Thanks for bringing them all home safe and sound."

The girls came near.

"Uncle Mark, meet Katrine." Maeve rocked on her heels and grinned like it was her tenth birthday all over again. Rachel had to smile.

Mark took Katrine's hand as if touching fine crystal. Rachel was sure he'd never given such a weak handshake to an adult in his life. He caught Rachel's eye and raised a brow in a "what's up with her" sign. She shook her head faintly.

"We're, like, half-sisters, Uncle Mark. Gervas is her father too."

"I am pleased to meet you, Mr. Roth," Katrine said in a higher pitch that sounded less grating.

Mark plastered on a quick warm smile. "Welcome to the United States."

"Nice guards," Rachel whispered to Mark as she passed to head inside. At his fake innocent puzzled face, she mouthed "Dog. Fuzz."

Ann met them in the foyer. The introductions were repeated and they were invited into the living room.

"Bathroom first, Auntie Ann," Maeve announced and hauled Katrine by the hand toward the stairs. "We'll be right back."

"Where's Gervas," Ann said.

"Oh, he'll be along at some point. He ended up on a different flight. How are you feeling?" Rachel asked. "You look fantastic. All glowy."

Wilhelm sat awkwardly on the peacock feather chair and looked around while Mark went to bring in refreshments.

Ann preened. "Thanks. I feel okay. I'm sorry you had to come back so early." She glanced at Wilhelm. "We can talk later."

"Yes. I want to hear more about the break in."

"They didn't actually get inside," Ann said.

"Do the police have any leads?"

"Not really."

Mark came in with a tray of soft drinks with a plate of cookies balanced on top. "We're pretty sure they were after the ring. The crook only got to the porch before the alarms went off and the guard caught him."

"So he—it was a he?—was caught? Who is it?"

"We don't know," Ann said. "And yes, a him."

"Probably someone Manheim hired," Rachel said in a low voice. "I'm sorry for all this trouble. I had the stupid thing for over twenty years and nobody cared then. What a mess."

Mark handed Wilhelm his drink of choice then sat next to Ann and put his arm around her. No one said anything else until the girls waltzed into the room. Katrine was a few years older than Maeve, maybe even close to thirty, but Rachel couldn't stop thinking of them as "girls."

"Everything good?" Rachel asked Maeve.

"Yeah. It sure was exciting when the cops arrived to take the creep away after the attempted break in," Maeve said, helping herself to a cookie and offering one to Katrine, who took it with a wary look and nibbled a small corner.

"The neighbors weren't happy," Ann said. "I think they're planning to run us off the block."

"They're fine, Aunt Ann," Maeve said. "Mark and I'll talk to them. I mean, it's like a once in a lifetime opportunity to get up close to international espionage but stay safe."

"Hmm." Ann pursed her lips. "So, Katrine. It's lovely to meet you. Tell us a bit about yourself."

Katrine looked not exactly shell-shocked but a bit faded around the edges and had dark circles under her eyes. "I haff some troubles with the voice." She pointed to her throat. "Forgive. Thank you for having me." She swallowed. "Mein father, you know, is Gervas Friedemann. Mein mutter, she is…unwell. Mein bruder, Max, and his fiancé, they care for her." She sipped from the bottle of water Maeve handed her with a smile of encouragement.

Rachel was proud of her daughter. She'd been certain Maeve would barge in and talk for Katrine.

"I haf sick… an illness from born time." Katrine lowered her face as if ashamed. "Makes for growths. I haf this cut out." She touched her throat. "I studied at University. Business. I finish the school, but help only wid household management now times."

"You live in a big place, though, right, Katrine?" Maeve cut in. "And with your brother gone a lot on his engineering work and your mom not able, there's a lot to do. You have, like animals and stuff, too."

Katrine blinked and looked in askance at Wilhelm. They conversed for a minute in German.

"I sorry for this…" Katrine said afterward. "This German speak."

"That's quite all right," Ann told her.

"Yes, we haf small estate wid plants…garden? Large. Sell some produce. Und farm animals. Grow also harts…deers and birds…" She spoke a couple of words in German to Wilhelm, who translated "game cock."

"Game cock," Katrine repeated in her gravelly voice, "for the hunting."

"And she takes care of the records and orders," Maeve said. "They live near the Black Forest, you know."

"Your father said he had some thoughts about staying at your place," Rachel said to Maeve. It was the closest to an accusation of her daughter not sharing the Katrine secret Rachel could say in public.

"Um, well, he did call and ask how I'd feel about having Katrine stay with me while she's…visiting."

Again that little hesitation Rachel picked up. Something else Maeve knew that she wasn't sharing. When had Rachel become so untrustworthy that people had to keep secrets around her? The nibble of hurt stung.

A harsh yowl from Katrine's purse made Rachel jump. She wasn't the only one, as she saw Mark pat Ann's arm.

"Excuse, please!" Katrine rose and walked to the hall, phone against her ear. She returned shortly. "Mein fadder has arrived."

Wilhelm jumped up and bobbed his head. "Thank you. I go now to meet."

<>

The story of potential European anarchy from a terrorist organization well-planned to undermine the euro and strip the Union of power made for a couple of AP paragraphs on page three. Arrests were imminent, and the German chancellor had already rearranged her ministerial cabinet. Manheim Friedemann's name was not even mentioned in the article.

Rachel lowered the morning paper she'd been reading over breakfast, alone at Ann's kitchen table on Friday. The girls and Ann were still in bed and Mark back at work. The past week of guards this and that covering their every move made Rachel's vacation unbearable. Gervas had been a guest of the State Department at some undisclosed location until last night, when he'd finally been released. To Rachel's house, supervised, while she was to stay here and coddle Ann.

She still wasn't sure how long Katrine and Gervas were staying in the States, or what, exactly, was going on at University Hospital.

"Good morning." Ann shuffled in on bare feet, hair perfect, a delicate white flowered robe flowing around her.

Rachel squelched a looming ill-natured thought toward her sister who looked beautiful even first thing upon rising while she felt dumpy in sweats. "Morning. How are you feeling today?"

Ann reached for a cup to make tea and smiled. "Crackers first. Helps." She waved at the paper. "Anything new in the world?"

"Apparently the downfall of the civilized world has been averted. Page three."

"That important? Gervas must be devastated."

"Yeah. Why don't you sit? I'll get the water for you." Rachel dropped the paper and went to fill the kettle. "Thank goodness for Mark being able to help sort things out." Rachel nursed her cold coffee and refused to meet her sister's knowing eye.

"I'm thankful for Mark every day. No news about Warfield yet? Who'd a guessed."

Indeed. "I sure know how to pick 'em, don't I? The State Department thinks he left the country, so they called off their watch."

"Oh?"

"That's why we came home early. They said he was on his way to Europe. I hope they caught him and arrested him." Rachel glanced at the new cell phone. She had yet to personalize the instrument with her favorite ring tones and calendar. "You still want to try for a couple of days in Door County before I go back to work?"

"The State Department might think we're safe, but I'm not sure Mark will agree. We can ask. Besides, I should think you'd rather spend time with Gervas. Are you still seeing him today?"

"I hope so. He's taking Katrine for tests, then we're meeting for lunch downtown."

"Poor girl. Her doctors must not have been able to do anything else for her in Germany." Ann put her hand over her still-flat stomach. "Did she want to talk much about it when you were traveling with her?"

"We didn't discuss it." Rachel turned when the tea kettle started spitting steam and shut off the stove burner. "She wanted to practice her English, so we did that. Though she slept a lot. I was tired, too."

Rachel brought Ann's cup to the table. "It could be Maeve who was sick. I keep thinking that. He's her father, too."

"I guess you didn't know about this before you went to Germany."

Ann's astute assessment made Rachel purse her mouth. "There was a lot going on. We need time to figure out where we're headed. And we only got a chance to talk briefly last night."

She set her cup in the sink and headed for the stairs and her room. As she passed, Ann touched her arm.

"You've had to put up with so much these past few weeks. I know you. It's not easy giving up your personal space like that. I'm glad you've been here for me, though."

Rachel bent to hug her sister's shoulders. "Me too," she whispered.

<>

Gervas tidied Rachel's narrow kitchen after breakfast. Today was the first he could spend in some peace after the debriefings on his brother's activities. He still wasn't certain which of Mark Roth's colleague's arguments had convinced them of his innocence. Having an attorney in the family had been a blessing. Although he'd desperately wanted to see the girls and Rachel last night, it had been after midnight before he'd arrived back in Madison. A phone call to them in between flights, at nine, had to suffice. Katrine had trouble adjusting to the time shift, she said, so he'd pick her up without too much time to spare for her evaluation at the clinic.

While navigating the mid-morning Madison traffic in Rachel's automobile, he wondered what kind of life this future held. He loved Germany, but Manheim had destroyed everything that had been good about living there. Perhaps he needed to emigrate. He could write and research anywhere for his books.

And Katrine? He hoped she lived long enough to create her own destiny.

29

A late morning rain shower made the sidewalks of State Street steam. Rachel strolled along with Gervas, hips touching as they looked for a free lunch table. She wasn't that hungry and simply enjoyed being with him. They'd exchanged only a brief hug earlier when he came for Katrine, not enough to make up for their separation.

"She was diagnosed with leukemia when she was six," Gervas said quietly. "It has a rare element called Fanconi syndrome."

Rachel listened as he rambled about his older daughter after their initial greeting.

"We knew she was delicate from birth." Gervas leaned his head against hers briefly. "Like an angel. Sylvie blamed the old house for her many childhood ailments and took the children on trips to warm places often while I traveled."

"You missed a lot, didn't you? Of their growing-up years?"

"We had staff, a nanny. In our set it was not typical to be so available to our children's needs." He stared at a double stroller in front of a grinning mom on roller blades.

"Here." Rachel stopped before a red and white-striped umbrella over a metal table being cleared by a young man wrapped in an apron. "Can we take this table?"

The waiter nodded. "I'll bring you menus."

Gervas put his fingers on his cheek, then moved them to the tabletop. "What have you been doing these past days?"

Waiting. Worrying. "Practicing English with Katrine.

Shopping with her and Ann. Maeve's been popping in and out. I warned her about her job."

"As any good mother would do."

Rachel earned a smile and pat on the hand. She put on a cheeky grin and pulled a paper out of her purse and flourished it before him. "Surfing the internet."

He laughed at the picture of himself getting into the armored vehicle for a ride to the airport in Berlin.

"You told Katrine there'd been an accident and Viktor injured." His quick look made her flush at the gentle chide. "I know. I had no phone. But you're all right. How's Viktor?"

"He took glass from a shattered car window in the eyes. The doctors were able to remove the glass. His eyes are scratched. They will heal."

She caught the young waiter's approach and didn't reply. They gave their orders quickly since he stood there, pad in hand, waiting.

Rachel studied passersby, twitchy with being exposed yet unable to stand being cooped up anymore. Hence her suggestion of meeting on the busy and popular area. Strolling summer tourists replaced busy, noisy students. Gervas wouldn't be able to tell her much, if anything, about his debriefing. She decided to stick with the topic of Katrine. "How long will the clinical study go?" She really meant "How long are you staying?"

Gervas nodded as if hearing her unspoken question. "The trial is ongoing. Katrine will participate as long as the treatment shows promise." He thanked the waiter who brought their drinks and leaned forward to pick up his glass. "One other thing. We have agreed to speak about the disease to the local news. Katrine wants to raise awareness."

"That's brave of her." She examined his averted jaw,

grizzled with several days' beard. A faint scar that she hadn't noticed before showed underneath. He scratched at it and met her eyes.

"I don't want to miss more of my daughter's life, however long that might be."

The sting of his words pinched Rachel. "I'm sorry."

"Please don't be. We have always known the outcome. I shared with her of my desire to stay with her during her treatment since my obligations in Germany are reduced, shall we say."

Rachel's heartbeat sped up a notch.

"Your brother-in-law is quite resourceful, helping us. But we must find a place to live."

"I'm sure that won't be a problem." Rachel smiled, inventing all kinds of scenarios, most of which ended up with them being one happy little family in her house. But that was impossible. Too much time had passed. She dug into the chicken salad the waiter brought, content for the time being. Gervas wanted to stay. Maybe for Katrine, now. Maybe for her later.

Rachel couldn't live in Germany, not after what she'd gone through, even if they never set foot in Berlin. How hard would it be for Gervas to file for residency? Or emigrate? One way she knew for sure would allow him to stay. But they weren't ready for that kind of commitment yet. Were they?

<>

With Gervas and Katrine settled at her house for convenience sake, Rachel felt awkward, displaced. No one would have cared if Rachel had moved back home, but it felt too much like playing house and she couldn't trust herself so close to Gervas. When her sister started to have fainting spells, she decided to stay camped at Ann's house. It made her commute to work a little longer, but she'd deal with that next week when she went back.

"I think our Maeve is put out," Gervas said over the phone the next evening. "She tells Katrine of her envy over giving up her old room in her old house."

"Maeve is coming tomorrow too after church. We'll make dinner for all of us." Rachel curled her legs underneath her and switched hands holding the phone to her ear, excited at the prospect of cooking in her own kitchen.

"She told me, yes, but would not specify her news she wanted to share. Has she always been so?"

Rachel chuckled. "Yes. Always dramatic."

"I look forward to spending the day with you tomorrow."

"Me too. I'll have my own job to keep me busy after the weekend. I wish I didn't have to go back."

Maeve seemed ready to fly out of her skin as she hustled into the house on Sunday afternoon. Even Katrine seemed alarmed and stayed a few steps out of her sister's way. Rachel knew better than to slow her down and simply made room on the coffee table in the living room for her computer and satchel.

"Looks like you drove here, computer on?" Rachel asked her.

"Uh-huh. I had to check something," Maeve mumbled as her fingers flew across the keyboard. "Let me show you something." Maeve twisted the screen. "Here! On this online auction site. I was doing some research, um, you know, on Regenbogens. Just out of curiosity."

Rachel, next to Maeve on the couch, waited while Gervas and Katrine pulled chairs closer and studied the screen. Katrine looked puzzled as lines crossed her delicate forehead. She brushed her hair behind her ears and listened to her father talk quietly in German, gesturing once in a while. Rachel heard "Regenbogen" and "Juden."

Maeve waited as long as she could before pulling the screen around again. Gervas raised his brows and grinned at Rachel.

"There are some old reports on what they sent to museums in the past, what was reported stolen or missing. That kind of thing. Then, this other alert pops up—you know, like an ad, or something, for…ta da!" Maeve clicked on some more icons she'd bookmarked. Rachel watched pictures download from a site on antiquities. Then Maeve tilted the screen again toward Gervas and Katrine.

"A small, jeweled golden cup," Maeve said. "Look at the provenance listed."

"Last known owner, Eli Regenbogen, dealer, Baden, Germany, 1938," Gervas read out loud. He whistled. "List price, five million euros."

"There's more," Maeve said. "Jewelry, a couple of sculptures."

Rachel hurt at the stunned expression on Gervas's face. Katrine had gone paler.

"I wondered, so often these past few weeks," he said. "What Regenbogen, no Reitmann, was doing with the antiques. Or Manheim. How could we have missed this?"

"Missed, Father?" Katrine pulled on his sleeve.

"It is how your uncle financed his—" Gervas broke into German again, a stream of despair that sounded harsh in the guttural language. Maeve appeared to pick out some words and phrases as she watched her father's lips. Rachel just sat and prayed. When Gervas calmed again, he took a deep breath.

"He used the false threat of blackmail as a ruse. He must

have." Gervas rose and paced. "This Reitmann person must have been in on the scheme."

"I bet for a percentage," Maeve said and nodded. She pulled the computer closer and clicked away some more.

"He told us he needed the entire Etruscan collection returned to satisfy young Regenbogen. He must have been searching for years and then selling the pieces to finance his group. How could I have missed this?" he repeated.

"The initial listing didn't always include the name." Maeve looked at him. "Why would you have been looking online, anyway? It's not your fault."

Rachel stood to put her arm around his waist.

"We have to tell the authorities right away." Maeve reached for her phone.

"No, wait."

Rachel pulled away at Gervas's plea. "I have an idea."

<>

Gervas walked out of Mark's office on Monday evening grateful for the lack of censure on any part of the gathered professionals. The owner of the respected Friedrich Lehrner art gallery with branches in Madison and Chicago had been an auspicious find. Gratitude was a poor word to describe Gervas's appreciation for all that Rachel's brother-in-law and the international community was willing to do for him, personally, and for Germany.

"Ve are suffering enough, are ve not, from the ghost of our past?" Lehrner had said. "I will do all I can to rectify the wrongs done at the hands of megalomaniacs."

"No matter who, no matter when." Gervas had been firm in his discussing with the assembled group which included three international legal experts, the art dealer who would pose as a buyer, two Interpol officers, and Ambassador Schelling on a long-distance conference call. Not even Gervas's megalomaniac brother would get away with financing a group whose purpose was to disrupt the carefully stitched European Union. Manheim may have been dismissed from his post and awaited charges in Berlin, but he still controlled aspects of his personal life and the family estate. After tonight, he would be operating under the assumption he had control of the Etruscan jewelry collection.

Hope lightened Gervas's steps as evening grew. Their plan would work. Gervas attempted to conjure some compassion by hoping his brother would receive the care he obviously needed while spending the rest of his life in prison.

Katrine had received her first treatment late that morning. Gervas drove to the hospital in hopes of saying good night, where she was being held overnight for observation. Eventually she'd need a bone marrow transplant if a suitable donor could be found, which would necessitate another round of destroying her own immune system. She'd need to stay isolated then too. He tried not to allow sadness to overtake the positive feelings. Gervas didn't want her to pick up on anything but his fatherly love.

Upon collecting his parking stub he made his way through quiet corridors. After a few turns and elevator rides, questioning a staff worker about the correct direction, he finally approached her room. The door was half open, soft light puddling in a half moon on the floor. Voices tumbled out as well. Katrine's familiar growl and another he'd come to love so recently.

He should have known Maeve would come to share this time with her half-sister. It was good, this sibling connection. Katrine should know more love if she had little time left in this world. They all should. Gervas waited, leaning against the wall, eavesdropping without shame on their dreams shared in their peculiar mix of Deutch and English. Rachel would have loved this. At least she would be there to comfort him later, when Katrine's body failed. If only this treatment would work. But he had decided long ago not to put his faith in the intangible.

The word "father" piqued his attention and he moved closer.

"We have that in common, I guess," Maeve said. "But at least you know him and he loves you so much."

"Mein fadder goot, not perfect," Katrine said. "He liked play vid us when he vas home. He and Sylvie, then, they fight."

"You call her that? Not Mother?"

"Her more sick than me. In the head. Max and me—ve hide…secret, no? Gerta and Margo…"

A litany of caretakers, nannies, followed. Gervas felt his chest, rubbed at the ache there. He believed in the resiliency of childhood during those dark years he'd been refused access to Katrine and Max. Phone calls could not take the place of the times he had desperately wanted to see and hold them. He had not realized Sylvie had paraded men before the children. Their fights had always been about him and his absences, what she suspected and was sometimes true about his behavior when on tour. The articles and interviews that were always about him, and not her.

"Ven Max, he finds letters, envelopes teared in her waste bucket, he meet mail delivery first. Then ve get notes Father sends."

"Oh, how sad!" Maeve said. "To know your mother did that. Dad said he'd tried to contact my mom, too, but she never got his letters and calls. We think my mom's roommate got to them first. More stuff we have in common."

Gervas turned away, wishing he hadn't stayed so long

after their laughter turned to comparing such disturbing failures. Sylvie and Atwater weren't solely to blame for his inability to communicate with his family. His priorities had been different then, and he'd had no better example to show him a better way. Hopefully Rachel had believed him about the missed letters and calls. He'd probably never have a chance to confront her former roommate again, even though they might occasionally see each other if he and Rachel stayed together. At least Rachel could understand he'd tried to change the course of events.

<>

Rachel rubbed her neck while she waited for the delivery of her and Peggy's supper—a sandwich delivery. The long day, her first back at work, would not end at a typical time. She'd expected as much and told Ann she'd be late. Rachel pulled the blinds against the dark and listened to Peggy pay off the driver and walk toward the break room.

Over supper Rachel planned to bring up a personal matter that had been bothering her for weeks. Hopefully it wouldn't end their longstanding friendship. Gervas had not brought it up again, but that didn't mean she'd forgotten. She would let the matter of his lost letters and phone calls go when she knew the truth.

Alone at a small round table with the sound of the ice machine and the answering machine picking up the bleat of a call out front, Rachel unwrapped her sub. Italian dressing on the wilted lettuce and fake cheese smarted her nose and canceled her hunger. Peggy dug into her chicken salad so Rachel waited.

Without meeting Rachel's eyes, Peggy finally said, "You've been keeping it in the whole day. You might as well get it over with." She set her fork down and stared at bottle of water.

Rachel bit her lip. She'd been hiding her entire life, she knew that now. First, behind Ann, then Maeve and Peggy. Even this comfortable job that had become hateful over the past ten years. She was going to lose Peggy over this, she knew. Maybe it was time to crawl out from under her pity rock. "You owe me an explanation for returning Gervas's letters and not letting me talk to him when he called. Back before Maeve was born."

There. She'd said it. She even looked at Peggy.

Peggy narrowed her eyes. "He told you that?"

"He didn't know. We guessed it had to be you. Why?"

"You hated him. You called him every name under the sun. Said you were glad he never came back when he married that next young thing. You'd never, ever trust him with anyone you knew. You should be *thanking* me."

Rachel clasped her shaking hands together under the table and swallowed her anger. "I believe you thought you were doing the right thing. But you never gave me the chance to think about what could happen if I knew he'd wanted to talk to me. If I could have read one of his letters."

"What makes you think you were the only one? He wanted anything with brains and legs."

"That's not true."

"You said it."

"I was angry. And sick at the time."

"Come on, there was a reason you never wanted him to know about you and the baby all those years. You were so desperate to hide from him that you forced everyone on this campus to go along with your paranoia."

Spit gathered at the corner of Peggy's lips. Her eyes bulged in her round face under her limp hair. Rachel's heart pounded.

She'd avoided confrontation most of her life when she wasn't the one in charge. Peggy's anger made her uncertain she'd done the right thing by demanding an answer.

"What do you think those reasons were founded on, huh?" Peggy was practically screaming. "He's a creep and always will be."

Rachel made an attempt to salvage the situation. She gathered her calm. "He's changed."

Peggy sat back and folded her arms. She tossed her hair. "What was your first thought when you found out he'd gotten to Maeve? Be honest! He was just after another young skirt, right?"

"That's disgusting." Calm tossed overboard, Rachel leaned forward.

"He said he didn't know who she was. Or did he wonder, hmm? Maybe she was just as star-struck as you were at that age."

"Stop it, Peggy! I trusted you. You don't know anything."

"Who really wanted to keep their relationship a secret? Not to tell you. Why? Huh?"

"No!" Rachel kept repeating no as she ran for her purse and the keys to Ann's car she'd borrowed for the day. "No, no, no. It's not true." She cried as she drove a crooked path to Prairie du Sac and the only ones she could trust.

Gervas returned through the maze of long corridors and elevators, past darkened gift shop and coffee and juice bar, toward the parking structure. He was not alone, but thought little of it until he felt the presence of someone hurrying behind him. A prickle of fear heated the back of his neck and he quickened his own pace. The looming dark garage presented no advantage. The exit choices were an elevator with closed doors and a staircase behind glass doors. Pushing a button and waiting for the elevator was too unnerving and he pictured his broken body lying at the bottom of the stairs all night.

He fingered his cell phone in his pocket. Waiting for a response, or even longer for a rescue, weren't options if someone were determined to harm him here and now.

Who was making him so afraid? Manheim had been taken into custody, Onus exposed. Gervas was ready to take back his life and start new with something worth fighting for. Angered, he gripped Rachel's long, pointed car key and wished he hadn't laughed and removed the small charm with chemical spray. How could Americans bear to live in such a pervasive state of fear? He walked quickly under a light in the garage and turned to take a stand. Before he could think twice he yelled, "Stop right there!"

Gervas's voice echoed. Thankfully, he saw a woman two rows of automobiles over, a nurse judging by her weariness and knapsack in the act of unlocking her trunk, look up and over at him. By the way her eyes widened when she looked beyond him, he wondered just how much trouble he was in. She quickly got in her car. A camera was mounted on a nearby post. He hoped it worked.

Gervas turned.

Even though he stood just outside the range of full light, Gervas recognized the man. Scott Warfield had never left the country after all.

30

"**Y**ou wish this to be over as much as I do, don't you, Mr. Warfield?" Gervas asked, keeping his voice quieter so it wouldn't bounce or alarm anyone else in the parking garage. "The police are looking for you."

"Not really."

"Ha. I suppose you are going to tell me next the man you wounded while he was arresting you misunderstood the situation? Or perhaps you are a government spy. A double agent."

"Something like that. Listen to me. I know what you're up to and I'm warning you. Leave Rachel out of it. Her daughter doesn't deserve to be treated like spare parts."

"I do not understand." Gervas fought the urge to relax his vigilant stance. Warfield took him by surprise with his unexpected topic.

"Here. This hospital. Swapping one kid for the other."

"Mr. Warfield, although I have a fair understanding of English, it is not my native language. I do not understand what my personal life has to do with you or the terrorist operation you once represented. Onus is over, its leaders apprehended, its operations being shut down." A spark of realization relit his fear. "Please don't hurt my children. They are innocent."

"They were. You scum. If you cause Rachel any pain at all, if her daughter is harmed in any way, I will make you suffer."

Gervas lowered his arms to his sides. The work shift must have ended for several people came into the garage, chatting and laughing, or swiftly heading for their vehicles. He took three steps closer to Warfield. "I love Rachel. I always have. I would never hurt her. Or frighten her as you have. Please, leave us alone."

Warfield looked both ways. He hunched his shoulders. "I did my best to protect her," he muttered. "When your brother knew you'd found her and possibly the ring to complete the collection and get the money he needed, he amped the stakes."

Gervas did his best to keep up. "We know about the men who chased us. It is no secret."

Warfield's lips thinned. "I've lost my position because of this. You've hurt Rachel enough. She deserves someone better. It should have been me. Being here at Mendota with Rachel started out as a coincidence. We really wanted to have someone in place to monitor Freiburg University without looking suspicious. To watch for Onus activities and coordinate international events. Manheim knew you'd spent time in Wisconsin, so when he sent you—"

"He did no such thing!"

Warfield grinned. "You were so played, man. But you think you've come out on top. I will make sure she knows the real you."

A car horn honked beside Gervas. He turned to see the weary nurse he'd seen earlier pull up in her automobile. She held a cell phone. "Need any help?"

"Thank you. My colleague…" Gervas twisted his head to note that Warfield had vanished. "And I had some issues to discuss. All is well. Thank you for your trouble." He waved as she drove away.

His conversation with Warfield had no closure. Gervas puzzled at his meaning, of exchanging daughters. How could he assume such a thing? He tried to phone Rachel several times but got only a message that her voice mailbox had not been set up. Then he called the State Department.

<>

"There, there."

Rachel used to hate the helpless pats on the shoulder her mother gave after listening to her woes. This time Rachel just leaned over, put her head in her mom's lap and wept.

"It's so revolting," she sputtered between bouts. "Why would she talk like that? She was my best friend."

Her mom stroked her hair. Rachel pushed her knuckle against her teeth, trying to get a grip.

Mom's voice was gentle. "The real question is, why does such a baseless accusation upset you so much?"

Rachel inhaled in gasps. "It's just, just, been so good. I wanted so much to believe." She wiped more tears.

"And why can't you?"

"I was so angry. For so long. And then, when he came back and, and I saw him, and, and I fell all over again, it was just too good."

Rachel rolled a bit and tilted her head to soak up more of her mom's sympathy. "*He* was too good, and it seemed like everything I'd made myself believe about how bad he was and that he was never coming back, had never really wanted me in the first place, weren't true. And I didn't trust myself."

Rachel's dad came into the room and plopped onto his recliner. "She better?" He'd hightailed it out of there when he'd seen her near-hysteria.

"She will be," Mom said.

"What's it about?"

Rachel almost laughed at the way they were talking about her as if she wasn't there, or was six again.

"Her professor."

"Oh. I liked him. For a kraut." He picked up the evening paper and pulled the lever on the recliner.

Rachel studied her mother's expression. "Can you tell? Just by looking at someone?"

"And talking to him. He loves Maeve. And you."

Rachel sat up and wiped her eyes and blew her nose. "That's right. They visited."

"More 'n you," Dad cut in and shook the paper folds.

She smiled. "Sorry. Been pretty crazy."

Dad harrumphed. "Did he ever get that ring? The one he was so desperate about?"

"Yeah, Dad. He did."

<>

Rachel got up with the sunrise the next morning. She hadn't slept well, and after two coats of under eye makeup, gave up and drove to the campus. She could get a good pile of paperwork crossed off the list before Peggy came in and they had to be civil. Rachel would apologize but the thought held no joy, especially since she'd given the ugliness Peggy conjured a second thought. And a third one in her dreams last night. Even though not a shred of it could be true.

With her keycard in her mouth, purse in hand, and briefcase over her shoulder pulling her off balance, she was ready to prop the door open with her knee while she stowed her card when someone reached over her head to hold the door. Rachel dropped the card.

"Don't scream. Don't say anything. Just get inside."

She took in a breath, sure she'd choke. "Scott," she whispered.

He kept his eyes on her while he bent to pick up the keycard. "Inside. Now."

All the while she was hustling toward her office Rachel

tried and rejected escape plans. He probably wouldn't let her out of his sight, even for the restroom. If he wanted to kill her, why didn't he just do it?

She hesitated outside her door and quaked when he put his hand on her shoulder.

"Go ahead. You have to see something," he whispered harshly against her neck.

"I thought you-you were in Europe."

He ignored her and shut the door behind them once inside. He flourished a newspaper.

Rachel slowly lowered herself to her desk chair. She had no secret button under her desk to summon the police and thought maybe she'd put in a requisition. "A newspaper? You don't have to scare me half to death—"

"Wait until you read it." He spread the sheet open in front of her, knocking aside her neatly stacked piles of work.

That did it. Anger surged, propelling her to stand. She noted his wild, red-rimmed eyes and messed hair, not to mention sour body odor. "What are you doing? Are you crazy? The police are after you. I want you to leave. Right now."

"Sit and read the article. Hey, I'm not trying to be the bad guy here."

Rachel sat and stared at him, one brow quirked.

"I just need you to know what's going on. Your professor is not some saint."

"I know that."

"But do you? Really? Are you willing to bet your kid on it?"

The doubt she'd been trying to tamp reared up and tickled her. "Have you been talking to Peggy? Because—"

He stabbed his finger on the paper. "Read this!"

Rachel kept her eyes on his face as long as she could as

she bent to do as he demanded. A full color picture of Gervas and Katrine in front of University Hospital, looking excited yet determined, spread across six columns above the fold.

"So? They're trying to help Katrine. What's your point?"

"Read the headline."

She narrowed her eyes and refused to submit. "Something about a genetic disorder. Gervas already told me about it. She had leukemia." She wasn't sure how far she could push Scott. He seemed to have lost his sense of rationality.

"That's only part of the story. She has a rare blood disease. Leukemia is more like a symptom. Most people don't make it past their early thirties. How old is Katrine, again?"

"Twenty-seven," Rachel muttered.

"Don't you get it?"

Rachel pushed away from her desk and folded her arms. "No, I don't get it. I don't know why you're here, acting like a-a monster. I don't get why the police thought you were out of the country. I don't get why you're bothering me. Leave us alone, please!"

"I'm trying to save you. You and Maeve. Just like I did before."

His hands were shaking. Was he on drugs or something? He was still powerful enough to hurt her. Why had she chosen to get here so early? No one else would come in for another half hour, at the earliest. "Look, Scott—"

"All right! I'll tell you. The article says the Friedemanns wanted to bring awareness of her weird anemia disease and the research efforts to cure it and all conditions like it with innovative therapy."

He leaned over her desk like he might crawl over to get to her. Rachel shrank back.

"Innovative therapy. What are they known for? Taking

bits from one person, modifying them, and inserting it into another. They're like freakin' Frankenstein's monsters."

More fear raced along her spine. "You're crazy. You're making things up. I want you to leave."

He straightened. "People who've participated in this *innovative* therapy have died, or had their nervous systems irreparably damaged, their lives ruined. They've all suffered. You need to check it out. They'll hurt Maeve. He'll take her away from you yet. In ways you never imagined."

A sound from the front made Rachel melt in relief. She jumped to her feet. Before she could round her desk, he'd slipped out.

<>

Between the moment Rachel locked her office door after an agonizing day and when she slid behind the wheel of Ann's car, she changed her mind about her destination. She'd drive straight to Maeve's house.

Maeve had to be fine. Gervas's daughter was sick, not hers. Her daughter was whole, healthy, beautiful and strong. Katrine was sick, an anomaly, the product of unfortunate genes. Katrine might die anyway, that's what Gervas told her. Maybe her mother's mental defect contributed to the girl's problems. Rachel didn't understand what Scott had meant by his veiled hints about therapy. How had he known about it? Katrine's disease had a name Rachel couldn't remember. Something with anemia, like Scott said, which didn't sound that serious. She'd done some research about anemia on the internet at lunch time instead of talking to Peggy. A lot of young women had that trouble. They just needed to eat right and take iron. It had nothing to do with Maeve.

Fifteen minutes later, Rachel stood outside Maeve's door, knocking and ringing the bell. She had a key but needed an excuse to use it. She glanced at her watch. Quarter till six. Maeve should be home.

Rachel hunted for the keychain in the bottom of her purse. Along the way she groaned when she saw her phone blinking with unheard messages. Four calls from Gervas last night and today. Why hadn't she bothered to look earlier? She'd listen later.

She pounded once more and called, "Maeve!" As she brought the key to lock, the garage door rumbled. Rachel slipped the key back in her purse and lowered her arms.

Maeve stuck her head around the corner of the garage. "Hi, didn't expect you. Did I forget something?"

"No." Rachel walked toward her daughter. "I just wanted to see you."

"Okay." Maeve turned her back. "C'mon in."

Rachel caught her shifting a sweater over her arm and pushing the button to lower the garage door. Rachel scooted inside. Maeve didn't face her again but mumbled, "Make yourself at home, be right back," and hurried down the hall to her room. Rachel stared after her. Something was up.

Maeve changed into a long-sleeved shirt when she strolled back into the kitchen. She rolled the cuffs up, exposing her wrists. Rachel stared, thinking of Scott; of the way he wore his shirts and his accusations that morning.

"So, you want to have supper with me? I'm not sure what I have." Maeve opened the refrigerator door.

"I just haven't seen you that much lately." Rachel stood there, starting to feel foolish at how normal everything seemed.

Maeve grinned and set a carton of eggs and a wedge of yellow cheese on the counter. "Yeah. Miss you too. Omelet?"

"Uh, sure." Rachel stepped to the sink to wash her hands while Maeve reached for a skillet hanging nearby. The move exposed more of her arm. Rachel couldn't take her eyes away from the orange stain and bandage on the inside of Maeve's elbow.

"Maeve?"

Her daughter caught her stare and lowered her arm. "It's nothing, Mom. Don't worry."

Rachel's phone rang in the depths of her purse, an unfamiliar harsh burr on the new phone that made her grit her teeth. "I'm not worried. You can talk to me, you know."

"Aren't you going to get that?"

"After you explain your arm to me. What happened?" Fear again. "You're not…there's nothing wrong, is there? You're okay?"

Maeve wrinkled her brow. "Explain what? I'm fine. I just got tested for the National Bone Marrow Registry." She shrugged. "That's all."

"Bone marrow? But, why? And why keep it a secret?"

"I just didn't want you to worry." Maeve turned in a bit of a huff and reached for a bowl. "Like you always do."

"That's what mothers are supposed to do. Worry. Because we love you."

"Because you hope you aren't traumatizing your children for life, you mean."

"Well, that too."

"Like Katrine's wacko mother."

"I'm not like that."

"I didn't say you were."

"So, what's with the bone marrow deal?"

Maeve's phone rang. She held it up. "It's Dad. Just a sec."

Rachel slid a glance toward her purse. All those missed calls.

"Yes, she's here," Maeve said. "Sure. See you in a jiff."

She slipped the phone back in her pocket. "He's on his way."

"So, what's this about the registry?"

"You should get tested too. If everyone did, we'd all be able to help each other."

"You're avoiding the question. I thought we'd gotten past the secretive stage. If what you're doing is on the up and up, you have nothing to hide. Where did you hear about this?"

"At the hospital. It's no big deal."

Maeve opened the carton of eggs. Rachel watched her crack two while she started a slow seethe on top of the frazzle of remembering Scott's paranoia about "cutting out parts" and Peggy's wild taunts. "Bone marrow transplants are risky. Why would you just decide to do something like that out of the blue?"

"There's, like, zero risk anymore."

"Anymore?" Rachel raised her voice. "Who talked you into this? I didn't even know you were considering it. What are you thinking? You can save your half-sister? She's dying. She has a genetic disease that's incurable. And what about your past?"

Maeve twirled, holding a spatula. "My past what?"

"Don't make me say it."

At Maeve's accusing silence, Rachel blurted "drugs."

Maeve narrowed her eyes. "Two years ago. A little pot. No. Big. Deal. Finished?" She turned back and flipped the omelet edges with tense precision. "And she doesn't have to die. At least I care."

The doorbell rang. Rachel let Gervas in. With his first look at her glare, he refrained from kissing her. He shifted attention to the small kitchen and Maeve's rigid back.

"Mother-daughter, how is it? Spat?" His amber eyes did not crinkle into amusement as if he recognized the fight was no ordinary one.

"Not exactly." Rachel nodded at her purse. "I suppose all those calls were to inform me you'd talked *my* daughter into thinking she can save yours? That's why you came back, really, isn't it? Convenient of your brother to cause some problems in Europe at the same time, right?" Rachel took three steps backward and ran into the chair with her purse. She picked it up. "And us?" She didn't care that Gervas's face had gone pale plaster-colored and his mouth gaped like a broiled trout on a plate. "Collateral damage. Again. Just as long as you get what you want."

"Mother!" Maeve stood there, crowding the already small room. "What are you saying? He had nothing to do with this. It's my decision."

"She's going to give Katrine her bone marrow," Rachel spat. "You came to find her, not some artifact. Or me."

Gervas turned his head to stare at Maeve as if he didn't recognize her.

"Do you know what they do to you?" Rachel's voice seemed to leap from her without her permission. She felt as though standing beside herself listening to some demon shrieking nonsense just to be making noise. "They give you drugs first, to release more red cells. Then they take out pieces of your person, your marrow, and put it into someone else." No matter how hard the real Rachel tried to stop the demon Rachel from using Scott's absurd argument, she couldn't. She wouldn't have been surprised to wipe sweat of blood from her forehead. "They hurt you. It's a big needle. People have died, Gervas. People who they stick have permanent nerve damage. Or get infections that kill them."

He swallowed. Opened his mouth. Closed it.

"He's just using you, Maeve. It's not worth risking your

own health or future."

"You don't have any idea what you're talking about, Mom. I can't believe you'd be so callous about another human being's life. Katrine's my sister and if I can help her, I will. You should be so grateful you raised me right. In spite of not having a good man like Dad around. I think you'd better leave."

Rachel didn't just leave. She watched herself melt away.

31

Rachel put her hands over Ann's bulging tummy.

"Feel it? Here? She's kicking." Ann's smile lit her whole narrow face.

"She's strong." Rachel grinned back. Ann was on bed rest, or couch rest, as she liked to say. Mark had carried her downstairs before going to work that morning.

"Do I tell you enough?" Ann asked.

"What?"

"How glad I am you're here with me."

"You know I'd do anything for you."

Ann shifted under the light blanket across her legs.

Rachel went back to taking ornaments off the tree. "It was a nice Christmas this year, wasn't it? With little David and even Colleen's mom." She laughed. "Just think next Christmas with more babies."

"I hope so."

"Don't you get like that." Rachel shook her finger at Ann. "She'll be here soon enough, and she will be perfect."

"Thirty-four weeks. I never dreamed I'd make it this far." She looked past Rachel out the window. "The snow is so pretty."

Rachel shivered.

"No nibbles on your house? You're probably glad not to have to shovel to get out to work in time." Ann stroked her stomach.

"I still have to have some shoveling done so the house doesn't look vacant while it's for sale. The agency doesn't put up signs anymore."

"Right. I guess you don't want anyone think you're on vacation and break in."

"So, I'll be heading to work soon. Maeve is coming, right?"

"Of course. Stop being such a worrywart. You've made so many changes in a short time. Are you really as okay as you look?"

Rachel laughed. "I'm glad I look okay. It does seem like a lot all at once, but, honestly, the old job was souring on me. I needed to change, and I love working at the community services center. It's not too far from what I was doing, you know. Only I'm helping people with bigger needs than finding the right class to fill their schedules."

"That was important too."

"Sure it was." Rachel put the lid on a box of wooden ornaments Maeve and Ritchie had painted when they were little.

"Do you miss it sometimes?" At Ann's longing expression, Rachel knew she missed her own former work and life of church and volunteering before she'd been relegated to a prone position.

"I miss some of the action on campus," Rachel said. She missed having Peggy's ear once in a while. Peggy's betrayal and their rift had been too wide to bridge. Rachel had submitted her resignation before classes started last fall and never looked back. "I think the only reason I stayed so long was that it was a connection to Gervas. When I didn't need that anymore, I was able to be more objective about what I wanted to do with my life."

Ann played with fringe on the pink and gray plaid throw. "I'll be the first to admit I have way too much time on my hands these days."

Rachel groaned.

"Now, come on, it won't be that bad. This kid has me all full of motherly sloppy moods. I feel like I have a chance to do everything right that I messed up with Ritchie."

"He turned out okay."

"Not because of me. And I know I'll still make plenty of mistakes, some just because of habit. I refuse to let that define my parenting, or make me afraid of not being able to do the right thing." Ann swung her feet over the edge and patted the cushion next to her. "I promise not to go all tough love and kick you out." Ann looked up from under her eyelashes.

"Hope not, since I can go any old time and Mark's the one who's paying me to stay here and babysit. You might get stuck with Mom if you give me the boot." Rachel sat.

Ann gave a delicate shudder. "Love Mom and all."

"But," they chimed together.

Ann took Rachel's hand. "Losing Peggy, I understand. I know you've forgiven her and all, but I agree you're not obligated to resume your friendship."

"That's what the pastor said too."

"Don't you think about him? Gervas? Isn't it time yet? He talks to Maeve every day."

"From Germany."

"You know why he's there. He wants to help his brother."

"I do get that. Really. It's all right, Ann."

"He called a lot in the beginning, and you know he wanted to come when you were—"

"I know. Ann, you don't understand." Rachel rose and paced away. "I said some pretty terrible things. Thought some truly despicable things. I can't just drop it. And I can't relive it every time I look at him and remember what I did. You didn't see the look on his face. I'll never be able to forget that."

"Then see him again so you can think of him with a new expression. You don't have to do everything on your own, you know. Maeve forgave you."

"She had to." Rachel forced a humorless laugh.

"She didn't have to, Rach. And you see her often. You've learned not to beat yourself up every time you're with her. We've all done things and said things we're ashamed of. Even Gervas. You can make this last hurdle of getting your life back. He needs you as much as you need him. He's hurting too."

"I forgave him."

"In your heart. He needs to hear it. And you need to let him forgive you."

"I'm working on it. Promise."

Ann thankfully let it drop, but Rachel let the words swirl through her conscience while she finished putting the holiday trimmings away. She stacked the boxes near the basement stairs for Maeve and Mark to store later, then went to putter in the kitchen.

Maeve rushed in through the garage door while Rachel was filling the slow cooker with potatoes and carrots on top of a roast.

"You'll never guess what I read." Maeve waved a color printout as she shed her coat and scarf on to the chair by the kitchen desk.

Rachel held up her hands. "I give."

"Spoilsport. How's Ann today?"

"Good. Baby's kicking up a storm. So?" Rachel winked at the paper in her daughter's hand.

"I just printed it off before I came over." Maeve handed it over and went to check on Rachel's meal preparation.

"A fire?" The picture showed a beautiful home flaming

while multiple firefighters streamed water over it. Rachel squinted. "In Baden? Freiburg? Oh, no." The Freidemann home and several outbuildings burned shortly after the new year. "Arson?"

"Yep."

"Anyone hurt?" Rachel clutched the page. Her heart fluttered. "I never even got to visit." She examined Maeve's averted face.

"Well, actually, Dad called about it. He didn't want us to see it and get all alarmed. His first wife, the crazy one—"

"Sylvie."

"Right. Well, she somehow got out of the loony bin," her swift glance up made Rachel chuckle, "sorry, Mom, and torched the place. She died, but Max and his wife got out okay."

"What a tragic way to go."

"You're not kidding."

"Hey!" Ann's voice rang from the family room. "Lonesome in here."

"Sorry!" Maeve shouted past Rachel's ear. "To you too," she whispered as went past.

Rachel grabbed her reading glasses and read more of the article. Max Friedemann, son of Gervas and the late Sylvie Von Hinckle Friedemann, "Except he really isn't," Rachel said, was the last remaining member of the family on the estate that raised game animals and birds. They planned to tear down the damaged structures and put the property up for sale.

"And so ends the legacy."

Maeve returned with used teacups.

"I could have gotten that."

Maeve shrugged. "I'm good."

"How did he feel about this?" Rachel indicated the article.

"Why don't you ask him?"

One point they'd never agreed on was the motivation for Gervas's return and finding Maeve. Rachel knew she was being unreasonable. In her heart she believed Gervas had not known about Maeve when he first came to the States, and that he'd never use one daughter to save another. Nor was he the monster Scott and Peggy made him out to be. Rachel needed to hang on to the threads of that belief while she worked through the outrage and the devastation of what seemed her whole life purpose: to protect her daughter. When that need had been so easily overrun, the clumsy scaffolding of her existence crumbled.

Sixty days of intense therapy in a "spa" Mark found for her in Colorado put the pieces back together. She just wasn't ready to see Gervas, as she told her sister. Yet.

"He still asks about you every day," Maeve said over her shoulder. She chopped up chives and added them to the cooker. "We talk more about you than Katrine. Or me."

Rachel nodded. She returned the glasses to their case.

"He's coming next month. For our birthdays," Maeve said, her nonchalance too studied.

Among other things the girls liked to say they had in common was a birthday two days apart in the first weeks of February. It wasn't the same date, Rachel said, to no avail. Since the successful bone marrow transplant and positive treatment, Katrine had gone into a kind of remission. There were no guarantees of a longer life or that the disease wouldn't return to ravage her blood and organs, but Katrine was satisfied and grateful. She moved in with Maeve and worked part time at an animal rescue and shelter. Loose ends of Katrine's life and death struggle were neatly woven, but Rachel had learned to be less cynical. She saw what Maeve did, especially on her new job, that helping others reaped a far better reward.

She started when Maeve put her arms around her. "You're doing so well. So much better, Mom. And you're strong. Don't you think it's time? He loves you so much. And I know you could love him if you let yourself."

Rachel hugged back and stepped away to look at the clock. "I have to go. But we can talk some more later."

"You have a half hour before you need to leave the house." Maeve leveled a look that made Rachel squirm. "Call him. Please."

"What? Now?"

"I sort of asked him if he'd be around about this time."

"Maeve. You guys are ganging up on me."

"He canceled some stuff so he'd be available." Maeve grabbed Rachel's phone and marched it to her. "Tough love time. Do you need me to push the buttons?"

"Ann told me she wasn't using tough love."

"Yeah, well, she's a pussycat compared to me. Don't make me dial."

<>

Rachel waited at the glassed in front door of her new condo. Fresh snow had renewed the neighborhood. She stood back so her breath wouldn't fog the window. Maeve and Katrine giggled like young girls over some mishap in the kitchen while decorating their Valentine's Day-themed chocolate birthday cake. In reality they were staying out of the way but not trying very hard. Rachel hugged herself and lowered her eyes. When she lifted them again, there he was.

She let him in, and tried to study his expression through the tears blurring her vision. "Gervas."

"Rachel, Rachel. At last." He dropped the bag he was

carrying and set a cut bouquet of flowers on the little table she kept in the entryway. They clung to each other and she cried.

When she could breathe again, she kissed him. Phone forgiveness wasn't enough. "I'm so sorry. I can't believe I ever let you go." She fingered a trickle of tear alongside his nose.

Gervas touched her hair and cheeks and kissed her fingers. "I think we needed some time. A chance to close matters of our past." He tipped her chin to look in her eyes. "Every day I thought of you, of what you were going through. You are truly well? I wanted to be here for you, but they said it was better to stay away."

He meant those dark months in Colorado, and they were right. "I needed to be on my own then, to conquer my problems." She'd won, she'd healed. And she was ready to move forward. "But I-I am glad you were there in spirit. Sometimes I was too ashamed to think of you, of what I said and what I believed, but most of the time I could feel you there in my heart."

He kissed her again and just held her.

Rachel lifted her head after a minute. It was suspiciously quiet. She turned her face toward the kitchen. "Aha!"

Gervas looked in the same direction and then back with a big grin.

"Our daughters, the optimists," Gervas said.

"Well, except for Max and Justine, Aunt Ann and Mark and Stella, and David, Ritchie, Colleen—"

"We get it!" Rachel held up her hands. "Soon as Ann's recovered a little more, we'll work something out." Before eating, Rachel and Maeve gave Gervas and Katrine some private time to discuss the fire and Sylvie's death.

"Katrine was home for the funeral, wasn't she?" Rachel asked.

"Just four days, and two of them were travel. She didn't want to miss work, and Dad wasn't around much for her. The trial, you know."

"Right." Rachel hadn't forgotten about Manheim, but since she hadn't even gotten to meet him, her own few days last summer in Berlin and the international scandal seemed surreal. Scott hadn't shown up again. To Rachel, he was a broken part of her soul she'd used to avoid blaming herself for her meltdown. She no longer needed that crutch and when she learned he really had been in the CIA on assignment to watch Onus, she let his power over her go. Maybe they could have been a couple if he hadn't become so obsessive. Was it her fault things had gotten out of control? Had she teased him?

"Don't start feeling bad about stuff, Mom," Maeve said. "Dad's here now and everything's going to be all right. Better than all right!"

"You are the cheery one, aren't you?" She looked at her daughter's faux innocence. "You better not be up to something embarrassing."

"Who me? Hey, I hear them. Let's go. And I hope you don't mind, but I invited two more guests."

"You did? Do we have enough food? I wasn't planning on a houseful of guests tonight. Really, you should have—"

"Don't sweat it, Mom. You'll approve. C'mon!"

Rachel allowed herself to be pulled along from her home office back to the living area. She was so happy with her choice of house all over again. Placed at the edge of the development, she had a nice view of a small stand of trees. And she didn't have to shovel. She went to Gervas's side and smiled at Katrine, who sniffed as she looked over the contents of a jewelry box.

"Danke, Father." She let Maeve rifle through an

assortment of cocktail rings and earrings.

"From her mother?" Rachel looked over the girls' shoulders.

"Yes. Some I gave to Max's wife, but these are hers to do with as she pleases."

"I was sorry to hear about the fire and her death."

"A sad end, to be sure." Gervas squeezed her arm. "But we are here to celebrate, yes?"

A knock sent Maeve scurrying to the front door. She returned with her grandparents.

"Oh! I should have asked you myself, shouldn't I?" Rachel helped her mom with her coat and hung it in the closet.

"That's quite all right, dear. We've been meaning to come over and see your new place anyway. We know it's only been a week and a half."

<>

Gervas stood to the side, watching Rachel, aching for her and all that had happened to her since he'd first come to the States last July. Like her, he couldn't blame himself for things her well-meaning friends and family had done, and he was proud that she had overcome the lies of others. Fortuitous her parents were here tonight, which meant he didn't have to wait another day.

He looked at his bag and the box it held. He'd bring it out later when he and Rachel would decide together what to do with its contents.

"So, couldn't get rid of you, could she?" Mr. Michaels grabbed Gervas's hand with some strength. With his other gnarled hand, Mr. Michaels clapped Gervas's shoulder. "Glad to see you, son. Awful glad."

"Thank you, sir."

"Ray. Call me Ray."

"Ray, I'd like to speak privately to you, perhaps after the meal."

The elderly man gave Gervas a knowing look. "Sure, son. Sure." He shifted his glace toward the women, his wife, daughter, and granddaughter. "Good girls, them." He snuffled and moved to sit in a chair.

Gervas rubbed his palms, sweaty with an unusual attack of nerves. He was about to do something for the first and last time, something it had taken him a lifetime to prepare for, and he didn't want to mess up.

He watched his family enjoy the simple meal of sauerbraten which Katrine had taught Maeve and Rachel to make. Some of their laughter was over Katrine's instructions and the subsequent interpretation. They should have had these experiences while growing up together, but he refused to look over his shoulder.

While the ladies were cleaning up in the kitchen after eating, Ray settled in a wide chair draped in the knitted blanket Gervas remembered from Rachel's other house. "I suspect I can guess your question, son. Ann's husband, now there's a classy fella, he done the same. You're kinda old for my other girl, aincha? Odd that Mark, now, he's so young." Ray laughed and slapped his knee. "Between ya two, ya average out. But who'm I to argue with love. Been loving on that Alice in there for more than fifty years."

Gervas had wondered at the youth of Mark Roth, Ann's husband. "I can't expect fifty years of marriage with Rachel if I have your blessing to ask for her hand. But I can assure you that I have loved her for more than twenty years already."

"Shame you didn't get back together those twenty years ago for our dear Maeve. But she turned out all right. So did Rachel. Learn things, I guess, about your strengths when you have to rely on your own wits." Ray looked Gervas up and down. "Be good to have smart fellas take care of my girls. If she'll have you, you got my permission. And my blessing. O 'course Alice might have more to say than me. But she dotes on that girl of yours already. You going to take Rachel away to Germany? I'm not sure we'd like that so much."

"Thank you, Ray. I do not plan to return to Germany but for visits from time to time. My life is here in the States now."

"Good."

There was no easy part to the equation of proposing marriage. Asking Ray was less daunting than Gervas had feared. He had tried to prepare himself emotionally for any kind of answer from both Ray and Rachel. He hoped.

Gervas dipped into the large square of red and pink frosted cake he was served. The chocolate interior was delectable, but he left a good deal of frosting on the side of the plate. He watched Rachel chat with the others, occasionally meeting his eyes and smiling with an endearing shyness he had not seen before. Gifts were exchanged and exclaimed over and not long afterward, he and Rachel waved farewell first to Ray and Alice, and then the girls.

"You did a wonderful job hosting this party tonight," he told Rachel.

"Thanks. The girls actually took care of pretty much everything."

"This is a nice house, a condominium, yes?"

"Yes, and I like it."

"Before I leave too, I—" At the hint of uncertainty and sorrow in Rachel's eyes, he quickly amended his statement. "I have a room in a nearby motel, that's all, Rachel. I am not going far. I have something to discuss, to ask of you, in a while, but first, may we sit?"

He brought his bag over to the coffee table in front of the sofa, sat beside her and reached to remove the clear case. Rachel's eyes widened.

"Oh, you have them all together again. You stopped to get the ring from Mark's safe deposit box?"

"Yes."

"They're beautiful all together. A necklace." Rachel put her finger on the top of the case. "These earrings are so dainty. This is a pin? With gold filigree and blue stones?"

He held out a key.

"No. I'd rather just look. What are you going to do with them?

"That's one thing I wanted to discuss with you. I want us to make the decision together."

Rachel shied away. "I don't think so. I stole the ring from you."

"It wasn't really mine."

"I guess I know that, but I'm still ashamed of taking it."

Gervas took her hands and held them to his face. "The ring brought us together. I want to share this responsibility with you. If you want to keep them with us, or even want to keep the ring, I will honor your wish."

"I read an article about what you did with the other things, how you donated them to museums of their country of origin when that other man was arrested for fraud."

His cheeks warmed and he clasped her hands to cup his face.

"That was the right thing to do," Rachel whispered. "I think you, we, should make these items available for others to see in a museum."

He stared into her eyes. "It will be done."

Rachel sighed and sat back. "That felt good. Like I

dropped the last remaining rock I've been carrying."

Gervas shifted so he turned to face her. He should drop to his knee, shouldn't he? He reached in his pocket for the other ring he'd brought tonight, a square cut diamond on a band of white gold. He opted instead to slide closer beside her and put his arm around her. "I have something else to ask you."

"Oh?" Rachel raised her brow and smiled tremulously.

"I have asked your father for his blessing." He cleared his throat and flexed his fingers. "I haf—have—never before, nor never will again, ask a woman to be my wife. Rachel, will you marry me?"

"Really? You've never asked anyone? You've been married twice? Julianne?"

Gervas shrugged. "She asked me. I was amused."

"Sylvie?"

"It was expected. We merely had the civil ceremony, then a wedding in the chapel and reception." He looked at Rachel steadily, waiting and hoping.

"This is my first proposal," she mused.

"Do you want me to kneel?"

"It is the only time I've ever been asked. Maybe you should."

When he moved away to do so, she took his hand. "No, you don't need to. I was teasing. What did my father say? Is that what you two were talking about after we ate?"

"Yes. He was quite entertained at the fact that Mark is so much younger than your sister and I am so much older than you. Can you take such an elderly gentleman for your husband?"

"You will never be old, Gervas. Are you sure you want me? After all—"

He touched her lips. "Yes, after all. I have always wanted you, even when I thought you'd rejected me. Even though I hesitate to give you such a tainted name. Together we will move into a brighter future. So. Will you be my wife?"

"Yes."

Simple and perfect. Relief led to a simmering kiss.

Later, he picked up the case of jewelry to return to his bag. "We can finally put this to rest. It's been seventy-four years since the Regenbogens were forced out of their home in Freiburg and trusted the Friedemanns with their precious artifacts."

Rachel put her hand over his. "I think they would be pleased."

"I agree. Rachel, I love you so much."

"I believe. I couldn't understand it before, but now I'm at peace. And I love you too."

"We can marry soon?"

"Plan on it. This is going to be a very good year. We'll figure the rest as we go."

Gervas was finally home. He agreed, this next year would be very good.

For Thought

Rachel struggles with self-identity, as much as with her youthful indiscretion. What do you think of the way she handled her lifestyle choices?

Gervas, on the other hand, seems overconfident and even cold. What was he trying to hide?

Maeve grew up knowing she was different from other kids who had both mother and father. How did Maeve learn the truth about her "cyberstalker"? How did she react? Have you ever experienced stalking or unwanted attention in any form, and if so, what did you do?

Why does Gervas choose to remain in the States even after he gave up his search for the antique his brother was desperate to obtain?

How does Scott, the man in the Information Technology department who was interested in dating Rachel, get involved in her problem with Gervas and Maeve? What role did he ultimately play in her life? What do you think truly drove him?

What secret does Maeve want to keep from her mother? Do you agree with her? Why did Gervas play along?

Everyone in **Centrifugal Force** has a secret, and is or becomes adept at keeping the truth hidden. What were Rachel's and Gervas's secrets? Rachel's friend Peggy was a huge part of her support when she was a struggling single mom and later in life. What secret did Peggy keep and how do you think it changed Rachel's life?

Gervas's brother is in a position of power in Germany, and ultimately the European Union of 2011. What secrets did he have and how did he use them to wield his power over others?

This story was written before Great Britain voted to exit the European Union in June of 2016. What effect did that decision have on world events?

Forgiveness in order to move forward is a central theme in the book. In what ways did each of the principal characters need to forgive and accept forgiveness? How did doing so, or not doing so, affect their lives?

What control, truly, did each of the central characters in **Centrifugal Force** have over their own lives? How did the illusion of centrifugal force draw them together while thrusting them apart? Is control in life always a good thing?

Thank you for reading *Centrifugal Force*. If you enjoyed the book, will you take a moment to leave a review or share your thoughts with others who might like to read the book?